Daniel g

He planted b   hands on the steering wheel, then stepped away. Maria stood with her profile to him.

She pushed her glasses onto the bridge of her nose in a nervous gesture.

He placed a hand over hers and moved the wheel, adjusting their heading. Then he moved closer, his chest pressing against her left arm. Her warm, sweet scent mixed with coconut sunscreen invaded his senses and his next thought flew out of his head.

Wanting to be closer, he moved behind her, wrapping his arms around her body. Together they moved the wheel. The heat from her skin blended with his, weaving some intoxicating thread around them. Did she feel the wind funneling through the sails and over their bodies?

Yeah, she did.

He indulged the luxury of closing his eyes to revel in her body heat and perfume. This moment was all too familiar...and Maria didn't even know.

Dear Reader,

I wish I knew you personally to thank you for purchasing my first Harlequin Superromance book! Writing *Where It Began* was dear to me because it was based on a trip to the Bahamas with my husband for our twenty-fifth wedding anniversary. The beauty of the Abacos, the reefs and the remote location acted as a catalyst for Daniel and Maria's love story.

Raised as a power-boat kid, transitioning to sailing after marriage proved more difficult than I imagined. In the power-boat world, a heeling (tilting) boat means trouble, and setting the boat in motion merely requires turning a key. Learning sailboat rigging and handling sails taught me much about the power of nature and the joy of harnessing the wind. Also, as in relationships, finally letting go of the boat's lifelines to enjoy the heeling sailboat literally taught me to let go of my need for control and enjoy life's surprises and adventures.

I became hooked on writing in eighth grade, when I discovered the power of words in a poem written by e. e. cummings. I hope my word-crafted worlds of triumph and love entertain you. Feel free to email me at Kathleen@KathleenPickering.com and let me know.

Happy reading!

Kathleen Pickering

Where It Began
Kathleen Pickering

TORONTO NEW YORK LONDON
AMSTERDAM PARIS SYDNEY HAMBURG
STOCKHOLM ATHENS TOKYO MILAN MADRID
PRAGUE WARSAW BUDAPEST AUCKLAND

Recycling programs
for this product may
not exist in your area.

ISBN-13: 978-0-373-71754-5

WHERE IT BEGAN

ABOUT THE AUTHOR

Kathleen Pickering, the author with more than just a story to tell, believes stories teach life lessons. The second oldest of eight siblings, Kathleen draws characters from people around her, like her artist sister whose talent drives her into seclusion, or her newlywed son and daughter-in-law whose love is so fresh and genuine. Kathleen also travels to research her work. So beware. If she meets you, you may wind up inspiring one of her novels!

To you, reader, for celebrating my first
Harlequin Superromance with me.
Thank you!

Acknowledgments

First and foremost, I'd like to acknowledge my
new editor, Wanda Ottewell, for having faith in
my work and a sense of humor that rivals mine!

I'd like to thank friend and fellow author,
Karen Kendall, for introducing me to Wanda at
Florida Romance Writers Cruise with
Your Muse Conference. (Long live balloon hats
and Mexican cantinas!)

I have also been blessed with an amazing friend
and mentor in Heather Graham, who has written
for almost every Harlequin line, including
launching the MIRA imprint. Heather also
introduced me to my agent, Lucy Childs, with
whom I am so thrilled to be associated.

I must add that my writing career began once I
became a member of Florida Romance Writers in
Fort Lauderdale, which is a chapter of Romance
Writers of America. I am grateful for the company
of fabulous authors whom I call friends, especially
the M&M's and the beautiful Traci Hall.

Thank you one and all for your kinship,
your guidance and for loving the writing world
as much as I do!

CHAPTER ONE

"I NEED ANSWERS," Maria Santiago said, keeping her voice calm when she wanted to scream.

She inhaled a soothing breath, grateful for these tranquil moments during dinner hour with Poppa. She could count on him to anchor her in the world she remembered.

She selected a roll and passed the basket to her right, ignoring the pleasant warmth from Daniel Murphy Del Rio's hands as he took it from her. She also ignored his gaze, which never failed to make her uncomfortable. He always seemed to be questioning her. Heaven knew, she had no idea why.

The evening's shadows were growing along the beach, but her cherished ocean view from Reefside's terrace did little to quell the tightness in her chest over this demand she was making. Until recently, she'd been content to hole up in her studio, or indulge in sunrise and sunset walks along the beach, but no longer. Her precious twin sister, whose memory she still grieved, had begun to haunt her dreams.

Dreams, no. Nightmares. Until the nightmares began, she'd held nothing but heartfelt, wonderful memories of Carmen. Now these gruesome nightmares of her sister began tormenting her waking hours.

Why now? Carmen had died a year ago.

Maria had done some investigating. The answers didn't

please her, but she no longer had a choice. Her father would indulge her demand. He had to.

If possible, she sat even straighter in the deep-cushioned bamboo chair and continued speaking, determined to have him agree before she lost her cool and started raising her voice.

"My doctor insists that a promising antidote for retrograde amnesia is to return to the place where it began. I would like to take the *Honora* back to the Abacos."

She spared a glance at Del Rio and smirked at the alarm in his eyes before continuing. "However, Poppa, I wanted to be sure you still had confidence in your captain, since the *Honora* is collecting barnacles at the dock."

Del Rio's hand stopped in midair. He opened that captivating mouth of his to speak, then frowned, changing his mind. Maria didn't miss the quelling look Poppa sent his way.

She'd learned from her father that Daniel Murphy Del Rio was talented and fearless at the helm. Yet, since she'd become aware of him, he hadn't taken the *Honora* out at all. The few times she'd questioned Poppa, he'd waved away her concern. Anytime she asked Del Rio, he merely said that Elias—her father—had no desire to go anywhere. There was no denying she had hit a raw nerve with the ship captain. His focus straight ahead, he tore the roll into small pieces and chewed them one after the other, without taking the time to add butter, even though he had already placed some on his plate.

Good. Poppa had a bad habit of treating hired help like family. It was understandable with good employees like their butler Eduardo, who had been around for years, but Del Rio was way too new to Reefside for her father to give him such honors.

At least he was too new for Maria. Poppa said Del Rio

was the son of his business partner, and now like a son to him, but Maria continued to relegate him to employee status. She simply could not remember him and didn't like the way he did little other than reside at Reefside and shadow Poppa.

She also didn't like the physical attraction she felt toward him. Something about him intimidated her. She'd mentioned this to Poppa and he'd quelled her concerns with amusement. She had to trust her father's judgment, as she couldn't trust her own since her memory loss. However, she could mentally shelve the man where he belonged: on the *Honora*.

Del Rio was not among the earlier memories that had returned after the accident. She'd remembered Poppa. Momma. Carmen. Eduardo, who ran the house. It boggled her mind that Poppa was so generous with Del Rio, including him in intimate conversations that should be restricted to family.

Now that their family had dwindled to just her and Poppa, she had no room for Del Rio. That was a fact. With his ultrahot body, wavy hair, deceptively charming Irish looks and easy smile, she found it even more important to ignore him. When she could not, she found fault. Sadly, she couldn't imagine why. He had been nothing but kind to her.

Elias Santiago adjusted himself in his wheelchair, his dark gaze sliding from Del Rio to her. "*Querida,* I do not think this is such a good undertaking. You may look like an adventurous, gypsy princess in your beautiful dress, but now you sound like one. I do not want you wandering away from me."

"You should have no worries, Poppa. My memory may be gone, but I still conduct myself well in public."

What she couldn't say was that she refused to go

through another day of nightmares. Afraid to go to Carmen's bedroom for fear that her twin would appear as she did in Maria's sleep: angry. Distorted. Lunging for her with fangs and claws until the two of them hurtled over the balcony into a dark, foul-smelling abyss and Maria's screams jolted her awake....

She was exhausted. She needed answers.

Calming her thoughts, she summoned all her willpower to keep a smooth, even tone when she spoke. She had to know why Carmen was haunting her.

"Besides, I'm not wandering, Poppa. I'm focused on a goal—going back to the scene of the accident. My memory is missing, but I hope that will change with this trip."

Elias's raven eyebrows slashed into a frown. Planting both hands on the table to emphasize his lack of mobility, he said, "But I am unable to accompany you."

"Which is why I must go now, Poppa. I want to be well quickly, so that I can be here to help you."

"I suggest you fly over." Del Rio's soothing voice invaded the conversation. "Take your doctor. You'll be there in forty-five minutes and can hire a boat."

She turned to meet his challenge. "What? You don't want to work, Del Rio?"

His laugh sounded mirthless. "Not any longer, Princess."

"*Hijos,* stop!" Poppa's concern drew her attention from Del Rio's challenging blue eyes.

"*We* are not your children, Poppa."

"I think Elias means *we* are acting like children," Del Rio answered.

Eduardo arrived with their main course. Maria waited for everyone to be served before lobbying for her cause once more.

"Please, Poppa. This sail is vital. I have asked you for nothing else these past months."

Elias put down his fork. "And why not? Because you stay locked in your studio, day after day."

She winced as the accusation hit home. She'd been afraid of the darkness that shrouded her thoughts since awakening in the hospital. Not knowing answers to questions or recognizing people she should know sent her scrambling for solitude. If she were alone, she couldn't make any social blunders or look as foolish and frightened as she felt.

Also, the devastation of learning that Momma and Carmen had perished in the accident that robbed her memory had left a hole in her so deep she didn't think she could ever climb out. She'd behaved cowardly, immersing herself in her misery, leaving Poppa to mourn alone.

She soon discovered her best escape was her art, which seemed to be selling faster than she could create it. But now, even that could not distract her. Matters had gotten out of hand. Reefside, a private estate in the heart of Fort Lauderdale's metropolis, had become too quiet. In this beachside oasis her nightmares had become more frightening than ever. It was time to heal, especially with Poppa becoming weaker with diabetes. She had precious little time to waste, no matter how daunting this self-imposed task might seem. Poppa needed her. She was all he had left.

By some odd quirk of fate, she had decided that having Del Rio take her to the Abacos in the Bahamas on her father's ship was the answer. The doctor said retracing the steps up to the accident could jar her memory. Yet, something about Del Rio chafed at her. No doubt it was his bond with Poppa. Why else would the darkness in her mind rise fast, practically buzzing through her head, whenever she was in Del Rio's presence? She needed to conquer that silly sensation, as well.

Besides, Poppa said Del Rio was the finest sailor he'd ever known. Coming from Elias Santiago, that was high praise. Sailing on the *Honora* would get them to the Abacos fast enough while giving her time to adjust to the possibility of regaining her memory, of recovering all the details she suspected were so painful she'd blocked them. Here lay her dilemma. She wanted answers, but was unsure if she could handle them in one windfall. The *Honora* would carry her to her destination fast enough while giving her time to accept what she would learn. It was time to discover the facts behind her mother's and sister's deaths. It was time to embrace her life in its entirety and stop merely existing.

She raised her chin a notch higher. "I am out of my studio now, am I not?" She shook her head. "I have wasted too much time. I am ready to fight this black monster in my mind. Permit me use of the *Honora,* although God knows the thought of stepping on a ship again makes my knees quake."

Elias frowned. "Then you must not go."

"No, Poppa, you are wrong." Her voice dropped in desperation. She fought to keep the tears and the tremor from her words. "I can no longer live not knowing. Nothing will stop me."

Elias was a bear of a man whom few people crossed. His disease had ruined the joints in his ankles, yet his imposing frame continued to belie his useless legs. A silver mane of hair softened his dark, noble Latino looks. He wore his usual linen shirt and pants, white cotton socks to keep his swollen feet warm, even in the balmy, tropical evening. Elias still enjoyed good days, despite his wheelchair, but Maria had observed the signs of distress that seemed to occur more frequently. Besides her own over-whelming need to reclaim peace from these nightmares, she wanted to regain her memory so that she would be prepared for Poppa when he needed her. His blustering would do little to dissuade her.

Del Rio stood in the silence that had fallen, his plate untouched. He bowed slightly toward Maria, his spicy-warm, masculine scent filling her senses, before focusing his attention on Elias. "I cannot listen to this discussion. I seem to have lost my appetite. If you will excuse me."

Maria looked straight ahead, refusing to watch the man's exit. Del Rio might be thinking that his leaving could sway Poppa to deny her wishes, but she knew better. His absence would improve her chances to persuade her father of her plan. Elias added a splash of wine to his glass, which the doctor had forbidden.

She lifted her own glass. As he filled it, she offered Poppa an amused look. "Now that we are alone, I can ex-plain myself more freely, Poppa. Here's why I must leave as soon as possible…"

DANIEL STOOD IN THE TROPICAL morning sun, his world crashing around him like the surf hitting the beach stretch-ing behind the villa.

He stared dumbfounded at Elias, this man who was like a second father to him while growing up, and now, since his parents' death six years ago, his only father. Heat seared his back through his T-shirt as if exaggerating the hotbed from which neither he nor Elias had managed to extract themselves last night.

"Don't ask me to do this, Elias. Not when you know I've decided to leave."

Elias's request—or should he say, demand—to take the reclusive Maria to the Bahamas was tantamount to emotional suicide for Daniel. He'd waited around patiently this past year out of sheer love, letting his career slide in an attempt to recapture something that he'd finally come to terms with as irretrievable.

No way would Daniel comply.

The set of the older man's face made his intentions clear. This lion of industry might be restricted to a wheelchair, but confinement did little to curb his will. Elias Santiago hadn't built his empire by backing down.

"I know you've made plans for Australia, Daniel. Please. Give me three more weeks."

"No. I would have said so last night. You know it's already been a year of hell."

Daniel needed closure. He needed to get away. Staying dockside aboard the *Honora* with his life on hold had eaten away at him like rats gnawing dock lines. Aware that Maria's studio balcony shadowed the patio behind them, he lowered his voice. "I have already waited too long. Maria doesn't remember. I have no reason to stay."

Seated at his table beneath an umbrella as he was every morning, cleanly shaved, wearing his crisp linen shirt and pants, his silver hair smoothed back and a pot of coffee steaming beside him, Elias spoke to Daniel as if he was holding a board meeting. The only difference was that his nurse, in her starched white uniform and sturdy shoes, sat beneath the shade of another umbrella, focused on a Heather Graham novel.

Unwavering, Elias held his gaze. "I think you are afraid."

There was that, as much as it chafed him to admit it. Daniel had avoided sailing the *Honora* all these months for a reason. Self-doubt had stolen his confidence despite a notoriety for racing mile upon mile on the open ocean. He'd become so balled up after the accident that he hardly knew himself. He'd lost his love of the water and the love of his life with the simple turn of a boat's wheel.

Since he had no control over his fate with the woman he loved, he'd decided to climb aboard another love and reclaim his power over the sea. Leaving for the Australian races had twin purposes. First, to get his sea legs acclimated once more, and second, to take him far, far away from Reefside and Maria.

Maria. She deserved the chance to reclaim her memory. This, he understood. But if he took her back to the islands, to the place where the boats crashed, and triggered her memory, would the most powerful love he'd ever experienced truly and finally end?

He ran a hand through his hair in exasperation. The old man wasn't thinking straight. "I'll be damned if I hurt her, Elias. Hire someone else if she's so pigheaded about going."

A knowing grin crossed the older man's face. "Ah, love."

"Don't taunt me, old man."

"You'll sail, Daniel. Tomorrow. You don't have to tell Maria anything. Actually, I would prefer if you did not. Let her find her way. You'll grant an ailing man this one wish."

"How can you ask me to do this?"

Elias waved a swarthy, veined hand. "I know you, Daniel. Don't let the dead kill the love you had. Take this one last chance and do as Maria asks."

"Did she ask for me to take her?"

A dusky voice answered from the balcony above. "Of course, I did. You should do something to earn the money my father has been wasting on your salary."

Daniel's back tightened at her insult. Refusing to respond, he held Elias's gaze as if to say, *See? It won't work.*

He'd never adjusted to Maria's critical, or worse, ambivalent, comments since the accident. In the beginning, Elias and the doctors wanted to give her time to heal from her trauma and instructed Daniel to remain silent about their relationship. His heart had ripped a bit more each day that Maria remembered nothing about him—about *them*—since the collision.

As the year wore on, he had lost hope of regaining her love, and she had become less and less tolerant of his relationship with Elias. It wasn't until a few short weeks ago that he became truly honest with himself. His desire to win her back had died. Her ambivalence was the gun that had killed it. She'd pulled the trigger too many times.

Maria had made it clear that she didn't believe her father should be so generous with the hired help. Ironically, it seemed Elias was depending on the "hired help" to take this last step to let his precious daughter regain her memory. Daniel had become a pawn in a chess match he was certain to lose.

Elias chuckled. "Late though she may be to our discussion, she has a point."

Daniel looked at Maria standing above him in the yellow, paint-stained sundress she wore when working: her black hair caught at her nape, her dark bedroom eyes assessing him as a mere mortal. The muscles in his neck tightened under her gaze as he realized this exotic, exciting woman no longer did so much as bat an eyelash in his direction. He could not stay another day—heck, another minute—being so close, yet oceans away from her.

Daniel threw up his hands. "You both have lost your minds."

"Captain." She captured his attention with that one word. She leaned over the balcony, unaware of the enticing view of her neckline she offered. "I will, indeed, lose my mind if I don't restore my memory once and for all."

The laserlike intensity in her eyes reflected the torment haunting her. Darkness, she called it, from loss of memory. Daniel knew it encompassed more: the loss of a cherished twin, a mother, a life of possibilities with him of which she remained totally unaware.

He wanted to pull her into his arms and promise her he could take away the pain, if not for her sake, then for his own. She wouldn't be in this state if it wasn't for him. But when she finally did learn the truth, she would never want to see him again, anyway. So why honor her request?

Perhaps he should agree to this suicide mission because he could finally end this fiasco. He'd already made other plans because he couldn't handle another day spent smoldering with the memory of her touch, her taste, her love, all the while pretending he'd never known her.

Maybe that had been his mistake from the start.

"So, you think your doctor's suggestion will jar your memory?" His question was laced with sarcasm.

She pulled a thin, ash-wood paintbrush from her haphazard bun of ebony hair. The motion ignited a powerful urge to run his hands through the heavy satin strands falling down her back. She pointed the tip of the brush at him, her dark eyes intent on her decision.

"Quite honestly, Captain, I could care less about your opinion. I'd like to leave tomorrow. I have already begun packing."

Daniel shrugged. "You must not have heard that my employment with your father has ended. You'll have to find another captain."

"Daniel."

Elias's objection vibrated right through him. Daniel closed his eyes for one blessed moment to enjoy the strength of his declaration, because his cause had been lost the moment he heard the desperation in Maria's haughty words.

Damn it all. They had shared the kind of love a person didn't find often. He really should try one last time to win her back, and yet, if there was no reaching her, he also wanted freedom from the memories. When Carmen died in the accident, it was as if her mean spirit had inhabited his sweet, affectionate Maria, erasing any trace of the woman he had loved more than life.

"Daniel, my son." Elias's voice dropped to a whisper. "In this terrible accident I have lost a wife and a daughter. Will you not honor me by taking this last chance?"

Daniel's blood grew hot. "You mean as penance for not stopping the thunder boat from ramming the skiff in the first place?"

Elias glanced toward the balcony, determined that Maria not hear their words. "I mean no such thing."

"Then why do you insist that I take her?"

The older man's gaze softened. He reached out a hand, letting it settle, palm down, on the glass table. "You think I do not know how you suffer, as well?"

"It's in the past."

"Nonsense. You breathe every moment of that accident, every day. I see it in your face when you think no one is watching."

Like a falling ax, the truth cleaved his emotions. He had decided to leave because he could not—no, would not—suffer this constant turmoil any longer. Either Maria loved him, or she did not. As of today, she did not. A year was a long time to torture a man.

"Then let the past die, Elias." Daniel ground out his quiet words. "I will return in six   onths to check on you both."

Elias pounded the table with his hand. "You do not run out on family."

He knew, without looking, that Maria had descended the balcony stairs to the patio. He heard the silent padding of her bare feet, felt her body heat. He crossed his arms, watching Elias's gaze warm as she approached. He didn't have to see to know she moved like a siren walking on air.

"So, *querida,* you join us for breakfast?"

She passed Daniel to kiss her father's cheek. "I couldn't work with you two arguing. I want to join this conversation."

Daniel's senses swelled with the citrusy scent clinging to her skin. The stains on her sundress reflected bright oil paint from canvases already finished and sold. The thin straps of the dress threatened to slide off her tanned shoulders, and his hand itched to push them farther down that soft skin with a finger.

He swallowed hard when she turned, her dark eyes grazing him with that curious but unfamiliar gaze that tore at his heart. Right now, losing her seemed like a life sentence. She and her stubborn father, more precious to him than anything in the world, were asking him to do something that would destroy everything he'd spent the past year trying to preserve.

He might be planning to move on with his life, but Elias and Maria Santiago were family. Nothing tied Daniel to the land like Reefside, the only home he now knew, and its inhabitants.

Before the disaster, Daniel and Maria had built dreams for their future. She would create canvases of international renown, while he raced closer to world cup status. When he had asked her to marry him, she had said yes, and compounded her acceptance with the sweetness of her body. That memory alone practically drove him to madness.

They had decided to make a home at Reefside, with Elias. Maria's father had shared their dreams. Blessed them. Then, their world shattered on one gorgeous, sun-filled afternoon, the aftermath of which still lingered today.

Since the accident, Daniel could not bring himself to sail. Meanwhile, Maria's career flourished, while she remained blissfully unaware that Daniel languished.

Daniel had doggedly followed every rule Elias and the doctors had set for helping Maria regain her memory. They had wanted him to go slowly—not upset her by trying to make her remember they were lovers. If she could not recall her previous life, anxiety might drive her deeper into herself. But their rules had fallen short. In a year, Maria had not remembered him. At all.

Now, with Elias's demand that he take her back to the Abacos, Daniel was terrified of what might happen if she did remember—out there. In Little Harbour. Not in the safety of her home.

If he were to agree to this mission, it would be out of kindness. He'd already told himself the two of them were finished. He'd welcome time alone with Maria. Taking her away was the right choice, but not to the Abacos. His throat tightened, making it hard to breathe. He shot Maria an impatient look that would have sent a lesser woman fleeing.

If Maria sensed his distress, she ignored it.

"Poppa offers you respect as a family member. Yet, you treat his gesture lightly." She laid a hand on her father's shoulder. "I told you, Poppa. He's playing you for a fool."

The only fool here is me, Daniel thought, *for wasting an entire year trying to reach her.* This was one insult he would not ignore. "You have no idea how wrong you are, Princess."

Her dark eyes snapped to attention. Her full lips compressed into a hard line. "How could I possibly know anything other than what I hear? And do *not* call me *Princess*."

Damn if his jaw didn't tighten so hard his back teeth hurt. He thumbed in the direction of the yacht docked on the Intracoastal side of the estate and asked her a question he didn't need answered, if only to reclaim some control over this situation. "Well then, tell me this...Maria. Do you even like to sail?"

He immediately regretted the confusion that clouded her eyes. She visibly struggled with his question until her resolve steeled. "There is only one way to know, Captain. Poppa says you are the best of the best, yet you've stayed landside for months. Would you dare take the *Honora* off shore to find your answer?"

Oh, he wanted the chance to find out, all right. A chance to woo her. Seduce her. Win her back. But on the *Honora*...where it all began? No way could she be aware of this one dangerous fact.

In his role as captain of the sloop he loved, he would be creating a facade that didn't exist on the last journey, almost a year ago to the date. As far as Maria knew, Daniel was hired help. Anonymous. Indifferent. Yet how long could he remain that way? Despite its fifty-foot waterline, the *Honora* would be tight quarters for the chemistry they still seemed to share.

Deep inside, he longed to be alone with her. To calm her, explain things to her. He believed she felt their bond, even though she ignored him. Dare he test her limits at sea? Away from Elias? Away from empty rooms that were once her mother's and her sister's? Should he try, one more time, to see if their love was strong enough to overcome the trauma of retrograde amnesia?

The chance to win her back, as a stranger, was cowardly, no matter how appealing. He'd be better off pursuing his new plans, away from Maria, especially with her in such a volatile, emotional state of mind.

She was out of reach now, but if she remembered the accident without the right people around her to help her understand? Then, for sure, she would be lost to him. He'd be better off leaving for Australia and starting a new life. If, in time, her memory returned and she was willing to forgive him, they could at least remain friends.

Sailing away with her tomorrow would simply make a bad situation intolerable. He should move on. After all, had she died in the accident, like the others, he would have had to start over. Her love would have remained an ache deep in his being—one he'd learn to live with. There wouldn't be much difference between that sad acceptance and the way he felt now at the lack of recognition that pooled in her eyes when she gazed at him.

Damn it all. While his heart tugged at him to take her away and make one last try, his mind demanded he run as fast as he could.

Elias watched him with hawklike calm. Daniel might fool Maria, but the older man knew. He recognized the depth of Daniel's love for his daughter. Elias had urged Daniel to overcome his fear of his own abilities to command a vessel.

Daniel met his gaze, silently pleading that this interview end. He needed to commit to the races in Australia. Winning was critical to cement himself in the sailing arena. The sponsorship calls and advertising contracts wouldn't be coming in forever. He only had a small window of time here to get back on track. Daniel had spent too many months wrestling with the guilt that had tied him to Reefside, day in and day out, and the need to ensure Elias and Maria fared well.

A sigh escaped his lips. Why the hell was he arguing with himself, anyway? Elias's look said it all. Daniel had no choice but to right the wrong that had begun with him. It was his fate to be ground zero when Maria exploded back to life. It just had never occurred to him, or Elias, that she would request to sail back to the place where it all began.

Daniel needed time to think.

"I have errands to do. I'll answer you in an hour."

He didn't even look back when Elias called out, "Be sure there is storage on the *Honora* for Maria's canvases."

CHAPTER TWO

AGAINST HER DECISION not to heed Del Rio at all, Maria watched his angry stride, infuriated at his rudeness. He had her full attention as he headed into the tropical overhang leading around the villa. His unwillingness to help confounded her. After refusing his attempts at conversation with her all these months, she finally needed him and he was dodging her.

It made no sense.

She'd avoided him most of this past year because a wave of anxiety would hit whenever he came around, rattling her right down to the bone. Then, his soothing, deep voice with its touch of laughter would lull and excite her at the same time. His concerned glances, as if he expected her to ask him a question at any moment, had left her feeling inadequate and foolish.

Recently, however, she'd felt differently. It occurred to her that her subconscious was prodding her. Perhaps Del Rio knew the answers to her questions. Instinct said that he was her ticket to regaining her memory, and every ounce of her being knew this to be true. If only she could calm down enough around him to stop being such a shrew, he might be inclined to help her.

The clang of iron from the side gate heralded his exit. She dropped into the seat across from Elias, aware her father watched her. Perhaps he was reassessing the wisdom of letting her leave. It didn't matter. She had to make this voyage. Nothing was going to stop her from retracing that trip to Little Harbour—unless Poppa was ill.

"You're angry with me," she said.

Elias shook his head, his rheumy brown gaze filled with intention. "No, *mi querida.* It hurts me to see what is left of our beautiful family quarreling."

"Del Rio is not family. He acts as if you and I belong hidden away like a couple of loony tunes in an asylum."

He gave her an indulgent smile. "You simply do not remember, Maria."

Her breath caught in her throat. Yes. Poppa was right. While a niggling thought teased that she knew Del Rio, he remained an enigma. That his family had been tied to hers for so many years made her wonder why she could remember nothing of this South American.

Yet, something about him disquieted her. Poppa had said Del Rio's mother was beautiful, his father a lifelong business partner. Elias had laughed, insisting that Del Rio had inherited his Irish father's renegade looks, while his blue eyes reflected the deep current of his mother's Chilean soul. Del Rio must have held a strong affection for his mother and her Chilean roots, because he used her last name more often than his surname. The man certainly showed a respect for family that Poppa more than once had openly admired.

Her father could keep his poetic musings to himself.

"I am so tired of not remembering, Poppa." Her tremulous words surprised her.

Elias turned his wheelchair to face her. With a slow shake of his head he said, "My beautiful Maria. You have been lost in your hideaway upstairs for too long. I am glad you have found strength to seek the answers you want. If it was in my power to accompany you, I would."

Her chest tightened with love for her father. She stood.

"Thank you, Poppa. You know I hate to leave you. I will be back as soon as possible."

Yes, Del Rio could go to the devil if he did not agree to take her to Little Harbour. It was as simple as that. She pressed her cheek to her father's, relishing the warmth, inhaling the familiar, soapy smell of his shaving lotion. Familiar scents had been triggers for her memory, and Poppa's was one of the first to bring her around. "I love you, Poppa. I trust you will ensure your captain cooperates."

He patted her back. "Have Enrique bring your things to the *Honora*."

Ascending her steps to the studio, Maria pushed thoughts of Del Rio away. A commissioned piece needed to be completed before morning. The easel holding a painting half her size stood by the open French doors to capture as much tropical light as possible.

She reclaimed her seat on the wooden stool splattered with various colors of dried paint. Her gaze rested on her current work, which a socialite from her mother's International Women's group had asked her to paint. The woman wanted the view from her Islamorada home to be painted like a dream.

Maria usually created only what arose in her imagination, but since this woman had been a friend of Momma's and offered to pay an outrageous price, Maria had accepted. She had laughed out loud when she saw the photo from which she would work. Living in the Florida Keys *was* like living a dream. Lately, daydreams came easily to Maria. Anything that promised escape—the slow burst of sunrise, birds flying over the sea, this photo of the view of Florida Bay from her client's window, all set her paintbrushes in motion. She'd created a technique of blending colors and images that left the viewer mesmerized and contemplative, just as the perfect dream might do. This commission had been simple to create.

Maria still couldn't believe that complete strangers sought out and paid huge sums for these canvases splayed with the surreal joys, sorrows and regrets of her soul that words could not describe. Heaven knew, even her nightmares made excellent subjects and sold fastest.

She marveled at the encouragement she received from art critics for indulging this exquisite escape from reality. Yet now, only reality stared back from the canvas in the form of Del Rio's face. He had mocked her when he asked her if she even liked to sail. He knew the answer. She didn't. And her inability to remember shook her to the core.

It was like being surrounded in complete gloom with no walls, no floor, no sound. No matter how much she reached out, how often she felt for footing, how hard she listened, nothing came. Only darkness. A darkness that spawned nightmares.

She had no memory of the accident; Poppa had told her about it. The only proof was the concussion, cuts and bruises she had sustained. Awakening in a hospital bed and not even knowing her own name had been terrifying. Elias was the one who'd rekindled her memory. By holding her hand and singing songs from her childhood, he had reached her.

Del Rio had been with Elias at the hospital. He had stood behind Poppa to support him. The two men had a bond. She remembered this fact. She also remembered her stunning twin, and their dark, elegant Latina mother, Rosalinda. When Maria and Carmen were young, their mother used to tease that no one could tell the twins apart. Maria remembered Elias saying he would always know the difference.

But what of Del Rio? He remained in her mind like Elias's shadow. Her father would have to reeducate her about his family, his past. Elias had said Del Rio was like a son to him, but Maria couldn't even bring herself to speak his first name.

Why?

The man was easy on the eyes. In fact, he was downright handsome. She didn't like the pull her body felt toward him when he was around. Somehow she'd managed to ignore him. If she kept treating him as an employee, she didn't have to consider the possibility that he might be more to her family. Because if he was simply the *Honora's* alluring captain, then Elias indulged him far more than necessary. And why would this distress her?

Shame tugged at her heart. She knew why, and was loath to admit it. Jealousy. As children, Carmen had been Poppa's favorite. Maria never quite minded because Carmen was irresistible, always quick to laugh and get into mischief. Maria had always been the "quiet" one of the two, so she was used to handing over the spotlight to her twin. Elias had indulged Carmen and Rosalinda equally because their personalities were so similar.

People used to joke that Carmen and Momma should have been the twins, not Maria and Carmen. The two were inseparable. Maria had felt like a spectator at their party, but she hadn't minded. Someone had to provide an audience for their antics.

Now, with Carmen gone, Del Rio had taken over that coveted spot in Elias's attention. If she were totally honest, Maria had been jealous of the love Elias poured on Carmen and their mother. He was always less enthusiastic—perhaps she'd call it softer—toward her. Did a vile part of her now hope that as the remaining child she would take first place in Poppa's eyes? Did she resent that Del Rio had filled that void instead of her?

Hurt squeezed her heart. Was she that shallow? She released the breath she'd been holding. No. Not shallow. Needy. Her amnesia had driven her into isolation. She felt so very alone in her darkness and had become a recluse. Painting day in and day out. Sometimes sleeping in her clothes.

She'd turned away lunch dates, since most of her friends were Carmen's and spoke only of her, deepening Maria's loss. She stopped attending gallery showings. Refused interviews. Her world had narrowed down to Reefside. This art studio. The silly monkeys in the banyans outside her front window. And Poppa.

With diabetes weakening her father each day, she worried that she'd made a hasty decision to leave him. Yet Poppa's longtime family physician said now was the perfect time to go.

She had to stop second-guessing her decision. It stressed her too much. Inhaling a deep, cleansing breath, she turned her focus on the canvas. By the time she lifted her brush, Poppa, the heart-stopping Daniel Murphy Del Rio and the world outside her balcony had vanished.

SHADOWS FELL ON THE PATIO as the sun climbed into the late-afternoon sky. Daniel took the last step up to Maria's balcony, enchanted, as always, by the Bohemian feel of her studio.

A chaise lounge scattered with turquoise pillows faced the ocean. Terra-cotta pots overflowing with flowers lined the marble balustrade. Sheer curtains inside the open doors fluttered easily in the onshore breeze, beckoning him to enter.

His eyes rested on the lounge chair and his heart started

knocking around his chest. Once upon a time, he and Maria had made good use of that chair on many a summer night. The last time, she had agreed to marry him. It had been a year since he'd been up here. He steeled himself as he stepped across the balcony. Once Maria realized he was present, she would ignore him and it was going to do damage to his already tormented heart.

That's how it was between them now. That's why he should be hightailing it to Brisbane.

She sat just inside the doors, her back to him. The clear acrylic palette splashed with colors lay nestled in the crook of her tanned arm as she leaned toward her work. She'd twisted her hair into a knot again, catching it with an extra paintbrush.

The brush in her left hand flitted across the canvas like a lively bird. Her sundress hugged the slender curves of her body—a body now off-limits to him. The soft cotton falling in waves against the chair gave way to a smooth length of shapely leg and bare feet entwined at the ankle. Damn. She even had white paint smeared across the top of her foot.

The scent of linseed oil and paint mingled with the sea air. The subtle incense of her perfume wafted across his senses like needed oxygen. This…this was the Maria he loved. This was the woman who had stolen his heart; not the frightened, angry woman who now inhabited her skin.

He watched a moment longer, unable to resist. Her artwork, vibrant and warm like her voice when she spoke to anyone other than him, lit the canvas like seductive fingers reaching to touch his aching heart. He lounged casually against the doorjamb if only to counteract every straining nerve in his body. Without a doubt, her eyes would flash with annoyance when she finally acknowledged his presence.

He wouldn't even flinch.

He resisted the urge to laugh out loud at the irony. Maria could not even remember why she avoided him. Nor did she remember she once loved him like a woman on fire.

Damn himself for agreeing. He'd decided to give Elias—and Maria—only three weeks. Would he be able to spend that much time alone with her without shooting off his mouth about what they had meant to each other and ruining everything?

He cleared his throat. "Maria."

Her paintbrush stopped moving, but she didn't turn her head. "I'm busy."

He shoved his hands into the pockets of his jeans rather than reach for her and demand she look at him.

"We have to talk."

She slapped the brush down, her concentration lost. "I think not, unless you have a question about tomorrow's sail."

Daniel waited until she turned to look at him, the defensiveness in her glance nerve-racking.

"My only question is whether you're sure this trip is something you want to do."

She opened her mouth to speak then hesitated. "Dr. Hernandez assures me Poppa is strong. Now is the best time to go."

"There's that, of course. I was thinking more along the lines of what you are looking for."

She tilted her head as if gauging his question. "Like will I fall apart if I don't remember anything?"

"Or more like, will you be able to hold it together if you *do* remember?"

With an impatient flick of her wrist, she dabbed the

brush in a jar of linseed oil before wiping it with a square of white towel streaked with colors.

"Oh, please. I think you are sidestepping the real question."

"Which is?"

She appraised him over her shoulder. "Are you reliable enough to take me across the Gulf Stream?"

Oh. Low blow, Maria. A comment like that makes me wonder why I'm even bothering. My *Maria was more careful with her words.*

Daniel inhaled a huge breath, his mind racing with retorts, but he held them back. He wouldn't let her get under his skin so fast, especially with that satisfied smirk on her gorgeous lips. "What, exactly, do you mean, Maria?"

Maria shrugged one shoulder, the gesture sexy as hell. "Poppa said you're a world-class sailor. Seems more to me like you've been hiding on his yacht."

Low blow number two. He stepped across the threshold, planting his feet firmly on the wide-planked flooring. His throat tightened with the urge to shout, *we never spoke like this to each other before Carmen came between us,* but instead, he shot a volley back, aiming straight for her heart.

He gestured to the room. "I could say the same for you in your studio, my dear. When was the last time you left Reefside?"

She swung on him. "Well, at least I'm taking my future into my hands. I'm willing to change my situation."

He leaned toward her. "I *had* made plans, my dear. I'm supposed to leave for Australia this weekend."

She pointed a finger, color rising in her cheeks. "You owe me this trip."

If she'd slapped him, she'd have elicited the same response. Suspicion furrowed his brow. He resisted pressing a hand to relieve the pressure. Had Elias betrayed his secret? He cleared his throat before he dared ask, "And just how is it that I owe you, Princess?"

She unhinged the painting from the easel, carrying it to the drying wall, then turned to face him.

"You've been lounging around Reefside on my father's dime for way too long. You owe it to him to postpone your plans and earn the salary you've collected by taking me."

Relief was so immediate, he almost laughed. He'd come up to tell her he'd agreed to take her, but seeing her at work had, once again, thrown him off balance. And here she thought his reluctance was about money. If she only knew.

Damn.

He tried to stare her down, but she wouldn't look away. He held up a hand in surrender. "Okay. Elias asked for three weeks. That's all you get. I'll leave for Australia when we return."

Did she flinch at the mention of his departure? Now, wouldn't that be something?

He took another step into the room. "Do you understand me, Princess?"

She retraced her steps to stand before him, hands on hips. He almost grinned at that stubborn, familiar I'll-argue-till-you-kiss-me-into-submission look. *Oh, yeah, Princess, give me a reason to reach for you.* He was nuts to think he'd make this trip unscathed.

Her pointed finger came within inches of his chest. He wondered if she dared not touch him for fear of where it would lead. Her nostrils flared in that ever-so-enticing way. "*Never* call me Princess, Del Rio. Just get me to Little Harbour as fast as you can."

DANIEL STOWED THE LAST of Maria's gear and climbed into the cockpit, wanting badly to break something. Elias's

words, *You don't run out on family*, prodded him like a
pitchfork. Family. What remained of his family was here
at Reefside. Yet living with Maria's emotional absence and
physical presence made this last task seem futile.

Even worse were the last words she'd fired at him
before the accident. Despite the exquisite love that bonded
them, she had chosen to mistrust him. The look in her eyes
when her accusations flew had branded his soul forever.
He had been so busy these past months, working with
Elias to restore Maria's memory, that he hadn't taken the
time to sift through his own emotions from that fateful
day.

Now they whipped around his head like a hurricane. If
he was successful in helping Maria restore her memory,
and *if* all became resolved between them, could he be safe
in her love, knowing she'd turned from him once before?

Grabbing a polishing cloth, he settled for wiping down
the pristine instrument panel at the helm one more time. If
they weren't scheduled to set sail in minutes, he'd guzzle
a beer. Hell, he might anyway. His mouth was drier than
the Tortugas.

Yanking open the door of the cockpit refrigerator, he
pulled out a bottle of water. He swigged a huge gulp, glaring down the waterway leading to the ocean but seeing
nothing.

A haze of guilt clouded his vision.

How could Elias expect him—trust him for God's
sake—to take Maria back to where all the trouble began?
He and the old man knew the story. They had a deal. Now
Elias had imposed his will, knowing Daniel could not
refuse Maria. Elias was breaking the promise he'd made
like some deity tossing a mere mortal from the clouds.
And Daniel had agreed. He would do it as a favor…but for
whom? Did he still harbor the hope of winning her back?

He slapped his forehead. What the devil was wrong with him? He was about to spend one long, sweet sail alone with her. Like a maiden voyage for both of them. A lot of ground could be covered in twenty-one days. This could be the opportunity he'd been waiting for. Seducing Maria could be a goddamn dream come true, if he could allow himself to trust her love once more. Quite an irony, since he'd spent a year ignoring the possibility that he might not want her love anymore. Up to this point, all he wanted was to have her wake up and remember him. Now he wondered what good it would do if she did.

The *Honora* would be a hotbed of emotions for him no matter what happened. If Maria were to fall in love with him once more, even without regaining her memory, he could seize the opportunity to teach her what they'd once shared. Best-case scenario was that she would remember the accident and still find her way to understand the truth—what really happened before the collision—and forgive Daniel. Then, their love might grow roots so deep, no one would ever be able to shake them apart.

But before he could claim her love again two things were needed: honesty and redemption. There had been no sign of either, but that could also have been because the opportunity had not arisen. Well, here he was, ready and waiting. The only woman who could bring about either possibility was Maria, and she didn't have a clue.

He had been shocked when his hands shook as he started the engine. Acknowledging the tension he felt leaving the dock was hard. No matter what the courts had said. No matter what he knew had happened on that boat, he had been responsible for the accident. He was a licensed captain. His lack of control had caused the death of two women.

Granted, he knew the mechanics of operating a vessel.

He understood the wind, the tides, could read the skies, understood navigation laws, but witnessing those broken bodies and the destruction of lives after the fact had crippled Daniel's faith in his abilities.

Who was he kidding? He needed healing as much as Maria. That one truth he would give to Elias. The older man, better than anyone, understood why Daniel had remained marooned at Reefside while Maria continued to dodge him. Sometimes he wondered if what was precious between them had been destroyed when she doubted his love at the worst possible moment before the collision.

No matter. What was done was done. Her world had been stripped bare. He had lost confidence, and her love. What a joke. Now he had to overcome his own fears in order to sail to the place where their lives had been ruined.

He hung his head, briefly closing his eyes. Sometimes, it was best leaving the dead buried. Maybe Maria was better off starting over without him; he should jump off the *Honora* and head to Australia before it was too late. After all, if one stepped beyond the point of no return, well, there simply was no return.

Did he care?

Hell yes.

Because Maria couldn't remember. It wasn't fair that he held all the cards, because he *did* remember.

A groan escaped his lips. Like it or not, he'd accepted a lose-lose situation. Screwed if she remembered. Screwed if she didn't. When all this was over, he'd head to those Brisbane races either a man redeemed, or a man doomed.

Well, his world had been ripped from him once before when his parents were killed in Chile. He understood how to live with loss. Maybe sacrificing his future with Maria was the price he'd pay for absolution.

So be it.

A motion on the green caught his eye. Maria stormed down the lawn toward the dock, her hair bouncing like a veil of midnight silk on her shoulders. Her dark, exotic eyes smoldered with a distress he could feel from where he stood, and she hadn't even spotted him yet.

"Shit. Here we go."

Her steps slowed to a cautious tread as she approached the wharf. She still hadn't noticed Daniel. Panic tightened her features as she stared at the dock.

She stopped as if an invisible wall blocked her passage. Her chest heaved in quick breaths, tightening the thin, crimson fabric of her halter top.

Daniel's gaze caressed her face then traveled slowly down her body, over the rise of her breasts, down to her waist, where an inch of tanned, flat stomach peeked out from the waistband of chino shorts. They stopped midthigh, exposing the long, tanned length of those unending legs that once knew the touch of his hand. Daniel stifled another groan as she jammed her paint-stained fists into her pockets and looked up, her eyes begging for help.

Her fear wrenched his heart. Damn his doubts. He bolted for the dock, and offered her a hand, a peace offering in more ways than one.

"Here, let me help you."

Like a finger snap, her panic disappeared. Maria raked him with her gaze, glanced at his hand and ignored it.

"Did you stow my art supplies?"

Daniel rolled his eyes, flattening his palm against his board shorts. "You bet, Princess. Your twenty tons of paints, brushes and canvases. I'm glad you thought to pack at least one bikini."

He headed back to the *Honora*. Over his shoulder he said, "Casting off in ten seconds, sweetheart."

MARIA STARED AT DEL RIO as if he spoke a foreign language. This trip had been *her* idea. Why was she so terrified? She couldn't move. Every muscle gripped her bones like a vise, refusing to yield. The sun burned hot on her head and shoulders. The monkeys laughing in the banyans around her studio called as if begging her to stay. The soft scent of grass blended with the brine of the Intracoastal as land feuded with water in her mind. Just watching the yacht sway at the dock made her stomach heave.

Her blood grew cold as the familiar rumble from the center of the sloop rose on the air. Oh, God. Del Rio already had the engine running. The acrid smell of exhaust churned her anxiety. She swallowed the lump in her throat as she watched him, one hundred percent pure, bona fide male, standing at the helm.

His colorful board shorts and a small rip in the shoulder of his sun-faded blue T-shirt made him look more like a surfer than the captain of the *Honora* as he checked the instruments. Poppa had reminded her that Daniel had sailed his entire life. Won awards for racing some of the most sophisticated sailboats. Oh, he could handle a helm all right. Those tanned hands looked more than capable. She just didn't like what the sight of those strong, slender fingers did to her belly.

Damn. This was not about Del Rio. Boarding this ship was about Carmen and Momma. Enough.

With not even a glance in her direction, Del Rio jumped onto the dock and began untying the bowline. Next, he'd work his way to the spring line, the stern line, and then he'd cast off.

"Hold on, Captain. Give me a minute."

Her palms itched. Perspiration drenched her, pissing her off royally. She didn't expect this reaction and needed a moment to collect herself.

He faced her, arms open. "I have to be in Australia in three weeks. Let's shove off."

Inhaling a searing breath of earth and sea, Maria bolted forward. She didn't stop to think until she was locked in her cabin, poised over the toilet, throwing up what little toast and tea she'd managed to eat at lunch.

The engine accelerated. They'd left the dock. The forward motion of the ship had her heaving again. She flushed the toilet and sat on the floor, her cheek pressed against the closed lid. Becoming panicked and ill had not been part of her plan.

She moaned as a thought occurred: maybe she hated sailing and Del Rio knew it. Maybe *that* was what he'd tried to tell her last night.

She slammed open the toilet lid and heaved once more.

DANIEL STRAINED TO HEAR any sound from below. He'd given Maria the bow cabin, which left him hard-pressed to hear anything, even through the open hatch topside. He hoped the snug but luxurious quarters would give her a sense of security since he felt her terror right down to his bones. Until she overcame that fear, they'd get nowhere. The familiar feel of the wheel beneath his hand sent a surge of pleasure through him. He'd be careful this time. He'd do everything by the book. Yet, no matter how sleek and fast the *Honora,* and how comfortable the wheel felt in his hands once more, the passage to the Bahamas would seem endless.

For both of them.

As the *Honora* glided down the waterway, Daniel glanced back at Reefside. Elias's shock of silver hair revealed his presence on the rooftop terrace. Of course, the old man chose to witness the beginning of the end. Daniel should have known better. Loyalty to family ruled a Latin

heart. Maria had to regain her memory before any of them
could move forward.

Damn the bastard for knowing exactly what needed to
be done.

CHAPTER THREE

THE RATTLING OF ANCHOR CHAIN woke Maria. She'd managed to move from the toilet to her bunk, more a bed in the center of the forward, V-shaped cabin, and fallen into a brief, dead sleep. She barely remembered flopping onto the bed. Somewhere in her haze she'd heard the three horn blasts signaling the bridge opening. But to drop anchor now meant they hadn't entered open water. What was Del Rio thinking?

She rolled off the bed, her knees like rubber. She'd never been seasick in her life—that she could remember. And they hadn't even left the Intracoastal.

Water. She needed water.

A bottle of mouthwash perched on the sink in the head. She rinsed her parched mouth, spitting out the burning liquid.

Her reflection in the mirror said she already looked like the dead. As she splashed water on her face, the gentle hum of the engine ceased. She stopped, listening. Why were they stopping? Maybe Del Rio had a change of heart. That had to be the answer. Not good. She might be sick, but she was determined to see this journey through. She opened the medicine cabinet, grateful to find the roll of antacids. Chewing two, she headed for the deck.

The warm, salt air caressed her face, a welcome change from the air-conditioning below. Del Rio had his back to her, snapping off the cap from a Modelo Especial. He tipped the beer to his lips and didn't even turn to greet her.

"Why have you stopped?"

The Hillsboro Inlet Bridge lay off the stern, the inlet a football field's distance off the bow. The ocean blanketed the horizon in turquoise luminescence beneath the setting sun. She looked back at Del Rio, his profile to her now as he gazed across the small harbor.

He took another swig. "I thought you might want a second chance to jump ship."

Her enthusiasm for getting out to sea overrode her disquiet at his arrogance. A glistening bottle of water stood in the beverage holder. Whether for her or not, she twisted off the cap and downed half the bottle before speaking.

"I'd like to get under way, if you have no objection."

The beer bottle stopped halfway to his lips. "Oh, I have an objection."

The heat of his gaze made her pulse leap. "Why are you drinking beer when we should be sailing?"

He moved around the deck table, his intentions like a heat wave. He stood close to her, a boa constrictor measuring its prey. His skin smelled of suntan lotion, his breath a sweet mixture of barley and hops. She refused to budge, though she ached to slap his concerned, irresistible face. Instead, she drank from the water bottle.

His gaze moved to her throat as she swallowed.

"We can't sail into West End in the dark. The reefs are too dangerous."

She didn't expect this answer. "For goodness' sake, then why did we leave so soon?"

Del Rio started to say something, but the words caught in his throat. He swallowed hard then managed to smile. "I thought it was a good idea for you to adjust your sea legs before we got too far."

Something told her that was not what he wanted to say, but given her queasy stomach, he might have a point. "You're worried for my welfare?"

He held her gaze a moment too long before a sheepish grin broke. "Nah. I just don't want you puking on my teak."

Under other circumstances, she might have laughed, but right now she suspected he meant it. She placed the bottle back into the holder.

"So, now we just wait?"

Daniel nodded. "It's only a couple of hours. How about we put together some nachos, enjoy the breeze and chat?"

Suddenly, going below with Del Rio at her heels was the last thing she wanted, especially with nothing to do for hours. Why hadn't she taken the time to reason what it would be like to be alone with him on the *Honora*? Lord. It felt way more intimate that she had expected. She had been so focused on making her plans happen, that she hadn't given any thought to the notion of them being isolated together. And damn if close proximity to this man didn't set her nerve endings tingling. Now turning back was too late.

Months ago, she'd refused to feel attracted to this man, who only seemed concerned with playing shadow to Poppa while leaving her to find her own way back to sanity. Yesterday, she'd told herself that if he truly cared about her, he would have jumped at the chance to help her recover her memory. But no. Clearly, he was too self-serving, which made his physical appeal totally unfair.

She pushed past him, planting herself on a cockpit cushion, her fingers curling around the lifeline for more reasons than the ship's sway. She closed her eyes, her stomach starting to roil with the rocking.

"I'd prefer to stay in the cockpit. I need air."

He returned to the helm, sitting on the cushion inches away from her, and took another sip of Modelo. Silent, concerned, he glanced at her as if he sensed her disquiet. She didn't want his understanding right now; just his compliance. She had a task to fulfill. She didn't like the reaction her body was having to him.

A flush heated her cheeks at his nearness. "And what exactly is your schedule, *Captain*?" She couldn't help the edge in her question.

He shrugged. "To take you to Little Harbour."

Impatience snapped at her heels like a nasty dog. She wanted to be there *yesterday*. "When will we sail?"

He glanced at his watch, at the sun low in the western sky, then at her.

"After midnight. Maybe 2:00 or 3:00 a.m."

His blue eyes matched the damned glorious sky behind him, wreaking havoc with her pulse and making her want to paint an abstract of them on her soul.

Her body froze. Where did that thought come from? With only three weeks to accomplish her goal, she had no time to explore her attraction to a man who had agreed to help her only to please her father. A thought struck: perhaps Del Rio was a gold digger. Perhaps it was Reefside he was after. Maybe this rudderless ship's captain hoped to gain a home through Poppa, so he'd canceled his Australian plans to accommodate her.

Not while I live and breathe.

If that were true, then Del Rio was truly despicable. With that thought, she unceremoniously quashed any attraction she might feel for this man. He had one, and only one, purpose: take her to Little Harbour. Other than his ability to captain the *Honora,* she had no use for Daniel Murphy Del Rio.

She breathed in the sea air, feeling infinitely restored. "So what do you figure? Four days to Little Harbour?"

He compressed his lips as if calculating. Given his experience, he should know the answer, immediately.

"I estimate six, maybe seven, days."

Suspicion narrowed her eyes, and she realized she could use her sunglasses right about now. "I have a travel book, Captain. It says a yacht of this size can make the journey in three to four days."

He took another swig of beer. "That's if you hurry."

Her temper started simmering. "You know I don't want to waste any time."

"You want your memory back?"

The question seemed to upset him. She answered slowly, trying to determine his intent. "Of course. Why else would I be here?"

His gaze held hers. "Then we should retrace the same journey you originally took to get to Little Harbour."

She didn't like where this conversation was leading. "How do you know how I got there?"

He looked past her to the horizon. "You'd be surprised what I know, Princess." Frowning, he dropped his voice almost to a whisper. He leaned against the cushions and slugged the rest of his beer. "So, how about those nachos?"

"Oh, just like that, you criticize my lack of memory then ask me to wait on you? Have you lost your mind, Captain?"

Once again, here she was with no recall, while Del Rio smugly sounded like he knew all the answers. It was on the tip of her tongue to ask what, exactly, he did know, but she refrained. That would make her vulnerable and reliant on him. She hadn't been prepared for that possibility.

His job was to take her to Little Harbour. Period.

Maybe that was the problem. Maybe he didn't want to

take her to the Abacos. Because of her, his departure to Australia had been delayed another month. No time to train. No time to organize a crew. Maybe he was taunting her because he just did not want to be here. Whatever the reason, a conversation with so much volatility within the first hour was not a good way to begin a voyage.

She studied his profile. What was it about this man that made her want to keep him at arm's length, preferably like an employee? She knew he had an excellent rapport with Poppa. But with her he was an arrogant, sexy, rogue pirate with a quick laugh, whose gaze alone promised a seduction that would fulfill a woman's deepest fantasy. She was quite certain any woman would relish three weeks on a ship with this man in charge. So, why not her?

She knew the answer. This sail was for her sister and mother. It was to stop the nightmares. Unearth answers. It had nothing to do with her and Del Rio.

Although she trusted her own gut and Poppa's faith in the man's ability to get her safely to her destination, she distrusted Del Rio because she could remember nothing about him.

He had proved to be the perfect gentleman over the past year. Yet with one look from him, her insides fluttered with a vague sense of knowing him, or wanting to know him, intimately, and that terrified her. She felt as if she were walking a high-wire blindfolded. She did not want to take another step.

She stood, hoping her glare would silence him. "Nice of you to offer, but *I* am not hungry. I'm going below. Don't worry about making dinner for me."

FROM WHERE HE SAT, DANIEL could hear Maria's cabin door slam, the tremor vibrating through the ship's hull.

Yep. This was going to be one hell of a trip.

He needed to do some final soul-searching here before leaving Fort Lauderdale. He was a man who few, if any, people could tell what to do. So, he had to admit taking this trip was something he wanted. But really. Why?

His life before meeting Maria had been chaotic, thrilling, prestigious. He'd been on the cover of sailing magazines. Earned enough money to run a small country. Dated beautiful women from Buenos Aires, Santiago, Monaco. Yet, while his life had never been more full, it had never seemed so empty.

He had lost both parents in a Chilean political coup when he was a young boy and had been exiled from his home country. Elias and Rosalinda had rescued him. Daniel had discovered racing helped to heal his broken heart, and gave him a chance to fly with the wind when memories of the demons that destroyed his world returned to haunt him.

Daniel attended the best American boarding schools. After his parents' disappearance, Elias brought him home to Reefside for vacations whenever he was not racing somewhere in the world. Of course, he hardly saw Maria or Carmen in their teenage years. Rosalinda used to whisk them away to Chile or Paris during school breaks.

Daniel soon made a name for himself as a helmsman and was asked to captain corporate-sponsored boats. He loved the sea, racked up the trophies, but those distant horizons made a man eventually understand how alone he could be in the world.

While he had seen Maria's artwork in celebrity homes where he partied, the woman herself had always managed to elude him. Her twin, Carmen, was the Santiago darling, running the club circuit, often accompanied by Rosalinda. Word in the clubs was that Maria preferred the solitude of her studio to the company of others. He could understand why. The depth, colors and questions in her paintings had seduced him in a way no woman ever could. He secretly harbored the hope of seeing Maria as soon as possible at Reefside and always accepted Elias's invitations to come home.

He would never forget the first time he finally saw her. Elias had asked him to come celebrate the twins' twenty-fifth birthday. Carmen and Rosalinda were spending the morning at the spa. Daniel had just finished lunch on the patio with Elias, drinking mohitos. Elias was enjoying a cigar when Maria descended her studio stairs in a big straw hat, a braid running down her shoulder and a bikini. Her tanned, smooth skin had glistened with suntan oil, her hypnotic eyes were shielded by a pair of sunglasses, and those full sweet lips were soft natural pink. Her ocean-blue bikini looked like Neptune's mermaids had sewn the tiny strings and scraps of fabric to magically mold her luscious body.

Elias had chuckled at Daniel's jaw-dropping reaction to Maria, and murmured, "I know, son."

Daniel had asked to accompany her down to the beach. She had smiled, taken his hand, and from that day forward, had never let it go.

Then, there was Carmen. How twins could be so diametrically opposed boggled his mind. While Maria was sweet, sensual and loyal, Carmen was like a viper. Beautiful and dangerous. Any man who came into her sights was not long for this world. At least, that's how Daniel perceived her.

Carmen had spent way too much time with her mother. Daniel suspected that the charming and seductive Rosalinda indulged in a few secret indiscretions, but that was no business of his. What was his business, however, was Maria. He had seen, firsthand, how his girlfriend's naïveté shielded her from her coldhearted sister and calculating mother. Daniel had pegged both women as poisonous from his first encounters.

While he would always be grateful for Rosalinda's generosity in bringing him into her home, he never extended himself past everyday courtesies or brief conversations. After he'd become older, Rosalinda's gaze seemed to offer far more than a mother figure should. He'd always wondered why Maria and Elias couldn't see this behavior in the other two women. He never acknowledged his own discomfort, not when Maria seemed happy.

He only wished he had known back then what he knew now. Perhaps he wouldn't be sitting in this cockpit, anxious to restart his life while the woman of his dreams stormed below in a huff, wishing anyone, other than he, was on the *Honora*.

Literally. This trip was going to be hell.

THREE A.M. ARRIVED WITHOUT a sound. Daniel stretched on his bunk, immediately awake as if the water lapping the hull had caressed his senses alive. Years of sailboat racing had his internal clock set for the changing tide. Other than Maria, nothing appealed to him more than manning a ship under sail.

The heat of adrenaline surged through his veins at the prospect of running the *Honora* across the Gulf Stream. Clearly, it had been too long since he'd felt the sea beneath him. He could look at this trip as a shakedown for his confidence. Test the waters. Test his skills. Recapture faith in his vocation.

He was going to make this trip his way. Safely. Getting them there and back without a hitch. He'd clocked too many miles on a sailboat to let one accident, no matter how terrible, stop him from knowing exactly how to run a ship under any conditions. Besides, overcoming this hurdle would set several serious wrongs to right. He had made this promise to himself, to Carmen, to Rosalinda.

Making this run across the Gulf Stream would also help cleanse the poison in his heart that was filled by the Santiago women. He'd given up way too much for love. And though there was a very real chance that Maria might return once more to his arms, he needed this trek to reveal his own desires. Since the accident, Maria seemed more callous, the way Carmen used to be. Yet, Maria's doctor assured him her behavior was a symptom of the amnesia. Fear often caused an amnesia victim to withdraw, or lash out, whichever reaction made them feel safer.

Once they reached the Bahamas, he and Maria might manage to enjoy the journey, as long as he ceased doubting his own abilities and helped Maria to feel safe.

He shook his head. At the rate yesterday afternoon had gone, fat freaking chance. Already his bravado was wavering. She had spoken to him more since boarding the ship than she had in a year, even if it had upset him. He'd almost forgotten how her sultry voice stirred his blood. Maybe if he played the role of a jerk, he could keep the animosity going and not worry about trying to seduce her.

Right. Even if he enraged her, he'd want to test his skills at subduing her. Hell, he used to do it all the time with her hotheaded temperament. Yes, indeed. He was screwed, no matter how he played his hand.

Her cabin was quiet across the dark salon. It was time to sail. The only drawback to the location of her berth was that the rattling anchor chain might awaken her.

Would that be so bad?

A beautiful woman's company on a starlit morning with the trade winds pushing them across the Atlantic? Another impossible fantasy. Damn. So many dreams seemed just out of reach. Sighing, he climbed the companionway onto the deck.

She looked ethereal seated on the bow as moonlight mingled with the lantern light swaying above her head. The onboard breeze teased his senses with her perfume. Intent on the new creation coming to life on the easel, she didn't sense him this time.

He sent a grateful prayer skyward. He wanted to watch for as long as possible. When she painted, his beautiful, talented and emotionally driven lover came to life. As usual, watching her concentrate while she created made him want her even more. It always had.

The waning moon behind them cast the tall mast and deck in silver light and shadows. Anyone else would have been facing the moon, bathing an upturned face in its thin, seductive light. But not Maria. She'd turned her back on the obvious.

Instead, she painted like a woman purging a nightmare. Agitation seemed to flow through the bristles as she slashed the ink-black canvas with haphazard strokes. She changed brushes without looking, and slowed to concentrate on what resembled singed angel wings spiraling through the star-dotted canvas past a fine line delineating night from a hollow, indigo sea. The effect was alluring. Forbidding.

Maria seemed terrified.

His breath caught in his throat. He'd catch her if she fell. Didn't she know that? He drew closer, wanting only to comfort her.

With his first step, her head dropped.

"Why do you sneak up on me?"

The despair in her voice stung.

So, she wanted to cross swords. At least she was talking to him. "I like to see you jump, Princess. Nice to know you've still got a pulse."

"Don't be an idiot."

He waited, willing her to look at him. Not a chance. "I thought you were sleeping."

From the way her head dropped back, he could tell she closed her eyes, as if trying to gain patience with a buffoon. "I couldn't sleep."

"What are you painting?"

She scrunched a shoulder. "The moon."

He moved closer. Still no eye contact. "But the moon is behind us."

She lifted a hand toward the open sea. "Yes, but moonlight stains the sky and sea in pieces."

Despite the intermittent flash of the lighthouse on the point, the few boats at anchor reflected the moonlight in glittering silver.

"You see the moon in pieces?"

She slowly met his gaze, as if surprised by his question. "It didn't occur to me to think of it like that."

He pointed to the falling, moon-singed wings on the canvas. "And what are these?"

She remained quiet way too long before whispering, "Not what. Who."

"Oh."

She didn't need to say another word. He knew exactly who the wings represented. Carmen and Rosalinda. And now he felt like a loser of the highest order for pushing her anxiety.

Elias had told him Maria felt profound guilt that her sister and mother had died while she had not. This was too raw a subject to discuss so soon, especially while she had no faith in him. He scrambled to change the subject.

"I'll bet you'll earn a fortune for that one." He let admiration fill his voice. "It's haunting and beautiful."

"You would think of money, Del Rio."

Another insult. She sure knew how to push him. "Name's Daniel, if you'd care to use it."

She ignored the suggestion. "Know what this painting would fetch?" The anger in her eyes almost blinded him. What was he supposed to say? "With your charming wit right now? I don't think I care."

She shook her head. "You're right. Me neither."

Without breaking their gaze, she reached for the canvas and tossed it overboard, a simple splash confirming its destination.

"Now, it's fish food."

She'd tossed it overboard.

He wanted to shake her. That painting was beautiful. Damn his own foul temper. He sucked in a quick breath and glanced over the side. The canvas bobbed faceup in the moonlight. Slack tide. Good.

He mustered all the calm he could. "I guess that finishes one masterpiece."

She turned in her chair and started to recap her paints.

"Do you care what happens to it?" he asked.

She didn't look up. "I tossed it. Didn't I?"

"Then do you mind if I salvage it?"

Her glance shot to him. "I'm not surprised you would go after it. I'm beginning to think you're a bit of a gold digger."

Another low blow. He'd have to play along with this one. "Well, then you'll have to excuse me."

Slowly, he pulled his T-shirt up, only breaking eye contact long enough to tug the garment over his head. Then he went for the tie at his shorts.

She stood, panic and heat warring in her eyes. "What are you doing?"

He fought the impulse to move closer when her gaze roamed his chest in the familiar way that had usually left them sweaty and, damn him, satisfied.

He cleared his throat. "I'm going to retrieve my investment. If you don't want it, I'll consider it a bonus to my salary."

Disregarding his answer, she lifted her hand, fingers outstretched, her gaze falling to his stomach. Would she... touch him? Then, as if she were coming out of a trance, his words registered. Anger mingled with heat in her eyes. "That's my painting. You can't have it."

He chuckled to cover the groan rising in his throat. "Not anymore. Law of the sea. I keep anything I salvage." He couldn't help himself. "And that just might include you, Princess."

Not even bothering to finish sealing the paint tubes, she crammed them into the box, slamming the lid closed.

"Why don't you just drop dead, Del Rio?"

Daniel simply stared as she disappeared down the companionway, staggered at how empty the night felt with her absence. Once upon a time, her hands would have been all over him when he removed his shirt. How could he have hoped for her to touch him, again?

He moved toward the swim ladder. She'd forgotten the dinghy was launched. He'd pulled his shirt off just to rile her. He'd succeeded, all right. At the rate things were going, the water-drenched painting would be all of Maria Santiago he'd recover from this trip.

As he descended the ladder, he sighed, bone deep. Since the canvas depicted two souls falling to earth, no one deserved this painting more than he did.

THE WALLS OF MARIA'S CABIN closed in. How could the sight of Del Rio's bare chest make her think she had a right to touch him—or even want to. And, *Dios.* The draw of his skin had her fingers aching.

Imagine. Claiming he'd salvage her along with her painting when the look in his eyes said *ravage.* The thought intoxicated her senses. *Madre de Dios.* That tanned wall of muscle and perfection he called a chest tempted her too quickly. Instinct had her fingertips reaching to brush the dark hair dusting the middle of his chest. She'd caught the impulse in time and slammed the paint box closed. Had he noticed her original intent? Heaven help her. Not even hours from home and she was losing her grip. Was she that desperate to touch a man?

Or was it just Del Rio?

She opened the paint box, forcing herself to concentrate on the slow ritual of capping and arranging her paints and cleaning the brushes. The scent of the oils soothed her. She wiped the palette clean, her body silently thrumming, her focused mind suddenly considering the idea of painting Del Rio for the second time today. This time, naked from the hips up.

Her hands stopped in midair.

What was she thinking? The rush of adrenáline coursing through her body was the same familiar drive she felt when her inspiration needed an outlet. Emotional overload spilled out onto her canvases when her passions ran high. Why would she experience this familiar, welcoming rush with Del Rio? Were they emotionally linked, and she could not remember? *Dios,* no. She would not even consider such a possibility. Not when her mind darkened so completely every time she probed for some kind of recognition.

The breeze invading the hatch over her bed betrayed no sound of Del Rio from above. Probably rescuing what he believed to be another piece of the family fortune, if indeed he was brownnosing Poppa for some sort of inheritance. She made a mental note to question her father about this. She needed more negative points to tick off when it came to Del Rio. Oh, yes. His belligerence was insufferable, his cocky, proprietary attitude toward her infuriating. Concentrating on these reminders should help kill any attraction she felt for him. So why did his pirate smile keep rising in her mind?

She swallowed hard. Because, she had felt a pull toward him before they even boarded ship. She'd purposely spent as little time as possible in his company. Given this undeniable attraction and her inability to recognize him from earlier years, as Poppa seemed to think she should, this man intimidated her like none other. She was doomed.

Okay, it was time to reevaluate her position if she planned to continue this trip. Del Rio was attractive... downright seductive. She could acknowledge that point. There was no way around the fact she was trapped with this man for the next few weeks. Something good had to come of this expedition. She *would* remember; she held that belief deep inside. Reaching the truth was her sole purpose for climbing onto the *Honora*.

In the meantime, Del Rio was not open for exploration. No matter what her fascination with him, until her memory was restored she could not cross into new territory, even if it held a muscled, irresistible, gentlemanly rogue who seemed more than willing to cross boundaries with her. No. No. No. Especially when she still had doubts about who he was, and his motives for taking her to Little Harbour. She had to remember first. Until then, Del Rio's delectable body was off-limits. Period.

Instead, she'd journal her thoughts on canvas.

That was it. She'd paint her way to recovering her

memory. She'd create her own, personal artist's diary. This sail would offer therapy for channeling these disquieting thoughts and urges until she understood why they existed. There certainly were enough canvases in the guest cabin to accomplish the goal.

Satisfied with this decision, she felt confident she could remain in Del Rio's company as a passenger on her father's yacht.

Perfect.

Center ship, the engine rumbled to life. She closed her eyes, saying a prayer for strength. The thought of strength drew her mind to Poppa. The doctor had given her the okay to sail with the promise that Elias was strong. She wouldn't have set foot on the *Honora* if she hadn't gotten that guarantee.

After years of battling with diabetes, Elias was living on borrowed time. Diabetes was no simple disease. Her father had already progressed into advanced stages. His ankle joints had dissolved, although his feisty nature always had one believing he'd jump from his wheelchair at any moment. She suspected he had been seeking a way to keep her from witnessing his deterioration, especially his weakened heart. She would not have taken this trip if she did not believe she could recoup her memory and be fully present to help Poppa. If he worsened while she was away, there would be hell to pay.

She pushed the thought from her mind. Besides, a more immediate danger loomed. Captain Daniel Murphy Del Rio. How she'd manage keeping her distance from him on fifty feet of teak and mahogany presented a challenge. She'd pretend he didn't exist. After all, she suspected he was only doing her father's bidding. Arm's length was easy with hired help. That should roast Del Rio's pride until she could finish this voyage.

She'd push him to make Little Harbour in three days. The sooner this fiasco was finished, the better.

Settling herself at the small working table, she pulled out a sketch pad and some charcoals. Her sketches would keep her in the cabin until dawn. Daniel Del Rio could sail alone at that helm for the rest of the trip.

NOT EVEN A HALF HOUR outside the inlet, Maria bolted onto the deck, eyes wide. She clutched her stomach and lunged across the cushions wedging herself between the lifelines, her slim figure wrenching with dry heaves.

Daniel winced at her discomfort. "Didn't eat any dinner, eh?"

She shook her head. "I'm sooo sick."

Mal de mer brought the best men to their knees. He reached for his bottle of Gatorade and tossed it onto the seat beside her.

"Don't worry, Princess. In a day or two, it'll pass. In the meantime, sip that. It'll keep you hydrated."

She settled herself onto the cushion, sucking air deep into her lungs, too weak to object to his nickname for her.

"I could die."

Daniel chuckled. "And to think, a short while ago, you wanted that to happen to me."

She groaned. "Can you stop? Just for a moment?"

"The *Honora*?"

"No. The taunts. Pretend I'm not here. Okay?"

Like he could pretend not to breathe.

"Sure thing. I'll imagine it's just me and the sea on this amazing starlit night. No vomiting hottie leaning over the side, dirtying my teak while offering me a divine view of her stern."

She shot him a venomous glare, but it lasted only a

second. Like a rag doll she crumpled onto her back, covering her eyes with her arm.

"Oh, God. Can you stop this boat from rocking?"

His heart went out to her. This was not the sea-loving woman who would stay up with him during night crossings, turning her face into the wind while humming haunting songs or regaling him with childhood stories. His chest tightened. Would she ever change from the fragile, frightened woman she'd become? Would it help if he told her everything she was seeking so they could turn the ship around and not have to deal with her discomfort?

No. He'd promised Elias he'd hold his tongue and let her find her way. But this was taking things too far.

He leaned toward her. "Would it help to know you never got seasick before?"

It took only a moment to register what he meant by *before*. She glanced at him warily from under her arm.

"How do you know?" Accusation laced her words.

Oh, man. Maybe Elias was right. She wasn't ready to hear anything he knew.

He shrugged a careless shoulder. "There's a lot I know. Hang around. Maybe you'll learn something."

"I may have lost my memory, but there's nothing I want to learn from you." Her voice sounded bitter.

He shrugged again. "Probably right."

She leaned on one elbow to sip the Gatorade. "I'm going to make this trip. Even if it kills me."

Even if it kills me. Her words struck like a rogue wave. His hands gripped the wheel at the memory of her unconscious body floating facedown among the debris of a splintered speedboat while her twin and mother floated lifelessly nearby. A shudder ran through him. He could puke right beside her at the thought.

Reaching over her to trim the sails, he met her dark, challenging eyes and said, "I have an idea, Maria. Why don't you just stop talking?"

CHAPTER FOUR

THE LATE-MORNING SUN splashed clear to the sea bottom as Daniel negotiated the *Honora* through the shallow water of the Bahamas' West End and into the harbor without a hitch.

Maria had awakened and still lingered against the cockpit pillow, sipping coffee, her tanned feet peeking out from beneath the sheet. He'd suggested she sleep topside to keep the queasiness away. She'd slept within an arm's length of him through the night, like a talisman.

It hadn't taken long for Daniel to finally relax into sailing mode, aligning his body to the movement of the ocean, riding with the wind while his self-doubt disappeared behind the wake of the *Honora*. The sailboat skimming along alone in the night while Maria slept erased the last vestiges of fear he harbored about his ability to sail. While the seven-hour journey left him tired, he felt stronger than he had in a long time.

Earlier he had put the *Honora* on autopilot, hoisted the yellow quarantine flag for customs entry, brewed coffee in a thermos and buttered rolls to have waiting when Maria awoke. She wouldn't be seasick for long, but until her sea legs kicked in, he wanted to pamper her. Hell, nothing had changed for him. He wasn't the one who forgot they were lovers.

She yawned. "I'm feeling drowsy from the seasickness pill."

"It'll pass."

She slid her sunglasses on. "So, this is West End."

She spoke the words with open curiosity. West End boasted little more than an updated marina. The yellow, pink and turquoise buildings with aluminum roofs and white porches were recent additions.

Daniel pointed to the sun-drenched buildings along the beach. "That's the resort. If the *Honora* isn't comfortable for you, I can book you a room."

She shielded her eyes from the sun. "Looks sweet, but I'm fine on board."

Score one for the home team. "Well, then, other than a few packaged goods and supply stores, there's not much here."

Except for the large number of boats in the marina, West End seemed basically vacant. The flat sandy terrain, easy view of the water and the intense light of the Bahamian sun made this remote spit of land an oasis for weary sailors.

A smile creased those pouty lips. "I could paint this."

While Daniel docked the boat, secured the lines and jumped off to tip the dock attendant for his help, Maria had watched from the cockpit, looking distracted. Daniel wondered if the docking routine had seemed familiar to her.

He stepped up the gangplank. "If you get your passport, I'll clear us through customs. Until we're cleared, I'm the only one permitted ashore."

He found it interesting that she stayed put until he returned from below deck with his paperwork. He cooled his heels for five minutes, while she disappeared to retrieve hers.

"What? You didn't trust yourself to be alone with me

in the cabin?" He grinned when she climbed back to the cockpit.

"In your dreams, Captain," she said, handing him her passport.

"There's that." *Okay, friendly banter. So far, so good.*

She peered over his shoulder. "Where's customs?"

He pointed to a small coral-colored building with a slanting, shingled roof next to the fueling station. "There. I won't be long. If you want to freshen up, we can look around when I get back."

Thirty minutes later, quarantine flag down, Bahamian visitor's flag hoisted, Daniel offered Maria a hand as she descended the gangplank. To his surprise, she took it. He appreciated how the breeze teased the white embroidered sundress against her curves and showed lots of smooth, tanned leg. The white thong sandals looked sexy on her feet. She seemed glad to be on dry land, but remained silent.

He wouldn't question how relaxed she had become with him. He didn't want to disturb this fragile, unspoken truce.

She pulled her elbow from his grasp, wrapping her arms around her waist. "I could use a cola. My stomach needs bubbles."

He laughed. "Bubbles it is, then."

She turned to view the marina, the small harbor ringed by a stone jetty, the *Honora* rocking gently at the dock. She froze.

"What's wrong?"

She shook her head. "I feel odd. Like déjà vu. I can't seem to shake the feeling I've been here before."

Daniel sucked in a breath. He needed to say, *Yes, love. You've been here with me.* But the words died in his throat. Instead, he shrugged. "Maybe in a past life."

He gestured down the dock to an outdoor bar doing a

lively business serving brunch. "We'll get you a cola with no ice and an order of conch fritters. You'll feel better."

Surprise lit Maria's face as he realized his blunder. How would he know that conch fritters were her favorite, or that she drank soda with no ice?

He was grateful when a local woman approached carrying woven palm hats and shell bracelets. Seeing Maria's frown, she asked, "Been a long sail, has it?"

Maria waved a hand. "You can't imagine. I wanted to kiss solid ground."

The woman laughed. "That'd be why I'm here forever. Too long a stretch across that pretty water for my liking."

Daniel patted Maria's shoulder. "It won't take long before she finds her sea legs."

She shot Maria a laughing glance. "If I lost my sea legs with this captain, I'd have need of a lap to keep me safe."

Again, to his surprise, Maria laughed. "Oh, I managed without a lap. Sometimes we have to make sacrifices."

The woman appraised Daniel from head to foot as if inspecting goods to purchase, obviously liking what she saw. Her mouth twisted into a toothy smile. She winked at Maria.

"Well, you keep playing hard to get, sugar. He'll be taffy in your hands in no time."

Daniel and Maria groaned in harmony.

The woman chuckled, lifting her wares. "Would you like to buy a bracelet?"

Maria waved her away. "Perhaps on our way back."

The woman retreated, pointing to a beach chair beneath a palm tree with a tiny table holding palm fronds and small plastic boxes. "I'll be right over there, darlin'. Be sure to come see me."

Maria took the few steps to the edge of the dock and looked down. "She hasn't got a clue."

Daniel leaned closer, her soft powdery scent filling his senses, tossing him back to memories of her—here. "Maybe she's right."

She peered up at him over the rim of her sunglasses. "I can't imagine you soft enough for anyone to mold."

He laughed. "Oh, I don't know, Princess. I'm thinking your hands could drive a hard bargain with me."

Her gaze wandered to the grinning woman. She was close enough to catch every word. "I think I've heard enough, Captain."

Chuckling, he ushered her down the dock. "Let me treat you to that cola."

"Fine." Maria waved as they passed the woman. "I loved her island accent. Think I'll paint it."

Daniel fell into step next to her, welcoming the change in subject. "How do you paint an accent?"

"You give it color and form, of course. But you wouldn't have learned that in your fancy college."

Okay. So flirting had made her irritable. It didn't change the fact that it irked him that he'd earned his Yale degree to please his elders. He had never wanted any career but one that would allow him to work on the sea.

Maria knew this. At least, the old Maria knew this. She used to encourage him to chase his dreams rather than hone his skills in a boardroom, despite the fact that Daniel had already invested huge sums from his sailing promo ventures into his father and Elias's import-export businesses. Elias had the best entrepreneurs on his teams, so it wasn't as if Daniel was leaving the company in the lurch. Elias understood Daniel's hunger for the sea probably better than his own father would have. That was why he offered Daniel the "job" as captain of the *Honora* in between sailing gigs. But why should he explain himself?

Maria obviously enjoyed his annoyance. "What?"

The challenge goaded him beyond belief. He couldn't resist taking her down a notch, even though by admitting the truth, he'd make his own noose for hanging.

He shot off his mouth. "I'm thinking your nasty comment is because you can't remember facts and it bothers you."

She stopped walking. "What do you mean?"

"Come on, sweet pea. If you thought hard enough, you'd remember how I felt about college. Then you would realize you didn't insult me in the least."

"You act as if I should know all about you."

He watched a seabird land on a dock piling. *Don't say any more, Del Rio. You are already in too deep.* Elias had asked him to keep his own counsel, but she was being such a bitch.

No. Maybe the problem with Maria was that everyone had treaded lightly around her. Maybe she needed some direct hits to the memory bank to knock her out of her self-pity and get the juices flowing. That smug twist to her mouth sent him over the edge.

"Oh, you knew me inside and out, and loved every inch of me, Princess. You just can't friggin' remember."

Shock filled her face. "You lie."

God help him, he wanted to grab her and kiss her until she remembered. With every ounce of calm he could muster, he plunged his hands into his chino pockets and faced her.

"Think what you want. *You* are the reason I'm with you on this hell ride. I feel responsible to help you jog your memory. But believe me, I have everything to lose here. Nothing would please me more than for you to take your pretty little ass back to Florida, right about now."

Way to go, sport. Blow the whole trip at the first stop. Was he so raw that he was willing to hurt her like this?

"I'm here to regain my memory, Captain." Her instant anger was like a furnace blast. "It's mean-spirited and manipulative for you to toss lies at me." She gestured to the small restaurant by the marina. "Why don't you soak your head in a beer or something? I'll see you back at the *Honora*."

So, THIS WAS HER REWARD for letting her guard down with him. With willpower she didn't know she possessed, Maria sashayed her *pretty little ass* with slow, deliberate steps away from Del Rio while wanting to run screaming down the dock. *Oh, my God. Oh, my God. Oh, my God. Del Rio...lover? Oh. My. God!*

Were her suspicions true? Could she have forgotten such an earth-shattering fact? Try as she might to find a familiar thread to that memory, she drew a blank. That shadowy buzzing rose in her head, leaving her mind an empty slate where only an occasional glimmer of light fell. Sometimes a memory seemed within her grasp, only to disappear in the smudgy ether before it could take form.

Damn her retrograde amnesia.

She hadn't recognized her father when she first recovered consciousness, but he had held her hand and sung childhood songs until she recognized him. Within two weeks, memories of her mother and sister flooded back.

She remembered her childhood, and old friends who seemed to have fallen away over the past year, and everything that had happened since coming home from the hospital. But no memories of Del Rio—or the accident, or earlier times that Elias insisted they had shared. Del Rio's face rose in her mind; his mouth relaxed against a shadow of a beard, sexy as hell with sunglasses hiding those baby blues.

If what Del Rio had said was true, why couldn't she re-

member him in her life? Why couldn't she feel an inkling
of recognition at his declaration? Her hands began shaking. She needed a distraction before she broke into tears.
She ducked into the only shop on the quay, blindly skimming through the meager assortment of tourist tokens
while the possibility tortured her. Were they lovers? Was
that why his naked chest looked so enticing last night?
Had she once known the touch of his skin? The feel of his
body against hers? Those infuriating lips?

Had she loved him?

The thought stopped her cold. How could she love a
man with no drive or ambition igniting his passion? Poppa
said Del Rio raced sailboats, but past tense inferred that
the interest had waned.

So, what were the man's motives for taking her to Little
Harbour? If, and just *if*, they had been lovers before the
accident, had he thought his world was wrapped up in a
nice, tidy package? With her in tow, and Elias's blessing,
had he planned on living comfortably at Reefside for the
rest of his life? Did he intend to seduce her on this trip?
Was that how he hoped to secure his future?

A hot glow rose inside her that the sexiest and most
offensive man she'd ever encountered may have been her
heart's desire. Damn her blank mind.

She grew still.

Wait a minute. Del Rio could very well be lying. Maybe
he invented that story to catch her off guard, to get her to
ask questions. Questions only he could answer, any way
he chose, because *she could not remember*. How devious.
But Poppa would never have allowed her to sail with Del
Rio if he did not believe his captain had good intentions.
Perhaps Del Rio had deceived Poppa, as well. There was
only one way to know the truth.

She needed her goddamn memory.

If she only knew fact from fiction, she would have a defense against Del Rio's claims. If she remembered, she could see through his lies. She could remove him from Reefside with this new ammunition. Poppa would never tolerate deceit. Neither would she.

She exited the store. She spied Del Rio seated at a table near the bar, sipping a beer. In that brief glance she detected unhappiness as he sprawled in his chair, staring down.

Something unbidden tugged at her heart. What if she was wrong? His was not the face of a guilty man; more like a forlorn man.

She headed for the local woman, beckoning and holding up some of her jewelry, the rounded, powder-pink shells looking like pure fun. No doubt the woman had heard their exchange on the dock.

Maria slipped three bracelets onto her wrist, buying time to regain calm. "These are beautiful."

The woman offered a knowing smile. "Sometimes the sail over can be a long trip in more ways than one. Jewelry is the perfect antidote for an argument."

Maria laughed. "You must see plenty." She reached into the crocheted bag hanging on her shoulder. "And you're absolutely right. I'll buy these three."

Maria took her time walking along the docks. Folks on their boats waved hello. West End certainly attracted a friendly crowd. She sauntered down a finger pier, reading boat names, watching small fish skim along the surface of the water, all the while trying to make sense out of Del Rio's claims.

She stopped at the end of the dock, her gaze following the line of the stone jetty along the inlet back out to sea. The ocean, looking like a glittering blue blanket reaching across to the horizon, did nothing to alleviate her sense of being stranded.

How was she to deal with Del Rio?

Truth was, she would have to forgo her suspicions until she gathered facts. What was the legal term? Innocent until proven guilty? Her policy of "arm's length" with the boat captain seemed all the more mandatory now. She glanced in Del Rio's direction once more. He had spotted her and was watching. When their eyes met, he looked away.

Yep. The man was not happy. Good. He should feel like a slug for trying to manipulate her. He'd think twice next time before crossing the boundary of propriety she'd set before they sailed.

Her only hope for normalcy was to go back to business. She braced herself, since there was no chance of returning to Reefside at this point. She could accomplish her goal, as long as she maintained her own comfort level with Captain Del Rio.

She could do that.

She had no choice.

Just in case he was watching, she strolled along the dock pretending an interest in her surroundings, though her thoughts were elsewhere. The more she tried to focus, the darker her mind became. She could remember nothing. *Nada.* Certainly not an intimacy with Del Rio.

What had Poppa said? *"You just do not remember..."*

Realization hit. Did her father know?

Her breath caught in her throat. No. She could not think of this. No. No. No. This was wrong. Something about Del Rio spelled danger, especially when her body seemed to have a mind of its own whenever he was near. Heaven knew she fantasized about losing herself in his arms. That alone left her feeling as if she teetered on the edge of an abyss. Could she have loved someone so completely that even with amnesia, her body remembered? Yet Del Rio seemed so blunt and uncaring at times. Surely a man behaving as coolly as he did wouldn't share the same deep and hungry emotions that had begun gnawing at her. But then why would Poppa have said such a thing?

Try as she might, she could hardly breathe. She stared at the grain in the wood planks beneath her feet. The different patterns ignited her imagination as she walked. Trees had died to create this boardwalk. A transformation had taken place. The urge for her easel overwhelmed her like a drug addiction. If she painted, she could escape Del Rio, his words, and breathe.

She ran for the *Honora,* not caring how she appeared. She flew past the bar knowing full well Del Rio watched. She couldn't think about him now. Colors swirled in her head, the shapes taking hold in her mind. Her fingers itched for her paintbrush. She'd stay in the cabin and lock Del Rio out until she finished. Then she'd choose her tack more wisely the next time they spoke. She'd get to the bottom of his game. But first, she needed to paint.

DANIEL ORDERED ANOTHER BEER and sat at the table until the sun drifted low in the western sky. Yep, he'd blown that one like a double-barreled shotgun at short range. Scared the trust right out of Maria. He wanted to chase after her when she bolted for the sailboat, but decided she needed distance from him.

He released a pent-up sigh. He could use a nap. The trip across the Gulf Stream had taken its toll. Sailing the *Honora* for seven hours alone on his first run since the accident, compounded with his concern over Maria's seasickness, had kept his nerves on point for way too long.

Had he been less fatigued he would not have indulged

his urge to upset her. Man, when Maria said things that proved she had absolutely no clue who he was or what they had meant to each other, she pushed his buttons like no one in the world could.

Now, he'd completely jeopardized her trust. Bet she'd even decided he'd invented the story. Made him seem like a manipulative SOB. Not exactly the type of disclosure Elias had suggested. He shook his head. *Idiota.* It looked as if blowing each opportunity to reach her was going to become his modus operandi. Trying to pretend she didn't mean something to him was not going to work. Not when she could undo his composure with a glance.

Daniel's chest ached. This was his burden. He'd known when he accepted her demand to bring them here that this trip would be difficult. Bone-jarring. Heartbreaking. He'd accepted the task because Maria needed him to open her eyes. He had been the one who'd caused her distress in the first place. Plus, he needed to see with his own eyes whether the love would return when her mind cleared. He had to be there to see if she'd be strong enough to work through the hurt. Then he would know how to redirect his life when this ordeal finally ended.

He learned a valuable lesson today. Dropping bombs in her lap was not going to help open her mind. On the contrary, it drove her deeper into herself. Guess the doctors were right about that.

He sighed. Okay. He would be ground zero when she detonated. Until then, he would be more careful. He swallowed the last of his beer, a man with a sentence. He'd make dinner a peace offering. At least he'd eat well on this trip.

Daniel pushed away from the table and waved thanks to the waitress. A local fisherman lived behind the resort. Daniel headed there. He'd make Maria a meal she wouldn't forget. Hell, he'd make the same dish he'd prepared the last time they'd arrived here. She'd melted in his arms then. No chance this time. He'd grovel like an idiot tonight to gain her forgiveness, even if she remained grudging and mistrusting. He had no choice. Twenty more days lay ahead.

At the sound of the *Honora*'s engine rumbling to life, Maria broke out of her reverie. Leaving the dock so soon? Blinking, she viewed the nearly completed canvas, but couldn't appreciate it as the thud of lines tossed on board sifted down the companionway. She unlocked the salon door and bolted for the stairs as the boat moved in reverse.

"Where are we going?"

Daniel maneuvered the *Honora* with ease. "There are moorings in the marina. Thought we'd get off the dock and have dinner at anchor."

She slanted him a suspicious gaze. "Trying to keep me aboard?"

That blood-warming grin creased his lips. "You read my mind."

"Let's make this clear. I am not, and never was, your lover. Get *that* fact straight in your mind."

His gaze lazily took her in. "Decided to fight? Good."

"Did you hear me?"

"Each and every syllable, Princess." He tossed her a thin white bag knotted at the top. "Throw these babies on ice. I already put the wine in the fridge out here."

Spindly legs struggled against her grasp. Shrieking, she dropped the bag. "What is it?"

He laughed. "Lobsters. Don't hurt 'em. Just put them on ice. If you scare the wits out of 'em they won't taste as good."

With two fingers she picked up the bag by the knot and

held it at arm's length. Though disheveled, he looked incredibly beguiling.

"You're drunk."

"Not yet. It would take a cask of rum to get me as numb as I'd like."

She headed for the galley. Interesting words. Looked like his admission on the dock had upset him as much as it had her. After carefully placing the bag in the deep icebox, she returned to her easel. Del Rio's discomfort gave her an odd sense of release. At least she wasn't the only one battling misgivings. She'd have to think about how she'd handle the man later. Her painting was almost finished.

CHAPTER FIVE

STARS SWIRLED IN THE SKY by the time Maria completed the canvas, and she was starving. She peered out the companionway, but no Del Rio.

"Finished with today's masterpiece?"

Daniel reclined in a hammock suspended between the rigging in the bow. He lifted his hat from his face.

"I thought maybe you jumped ship."

"Nope. Too hungry to go anywhere."

Civility couldn't hurt at this point. The salty breeze smelled divine and the night sky was overwhelmingly beautiful.

"Where did all those stars come from?"

Del Rio rolled out of the hammock and stretched, offering a view of his flat abs while the T-shirt stretched against the planes of his chest.

She swallowed her next words. Damn. One fine specimen. She needed to cool off. "Hope you don't mind. I need a shower before dinner."

He opened his mouth to say something, but obviously thought better of it. "Don't mind at all."

A sudden visual of them showering together in the small stall suddenly filled her mind. Where did that come from? She needed to get a grip.

He sighed. "Listen, Maria. I apologize for upsetting you this afternoon."

She held up a hand, not ready to go there. "If you're

truly contrite for being such a moron, you can stow my supplies."

He stepped into the companionway, their bodies inches from each other. "Going to make me work for forgiveness?"

She wanted to grin, but couldn't go there, either. She descended the rest of the steps into the salon. Daniel followed close behind.

"Sweat is more like it. Now be a good slave and get out of my personal space."

His gaze slid past her to the painting she had perched on the salon table. "Holy smokes. How did you transform that lily-white canvas into a fantasy version of West End?"

In reality West End was a sun-drenched, tropical marina situated among the ruins of a barren, struggling island. Instead, Maria had painted trinket-laden vines growing from the docks with birds perched in windowsills with brilliant, peeling paint while a river flowed through the sky and cascaded past clouds into the tiny harbor, reflecting the local colors in its splashes.

A low whistle escaped his lips. "You caught the twin emotions of this island's plenty and poverty in tropical relief. You sure know how to capture the heart of a subject."

While his praise warmed her, she wasn't sure if he meant the compliment or not. "Um. Thank you?"

He met her gaze. "I'll buy that."

She stepped off the stairs into the salon, resisting the urge to whisk the painting into her cabin. "Sorry. Not for sale."

It wasn't just a painting, for heaven's sake. She'd created a release for the anxiety that had gnawed at her all afternoon and was peaceful once more. Her stress now lived in this rectangle of canvas. She had regained her equilibrium, at least for the moment. The last thing she'd do was sell her peace of mind to Del Rio when he'd caused the turbulence in the first place.

Heck, she might as well sell her body and soul. She hesitated, her hand on the doorknob of her cabin. "By the way, it wouldn't hurt you to clean up, either. You smell like those lobsters."

Laughter rose in his pirate eyes. "Is that an invitation?"

Bam. There was that visual again. "God, no."

She quickly disappeared behind her door, his chuckle loud and clear on the other side.

A HALF HOUR LATER, reggae music pulsed from the iPod. The aroma of freshly baked bread led her to the galley, where Del Rio worked, steam from the lobster pot clouding the air around him.

He'd cleaned up, as well. His damp, dark hair flowed back from his forehead. His eyes seemed to reflect the day, and his tanned face was now shaved smooth enough to touch. He swiped his forehead along the sleeve of his orange T-shirt, the motion engaging the network of muscles along his arm and shoulders. Even his feet were sculpted, sprinkled with tiny bronzed hairs that traveled up a pair of legs any woman would imagine climbing. And those chino shorts hung just right on his hips. Darn, she actually salivated.

Daniel Del Rio was too damn sexy for his own good. Since he'd planted the seed they had been lovers, she couldn't shake the image of him naked—or herself naked next to him. Showering alone had been torture.

Get a grip on yourself, Maria Santiago.

Del Rio looked up, a wince of disappointment creasing his eyes. "I was hoping for a halter top and a miniskirt."

Ouch. Well, she deserved the gibe. The shapeless,

coffee-colored sundress that showed no cleavage and stopped below her knees was intended as spite for his earlier comment. She'd brought the dress along in case she got sunburned. Unfortunately, the only thing that was burned at the moment was her pride. She aimed to get that back.

She shrugged. "When do we eat?"

Snapping his tongs, he pulled the lobsters from the pot. "Now, sweet cakes."

White linen covered the cockpit table. A hurricane lantern bathed the area in a soft glow. Porcelain dishes and sterling silver cutlery lay on linen napkins. A California Reserve chilled in a silver bucket. Crystal glasses sparkled in the light. Maria's painting rested against the lifelines across the stern of the boat, the greens, turquoises and reds like a Caribbean conspiracy in the candlelight.

She turned to Del Rio as he hefted a tray of food. "You did this?"

He glanced down the companionway. "Um, yeah. There's no one else here."

She refused to be impressed, ignoring the flood of warmth filling her. "Why is my painting out here?"

He met her gaze. "I like it."

She swallowed the *thanks* sitting on her tongue. The compliment surprisingly touched her, and she wasn't ready to call any truce until she found out the motive for his rudeness at lunch. "Okay. It needs to dry anyway."

She took a seat across from him, inwardly chanting the mantra she adopted while in the shower: *Del Rio. The liar.* Those four words effectively quashed any rising attraction. Now that she was calmer, her painting seemed almost foreign.

"Funny. The painting looks different now that I've finished." It always amazed her that after dumping her emotions onto a canvas, her mind cleared to the point where she forgot what drove her to create the scene in the first place.

Daniel placed a lobster on her plate, then his.

"What inspired you?"

Dare she be honest? She tilted her head as he poured wine. "Trying to discern truth from lies." There. She'd said it. She'd accused him of lying.

He held her gaze as if deciding whether to answer, then seemed to think better of it. He gestured to the table. "Well, then, we may as well eat."

His lack of response was not what she'd expected. It wasn't her intention to kill the conversation. She was looking for an explanation. Awkward silence fell between them. Luckily, they both had the distraction of delving into their lobster tails. The cracking sound of the shells mimicked the tension in the air between them.

Despite the strain at the table, hunger gnawed at her. No doubt, the salt air, the passing of her seasickness and an afternoon of painting had helped. She chewed her first morsel, savoring the briny lobster flavor. The dinner rolls melted on her tongue. The wine tasted of bright oak and the lightest fruit; the salad, sheer perfection.

Her smile of satisfaction earned a return smile from Del Rio. She wouldn't begrudge him her gratitude, for goodness' sake, though she still felt uncomfortable harboring her suspicions.

Since Daniel had turned off the iPod, sounds of nature had been the only music accompanying their dinner. A few night birds called to each other. Water lapped the hull beneath them. Halyards clanged on the breeze. A reggae rhythm rose from a bar somewhere on the quay. Despite the questions swirling in her head, Maria relaxed. She finished her wine, only to have Daniel pour more.

She met his quiet gaze. "Dinner is excellent. Thank you."

A curious smile twisted his lips as the honey-colored liquid bubbled into her glass. It was as if he held a secret. "My pleasure, entirely."

He sounded like he meant it. She inhaled a deep breath. Okay. Now, or never. She had to clear the air if they were to have any semblance of peace for the rest of the trip. "Why did you say it?"

He looked straight at her, knowing exactly what she meant, his blue eyes smoky with concern. "I wasn't lying, Maria."

Just like the man not to mince words. She took time to sip her wine, if only to swallow the knot rising in her throat.

His entire demeanor reflected both frustration and contentment as he watched her. Clearly, he was standing by his words.

"How can I know for sure?"

"You can trust me."

Like I can trust a shark. "Actually, I can't."

He looked out over the water. "I'd probably say the same thing if I was wearing your sandals." He leaned back into the cushions, holding his wine close to his chest. "How did you remember Elias? Or your sister? Or your mother?"

She had to swallow before speaking. His probing touched a personal chord. "Poppa's songs. They were familiar. Then other memories followed."

His gaze softened. "So, how about we chat? See if we trigger anything?"

She hesitated. Interesting invitation. Questions could go both ways. What was there to lose? Yet something in her urged her to refuse. She closed her eyes to collect herself.

She wanted answers. This was an easy way to find them. With one nod, she said, "Okay."

He smiled.

She couldn't.

He opened a palm in offering. "Would you like to ask a question, or should I just talk?"

"How long have you been captain of the *Honora*?"

"Four years."

"And you are...?"

"My age? Thirty-two. My heritage? Chilean mother. Irish father." He inclined his head. "Did you know that our fathers were best friends?"

She waved away the facts she already knew. "Poppa told me. I know they had an export business."

"Several businesses, actually. My father was part owner of a copper mine. Dad sent copper from Chile. Elias distributed the goods and shipped electronics back."

She grew still. "Poppa also said we knew each other as children."

He smiled. "Yes."

"I—I do not remember. At all."

He held out a hand. "That's perfectly understandable. I was not a memorable child."

She felt herself smile. It wasn't so bad, this small talk. She appreciated his willingness to answer her questions. She didn't think he'd lie to her on safe topics.

"You know my parents died." Sadness threaded through his voice.

She could feel his loss. "Yes. It must have been awful. Do you know what happened to them?"

He frowned. "No. My mother's brother and wife turned up dead in their home, so it was assumed the rest of the family met the same fate. We think it was a political attack, since my dad and mom were benefactors to one of the universities Pinochet targeted as subversive."

He shrugged. "You know how the Irish can be. Dad was pretty outspoken in his beliefs, and my mother with her hot temper wasn't far behind him. Between their wealth and their strong opinions about the political scene in Chile, they became a target for Pinochet's group."

He focused on her, loss so very clear in his eyes. "We just don't know how or why, for sure. All investigations were thwarted. We found nothing."

What a devastating experience it must have been for him. She remembered that Poppa said he and Momma had left Chile for America when the Marxist leader, Allende, had practically destroyed the Chilean economy. When General Pinochet seized power, he soon restored Chile's economic health, but ruled as a dictator for decades, torturing and murdering anyone he considered a threat to his regime, either politically or economically.

She hesitated to inquire further because his face clouded. He suddenly looked so lonely.

He seemed to understand. "What do you want to ask?"

"Where were you when this happened?"

"Boarding school. Massachusetts. Preparing for Yale, as my father wanted."

She winced at the resentment in his voice. That explained his cruel words on the dock. She almost reached a hand out to him, but resisted. "That must have been awful. If I had known, I wouldn't have been so unkind today."

He shrugged as if the afternoon hadn't affected him. "It's okay, Princess. It was a long time ago."

So far, nothing tapped a memory of this man in her life other than what Poppa had told her. "You have no siblings, correct?"

He nodded. "That's right."

Silence fell. With all the turmoil in Del Rio's life, she felt selfish for begrudging him her father's affection. "So, we share Elias."

"Maria, you mean more to him than anything in the world."

His words warmed her. "I'd like to believe that."

A self-deprecating chuckle rose in his throat. "Oh, believe it. I've spent enough time with him to know."

That stopped her. Had she been born a son, would she have been granted enough time in Poppa's world to know how he felt about people around him?

After a moment, he added, "So, is any of this sounding familiar?"

She shook her head. "No."

He released a held breath. "Okay. So we press on."

"I appreciate your willingness to stand interrogation like this."

"No worries. I'm sure we'll stumble over more issues before we reach Little Harbour."

Somehow she sensed there was an underlying message in that statement. "So, what next?"

He thought a moment, then turned to look at the canvas in the flickering candlelight. "Since you brought your supplies, we'll make this trip an art excursion. I'll take you to all the places I believe you need to see. And you paint whatever appeals to you."

"We can do that and get back to Elias on schedule?"

"I'll make it work."

He was being way too agreeable. She chuckled. Clearly, the wine had relaxed her. "So, what's in this arrangement for you?"

"Well, I get to revisit my sailing skills while watching you create masterpieces."

Again, silence. Maria reached for another dinner roll

to help absorb the wine now making Del Rio look more attractive than ever.

"That seems too easy."

He snapped his fingers. "You're right. There is one catch."

Uh-oh. She couldn't handle any more suggestions that they explore the possibility that they were lovers. "Please, don't make me uncomfortable with more innuendos," she said, chiding.

Laughter lit his eyes. "No. This is worse. I'm making you first mate."

Not in this lifetime. "What do you mean, first mate?"

"You know, follow my orders. Help run the *Honora.*"

She focused on the large steering wheel. "Like run the helm?"

"Sure. You should know how to raise the sails. Manage the helm. Read the charts. What if I fell overboard or something?"

She couldn't resist. "Like if I pushed you?"

This time he grinned. "Yeah. Something like that."

She crossed her arms. "I still can't help but feel you're omitting something here."

The heat of his gaze held hers for way too long. "You know, even in that ugly dress, you're gorgeous."

"Cut. It. Out."

He opened a palm. "What?"

She laughed. "Just stop flirting. Okay?"

"Okay."

"Now tell me. What's in this deal for you?"

"In plain English?"

She swallowed hard. Did she really want to know? "Hell, yes."

Exhaling a huge rush of air, he said, "I want you to like me."

He sat there, shaking his head ever so slightly, as if he couldn't believe he'd just said the words.

Wow. He sounded vulnerable, anxious for her to think well of him. That seemed so sexy. Was it the wine? Or the tragic story behind losing his family? Right at this moment, she could not bring herself to be unkind to him, no matter what lay between them. She waited until he looked at her again. It felt like forever.

"You seem like a very nice man. That's all I can say."

The softness in his gaze had her genuinely wishing she'd have some flash of memory about them as lovers. The urge to dive into his arms was pure torture. One brief, heartfelt discussion and the pull his body had on her was enough to make her cave to her impulse. But facts were facts. All she knew for sure was that he was a family friend. Employee of her father's. Nowhere in her memory was there a bond between the two of them. Even with the squeeze in her heart, she could offer him nothing more.

"Well, that's better than your attitude yesterday."

Time to end the one-on-one. "And I'll pass on the first mate idea." She stood. "You cooked. I'll do dishes. Then I'm going to bed."

"Um, actually, Princess, being first mate is not an option."

Maria laughed. "You work for me, remember?"

Daniel stood next to her. In the small area around the table they practically touched. The breeze lifted the hem of her dress against his legs, and her unconscious responded as if her spirit reached out to him. She held her breath, moving from the table before he could take the plates from her hands. Close quarters on this ship were rapidly taking on new meaning. They'd made a little headway tonight. Yet Del Rio was off-limits. Not being able to touch him might slowly drive her crazy. "Maria."

She stopped at the sound of his voice. Mischief lit his eyes, and she didn't like it one bit.

"There is one small fact Elias neglected to tell you."

She rolled her eyes. "Great. Here you go again."

"No. You can take this one to the bank."

"Okay, I'm all ears."

"The *Honora* is mine. I bought her two weeks ago. I don't work for anyone anymore."

CHAPTER SIX

DANIEL BOLTED FROM HIS BUNK at the sound of Maria's screams. He crashed through her cabin door half expecting she'd locked it and he'd have to break it down. Silver light from the waning moon lit the small room through the open hatch overhead. Maria thrashed beneath the sheets, breathing hard.

"Ah!"

Daniel grabbed her shoulders. "Maria. Wake up."

Her face was drenched, tendrils of dark hair sticking to her cheeks. Her pupils were wide and unfocused, telling him she wasn't yet awake. "Maria."

"Help!" She reached for him, pulling him down. He half fell on top of her before sliding to her side and gathering her against him. A cry began deep in her chest, releasing as a haunting sob. Tears followed as if she'd never stop crying.

"Shush, honey. Shush. You're okay."

He caressed her head against his shoulder, guilt squeezing his chest. Nightmares still tormented her. He closed his eyes, willing her fears away, if only to free himself from sharing her pain. Why couldn't their world spin backward just one goddamn year?

Her silky, ebony hair flowed through his fingers, calming his blistering nerves. She smelled powdery fresh, her skin sweet and warm like a baby's after waking from sleep. But there was no peace here. Maria trembled like a terrified child. He bundled her into his arms, willing his heart to slow enough to soothe hers.

She snuggled closer, her fingers digging into his T-shirt. He kept silent, afraid his voice would wake her up completely. So he held her, grateful for this chance. He'd craved the feel of her body against his for the longest time. For now, this was enough. Inhaling her scent felt like coming home.

After a while she fell quiet, his shirt still knotted in her fingers, her breathing the even rhythm of slumber. She'd entwined one leg with his, just as she used to do. He squeezed his eyes shut to keep control of his emotions. He pressed a kiss to her forehead. Maria felt perfect in his arms, as she always had. Hunger to make love to her was tempered by the serenity of her sleep.

She'd calmed. Her warmth filled him. This small satisfaction engulfed his entire body. God help him, he loved this woman. If she only knew how thoroughly and completely tethered he was to her.

What a goddamn mess this plan was. If and when this trip blew up in his face, walking away from Maria was going to be the hardest move of his life. All logic about living without her evaporated when he could touch her, smell her skin, listen to her easy breathing. He pulled her closer, if possible. He could only go moment to moment at this point. So for now, he dared not move. Only a few more hours remained before dawn. He may never get this chance to hold her, again.

MARIA COULDN'T REMEMBER the last time she slept so soundly. She felt like a baby in Poppa's arms. Wait. That scent. Salt air and soap, incense and warm skin.

Her eyes shot open. She stared face-to-chest with Del

Rio's T-shirt. One arm possessively claimed her while the other arm pillowed her head.

He slept. His breathing soft, even. This close, his dark lashes showed the tips lightly bleached from the sun. His chestnut hair curled haphazardly across his forehead, the shadow of a beard lined his jaw. The scent of his skin, so haunting, filled her nostrils like some exotic, tranquilizing perfume. Her initial urge to trace his jawbone with her finger was immediately replaced with the shock that they lay together.

"What are you doing in my bunk?" Pounding his chest, she chanted. "Out. Out. Out!"

Daniel jolted awake. "What? Easy, Princess. Ouch! Stop hitting me."

He rolled away, but didn't leave the bunk. "Hey. Get a hold of yourself. You were screaming in your sleep last night."

She stilled. The nightmare. That ghoulish spiral into a dark haze where devils and demons pulled her screaming twin down, down, down, while Maria grappled desperately to reach her sister, only to realize her hands had no fingers. Greedy teeth and sharp claws ripped at her back, neck, arms and torso, and she felt as if her body were being torn apart.

She shuddered. Would those images ever die?

"Well, you didn't have to climb into bed with me."

He poked her shoulder with his finger. "You pulled me onto the bunk. I just…accommodated you."

She pointed to the open cabin door. "Get out."

He didn't budge. "Tell me about your nightmare. You were crying."

For one blessed second as she gazed into his eyes, Maria considered sharing her torment. She kept these nightmares secret from everyone. Anyone who heard them would think she was crazy. Del Rio was not going to be her first confidant. She shook her head. "It's none of your business. Now get out."

"Maria, I can help you."

"I don't need your help, Del Rio."

He looked at his hands a long moment before releasing a surrendering breath. "Okay. I'll start coffee. We'll head out after we eat. Put on plenty of sunscreen, honey. You're getting your first sailing lesson this morning."

He stalked out, not even bothering to shut her door.

MARIA WOULD HAVE TRADED HER eyeteeth for the shower at home. She needed a pounding spray of hot water to flush the scent of Del Rio from her skin. Damn it all. Why was she so drawn to him?

Her stomach knotted at the thought, making her want to throw up, again. This voyage was all wrong. She should take the next flight back to Fort Lauderdale and forget the doctors' claim this journey would help recapture her memory. Her conflicting emotions about Del Rio were confusing her more than anything. This little game between her and Del Rio was one she didn't want to play any longer.

Dios. Did she have a choice? So much was at stake, including her sanity. She could not even manage to be angry with Del Rio any longer after their discussion last night. He was just another human being trying to make his way in a world that left him to crawl from the rubble. Learning that Elias had reached out and offered Del Rio family ties had earned her empathy. Not good when she wanted to keep her attraction to his animal magnetism caged.

The unbridled look of love on Del Rio's face when he asked her to tell him about her nightmare practically dismantled every defense she'd built up against him. He was just too darned smooth for her to resist. And resisting was the only way she'd reach her destination—and her goals. Some inner voice warned her that to attach herself to this man was to lose all she was, and perhaps be left with a broken heart.

She *needed* to remember.

She turned her face into the water as she lathered her hair. She'd start with a phone call. Del Rio had a satellite phone in the chart table. She'd nail Poppa for some insights before she made a fool of herself for good. If anyone knew whether she and Del Rio had been lovers, Poppa would.

MARIA APPEARED IN the companionway like a siren. Daniel was grateful for his sunglasses, because he couldn't help but gape at her from the helm. Her damp hair glistened in one long, dark braid falling across her shoulder. A visor shaded those velvet brown eyes hidden behind her Versace shades. Her lips, glossed with a candy apple color, made him want to devour them, slowly. The turquoise bikini top covered the luscious swell of her breasts, the color like a jewel against her tanned skin, glowing with sunscreen. His eyes traveled down to her flat stomach where a black Spanish sarong draped loosely across her hips and the string bikini bottom.

He wanted to throw back his head and howl like a wolf.

Maria's face scrunched with discomfort, yet she stayed unmoving in the companionway.

He crooked a finger at her. "You can come out. I won't bite."

She looked perplexed. "I can't stay below any longer. I'm getting queasy, again."

He patted the cushion next to him. "Have a seat."

"I need the phone. I want to call my father."

"It's in my cabin. If you take the helm, I'll get it for you."

She glanced at the wheel then the sails behind her, taut with wind. The corners of her mouth curled down in distaste.

"No. I'll wait until we stop."

"Okay, then come out, anyway."

Her nose wrinkled in that cute way he loved so much.

"Not so sure I want to be first mate, either."

He chuckled, moving his hands palm up as if weighing a situation. "Seasick. First mate. Seasick. First mate. Hmm. I'd think staying on deck wins."

She stepped into the cockpit, the motion of her long legs making Daniel's knees grow weak.

"On second thought, maybe you should stay below. You look good enough to eat."

She shot him an angry look. "Why don't you just stop talking?"

He gestured to the coffee thermos and pastries. "And that's the thanks I get for making breakfast."

He shook his head, his lips pursed to keep from laughing as she settled herself against the cushions, her back to the stern, legs full length on the seat like Cleopatra on a floating chaise. Daniel forced his eyes to the horizon despite the fact he wanted to engage the *Honora*'s autopilot and pay homage to those gorgeous legs.

Under full sail, the boat flew across the water. Daniel had raised the bimini cover over the cockpit so they enjoyed shade while the trade winds cooled the deck. Relieved to see her discomfort abating, he stole furtive glances her way, unable to ignore the rise of her bikini top as she inhaled the heated, salty air deep into her lungs.

"Look at all the different colors of blue layering the sky."

He focused where she pointed.

She leaned over the side, giving him a great view of her gorgeous figure. He shook his head. Heaven help him.

"Look. The darkest cobalt blue is at the sky's zenith. Then the colors lighten to the palest blue where the horizon meets the teal of the ocean surface."

Sunlight dappled the water from robin's egg blue to turquoise. White sand, brilliant in the sunlight, caressed the island in the distance, a striking contrast against the intensity of the sea's color. The view always seemed mystical, as if they'd chanced upon some enchanted legend suspended in time.

Her appreciation gave him a jolt of hope, at once bittersweet. She always used to comment on the intensity of the colors out here. She also loved sailing. Would the twin pleasures relax her enough to let memories slide in? Would she then turn to him and remember the accident, and her anger?

"What's making the water change color?" she asked,

He almost laughed at the basic question when he'd expected a death sentence. She knew the answer already. Yet, he was more than happy to indulge her.

"The sea bottom." He pointed to each area. "Royal blue is deeper water, the turquoise reflects a sandy bottom, and that blue-green shade means there's sea grass or reefs below."

He watched her fidget until she couldn't stay seated. She grabbed a rolled towel from the bench, headed for the bow and lay stomach down on it, her head perched over the side.

"You sick, again?"

She called over her shoulder. "No. I want to see the bottom." Her grin nearly undid him.

Maria had no idea she'd just claimed her favorite perch.

She had certainly discovered her sea legs. Whether aware or not, she was acting on memories. Chances were, it wouldn't be long until she had a breakthrough. As the *Honora* flew with wind-billowed sails, Daniel steered by instinct because he was focused on the emotional storm brewing just over the horizon.

NOW THAT MARIA'S SEASICKNESS had abated, sailing seemed glorious. She loved the feel of the boat rising and falling beneath her. The wind passing over the sails pulled them taut, pushing the *Honora* forward, the sea splashing against the hull as if laughing. The ever-changing colors, the rush of white water curling along the hull blended into a soothing music. Stress seemed to pour right out of her body. She felt boneless and giddy. She wondered why she had been afraid of sailing. This experience was nothing like the vague, haunting terror of the speedboat accident.

Suddenly, a shadow like a torpedo shot past the bow. Then another. And another. She propped herself up on her knees. Behind her Daniel laughed, but she didn't dare take her eyes off the sight to look at him. The torpedoes raced past once more, only to return and expose dorsal fins.

Daniel called, "Porpoises."

One gray-speckled creature rolled over on his side and looked back. The silly turn of his mouth resembled a smile. The animal surfed the waves off the bow, and soon, others followed. Before Maria could catch her breath, a pod of six dolphins cavorted in the water below, riding the bow waves as if the *Honora* was one of them.

Maria raced back to the cockpit, angling for the companionway. "I need my camera."

She disappeared below then shot back to the bow, leaning dangerously over the side to capture the moment on film. The creatures broke the surface, smiling up at her as she snapped their pictures until they grew bored and moved on.

Exhilarated, she sat back and welcomed Daniel's smile. "Wow."

Del Rio nodded. "That's the beauty of a sailboat. No motor. Just us, the wind and the tagalong surfers."

"I have to paint them as soon as we stop."

"No surprise there."

She was so filled with contentment from watching the porpoises that she didn't even mind his teasing.

DANIEL WAITED UNTIL SHE stopped fiddling with her camera. "Now, why don't you put your camera away and come on back here for your first sailing lesson?"

Her smile immediately faded. "You're doing fine without me."

"No. It's important you know how to handle the *Honora*."

She plopped down on her butt, obviously deflated. "That wasn't part of the deal."

He shrugged. "Doesn't matter. As captain of this vessel, I require everyone on a long-distance journey to learn the helm." He held out a beckoning hand. "Come on. You'll like taking control, as usual."

She shot him a pointed look. "Goading me?"

"Every chance I get, Princess. But, as first mate, you're responsible. Now come on."

Daniel chuckled to himself as minutes ticked by. She'd moved like greased lightning when the porpoise swam off the bow, but now you'd think she stood in dried cement. What could she possibly be thinking, rooted in one spot for all these minutes, supporting herself with the mast stays while watching the sails billow overhead?

Daniel's gaze devoured her. He could watch her forever.

"Hey. C'mon, slowpoke. At the rate you're moving we'll be there before you get here."

She made her way into the cockpit. "I was studying the sails. They'd look great painted."

So, she was nervous. He'd play along.

"Go right ahead. I'll auction them to the highest bidder." He wiggled his eyebrows. That should distract her.

Disapproval clouded her face. "Such an opportunist. You really must learn to make a living on your own."

Daniel's jaw dropped, but he caught himself before letting her insult even nick the surface of his skin. "Now, don't go flirting with me or I won't be able to concentrate on your sailing lesson."

Reaching over, he grabbed her wrist, gently pulling her to the helm. He stepped away, planting both her hands on the steering wheel. The *Honora* heeled to starboard, so he stood on the high side with Maria standing with her profile to him.

She pushed her glasses back onto the bridge of her nose in a nervous gesture. "The bow looks far away from here."

He followed her gaze. "You'll adjust. It's like learning the periphery of a car."

He placed a hand over hers and moved the wheel. "Okay, now if the sails are perfectly trimmed, there should be no pull on the steering."

Maria widened her stance to keep balance. "How can you tell if they're trimmed?"

Daniel pointed to the little red strips attached near the front of the mainsail and the jib. "See those telltales? When they're blowing straight, you know the sails are trimmed. If they begin to flutter, you've either strayed off course or the wind has shifted and you'll have to adjust the sheets."

He pointed to where the line from the end of the sail

ran along the top deck to a self-tailing winch on the side within easy reach of the helm.

"See? This line is called a sheet. You pull through this winch to tighten or loosen the sheet as you need."

Maria swallowed hard. "I'll be damned if I touch one of those…sheets."

"Oh, stop. You'll be a pro in no time."

Daniel moved closer, his chest pressing against her left arm. Her warm, sweet scent mixed with coconut sunscreen invaded his senses and his next thought flew out of his head. He leaned back a fraction so his mind could clear. Her impatient glance pulled him right back to his instructions. He cleared his throat and pointed to the red needle in the compass housed on the helm pedestal.

"See where this arrow points? That's our heading. You only need to adjust the steering slightly when the arrow moves off course."

She backed away. "I can't do this."

He gently led her back to the helm. "Sure you can, Princess."

He wanted to wipe away the perspiration beading on her upper lip…preferably with his mouth. "Just give yourself a minute to get a feel for the vessel. This isn't a contest of wills. The boat wants to move—you're just giving her direction."

Under the steady breeze, the ship rose and fell in an easy rhythm as she cut through the water. He'd be patient for as long as it took to get Maria comfortable. Comfortable with his ship. Comfortable with him. Her hesitant hold on the wheel let the boat veer into the wind. She seemed startled as the compass needle moved and she turned the wheel in the opposite direction, but too much. The *Honora* veered upwind, making the sails luff. She scrambled to turn the wheel back to its original place.

He had to give her credit for trying. Given her fears, she was one courageous woman. He moved behind her, wrapping his arms around her body to grasp her hands.

"Look. Gentle movements with the wheel. Give the boat a chance to respond. We're not speeding. You won't break anything."

He stood quietly behind her, moving the wheel beneath her hands until the *Honora* was again on course. His body so close to hers nearly had him trembling. The heat from her skin blended with his, weaving some intoxicating spell around them. The sensation seemed to heighten as the *Honora* rode the waves. Did she feel the wind funneling through the sails and over their bodies? Maria relaxed a bit. Yeah, she did.

He indulged in the luxury of closing his eyes so he could revel in his success at calming her enough to feel the movement of the ship and relax. The tension melted from her shoulders, and the small smile curling on her lips almost transformed her back into the playful Maria who'd enchanted him. They'd sailed like this countless times before, except she'd rest her back against his chest and they'd move with the rhythm of the waves and enjoy the wind in their faces. If she only knew how much she loved stolen hours like this at the helm. He swallowed. If she remembered sailing, then she'd recall everything. This moment could end on an entirely different note. Playing this goddamn charade was killing him.

WITH DEL RIO BEHIND HER, Maria once again felt an absurd sense of peace. The breeze blowing in her face, the *Honora* winging across the open water like some exotic sea creature, the heat of Del Rio's breath in her hair seemed absolutely perfect. Second nature. Yin and yang.

Something about being outdoors, using nature to propel

them to their destination, filled her with satisfaction and...
freedom. For this one moment her defenses dropped. She
inhaled deeply, willing herself to absorb the experience.

She would have to paint this, too.

The calm emanating from Del Rio's body encouraged
her to trust her instincts manning the helm. Soon she anticipated the motion of the ship beneath her feet and adjusted the course even before the *Honora* shifted direction.
The sensation felt akin to flying. Maria relaxed more, surprising herself when she leaned back into Del Rio's chest
as if into a familiar easy chair. She was grateful he didn't
move.

"Feels like flying, doesn't it?" His voice was low against
her ear.

A chuckle escaped her lips. "I was just thinking the
same thing."

"Do you like it?"

Grudgingly she had to admit the truth. "I could love
this."

The muscles in his arms and chest flexed against her
back as he sucked in a breath. "You always did."

Zing. Always did?

She twisted back to look at him. "I've done this before?"

He lifted his sunglasses to meet her gaze, the sadness
in his eyes soul-deep. "You wanted to retrace your steps,
so we've been on the exact same course as before."

Her brain felt as if it was short-circuiting. No matter
how she concentrated, nothing remotely familiar rose in
her mind. "I can't recall any of this. I feel as if I've never
been on the water before, even though I know that's not
true."

She tore herself from the circle of his arms and the heat
of his body, leaving him to steer. She sat at the farthest end

of the seat, placing her back against the bench, facing him as if fending off attack.

It was just like Del Rio's claim they'd been lovers. How would she know what he said was true? Granted, she'd survived a boating accident, but she had no idea how she got on that boat, where it sailed from or who owned it. For all she knew, she'd never set foot on the *Honora,* though the ship did feel familiar. She'd also understood how to steer the helm rather quickly, as if by instinct.

Not knowing left her feeling more helpless than she wanted to acknowledge. Having to trust Del Rio for the truth left her skittish. She'd suspected his motives until dinner last night. He seemed sincere, but what the hell were his intentions? She needed answers.

"Please, tell me you are lying."

He stood rock still. "Why would I lie, Maria?"

She said nothing, unwilling to share her thoughts.

"Speak! Why would I lie to you?"

Her gaze shot to his face at the vehemence in his voice. "Because I've been thinking."

"About what?"

"Your motive for taking me on this trip."

His expression softened. "I already told you why in West End."

She shook her head. "But how can I believe you?"

"What could I possibly gain from lying to you?"

She hated to state her suspicions out loud, but what else was there to say?

"You know that Elias is not well."

The look he gave her made it very clear he did not like the direction this conversation was taking. "And?"

She swallowed hard. "You have no family. I have no idea what your financial situation is. What if you're trying to cement your place in the Santiago legacy?"

"So, I seduce you, convince you to marry me and control your life because you have no memory."

She suddenly felt incredibly foolish. There was plenty of inheritance to go around, should Poppa bequeath anything to him, but she was operating on principle here. Moral standards against gold digging. She lifted her chin in defiance.

He shook his head. "And you suspect me of these intentions because…?"

Heck, she might as well finish this awful conversation. Ticking off reasons on each finger, she said, "For the past year I've watched you shadow Poppa. Don't get me wrong, I know he trusts you. But you have no job. No ambition. I can't remember you. Then what? No sooner have we landed in the Bahamas when you tell me we were lovers and that's why you're here. I can't remember. Next, you coerced me into manning the helm. Once I start to enjoy it, you drop the bomb that I've sailed this ship before. With you. I can't remember, and although I've recalled every member of my family, I don't remember you. So, what does that scenario look like to you?"

He stared at her a long moment from behind his sunglasses. A muscle worked along his jaw and she expected him to blow any second. Instead, that sexy pirate's grin broke across his lips. He threw his head back and howled with laughter.

Suddenly, the confines of the cockpit seemed way too small. She stood. "Don't mock me."

He pinched his forehead, shaking his head as if he'd heard the best joke of his life. "Oh, don't worry. I'm laughing at my own idiocy."

"What do you mean?"

He looked as if he'd just come to an unfortunate conclusion. "Never mind. Just don't worry, Princess. Your virtue and your inheritance are safe from me."

The awful sense of blackness closed in as she tried to retrieve a memory—any memory that linked them as a couple—while staring at this infuriating, incredibly sexy man.

Nothing.

From the way he looked at her now, she had hurt him very deeply. The only way she could learn the truth was by collecting facts. Elias had to know the answers. She'd suspected he had been shielding her all this time thinking it was in her best interest. Now, she needed facts.

She held out her hands in a gesture of truce. "Look. I can help solve this issue between us. I'll take the helm. I'd appreciate if you'd get me that damn cell phone. Now."

CHAPTER SEVEN

AT LEAST FIVE MINUTES PASSED. Del Rio was taking too long getting the phone. What was he doing down there?

Her nerves, already short-circuited from her sparring with Del Rio, couldn't take much more. The *Honora* sailed on course, the steady wind making it easy to keep the heading, but panic edged her confidence.

Balancing herself as a gust tilted the boat, she grimaced while adjusting course. Something didn't seem right here. Despite amnesia, she'd remembered her car and how to drive it. The same thing with her painting—the techniques had not been lost to her. Yet, if Daniel spoke the truth, handling the helm should feel familiar. It did not. Watching Del Rio sail the boat and dock in West End yesterday all seemed new to her.

Today, she discovered she liked steering the *Honora;* he'd been correct in that assumption. But for the life of her, she didn't know what to do with the sails and lines. If she truly was an experienced sailor, why did it not seem familiar?

She concentrated all her energy on remembering. She scanned the horizon, the sea, the shoreline to the south and recognized nothing.

The truth dawned. Of course. She remembered nothing because no memories existed. She and Del Rio had no shared past. The liar was manipulating her and doing a damned good job of it.

She needed to speak with Poppa to end this charade. Where was Del Rio? Had he fallen into the bilge?

"Hey, Captain. Where's that phone?"

Ahead of the boat, the water changed to that incredible turquoise she loved best. Her gaze followed the line of pale blue to where it darkened off to port.

Turquoise means sandy bottom. Royal means deeper water. Oh, *Dios.* They could run aground on this track. She knew enough to understand that at the speed they were going, the *Honora's* keel could sustain serious damage. Panic gripped her as tightly as she gripped the wheel.

"Get up here, Del Rio. Now!"

Panic filled her voice. Her immediate reaction was to untie the sheets and release the wind from the sails. She froze. Uncertain. She wanted to jump overboard.

"Del Rio."

No time left, she turned the wheel, pointing the bow toward the darker water. The action dumped the air from the sails. The boom slid above the companionway just as Del Rio emerged. He registered the motion and reacted fast enough to duck as the boom shifted, slamming to a stop with a thud that rattled the boat. The sheet Maria hadn't untied from the cleat kept the boom from jibing completely.

Daniel jumped into the cockpit.

"Look." Maria pointed to the shallow water. As she did, the *Honora* lurched, knocking them both off their feet. The wheel spun, turning the ship toward the shallow bank.

Daniel grabbed the wheel and spun it to port. The ship jolted as it skidded into the shallows. With lightning speed he released the sheets, the sails snapping angrily overhead.

Daniel pulled Maria back to the wheel. "Keep this course."

Holding the *Honora* steady was like wrestling a gorilla. The initial forward motion of the ship and the lack of wind gave Maria no power to command the boat's direction. Running aground had practically stopped the ship dead. Now, the *Honora* floundered, bouncing off the bottom with a deadening thud, over and over, while Daniel changed tack.

In mere seconds, he pulled the sheets on the port side until both mainsail and jib filled with air, tilting the boat in the opposite direction of the bank. With a shudder, it slid out of the sand, coasting toward deeper water.

Slowly, the vessel picked up speed, creating pressure against the wheel once more.

"Close one." He glanced at Maria. "Good job."

Maria's knees buckled. "Please take the helm." She dropped down on the bench, covering her face with her hands as the adrenaline surge subsided.

Daniel squeezed her shoulder. "You okay?"

Anger heated her words. "Don't ask me to steer anymore."

He looked surprised. "Why? You saw danger and reacted."

Her hands shook. She stuck them between her knees. "I almost knocked your head off."

He chuckled. "You did, at that."

She bit her lip in dismay. He'd made sailing look so easy. He'd expected her to know what to do. Perhaps she had indulged his expectation and taken the helm because Poppa always drew a line between the roles of men and women. He'd gone so far as to order Maria and Carmen to use chauffeurs instead of learning to drive because women were not meant to operate machinery.

Momma had prevailed, of course, in ensuring she and Carmen had driving classes, even tried flying. Maria felt driven to be accomplished in all the lessons she pursued as proof to Poppa that she was capable. To almost damage the ship and cause harm to Del Rio due to her lack of skill was seriously eroding her confidence.

He shook his head. "Maria. You reacted by instinct— maybe even memory. We could have been hard aground for hours."

Her chin trembled. "I didn't know what to do."

"No, Maria. Listen. You recognized trouble because you used to sail the *Honora* all the time. You didn't trust yourself to trim the sails, but that was the correct choice. Had you done that, we wouldn't have jibed or hit bottom."

She slapped her hands over her ears. "I can't hear this."

Ever so gently he lifted her chin with a finger. "Would you be willing to trust that I'm telling you the truth right now?"

Dropping her hands to her lap, she shook her head. "No."

MARIA LOOKED SO HELPLESS. He wrenched his gaze away to steer the *Honora* into the channel he'd neglected to point out to her before going below. He hadn't expected to be away from the cockpit so long. What he really felt like doing was pulling Maria into his arms and reassuring her.

Right. As if she'd permit him to touch her.

He shook his head, angry with himself. He'd been distracted by a brief conversation to update Elias before bringing the phone on deck. Now it would take another day or two to get Maria calmed down again. If only there was some boulder he could crawl under for upsetting her.

Reaching into the pocket of his board shorts, he pulled out the phone.

"I think you wanted this."

Listlessly she opened her palm. "Where is the seasickness medicine?"

He frowned at her distress. Opening a small locker, he tossed her the container of Bonine.

Maria retrieved a bottle of water from the fridge.

He watched in silence as she swallowed a pill.

"Sorry, Princess. I should have told you about the channel before going below."

She waved away his apology, tucked the phone in her bikini bottom and curled up beneath the towel.

"Wake me when we reach our destination."

He leaned closer. "Hey, I'd give my right arm to be that telephone right now."

"Oh, shut up."

She didn't even bother to look at him. With a cockpit cushion cradling her head, her hands tucked underneath her chin, one slender foot peeking out from beneath her sarong, she looked so fragile.

She'd removed her sunglasses and visor, giving him a clear view of the dark lashes fanning her upper cheeks. Her lips—relaxed, open slightly, and so damned kissable—caught his breath. He fisted his hand instead of running a finger over those lips just to feel the electricity of touching her. She lay so close yet was fathoms away from his reach. His head ached with unease. He'd blown his second attempt to jog her memory.

He glanced at her prone form. Her shallow, troubled breathing betrayed she wasn't asleep, but a tightness around her eyes showed she ached to be.

Daniel sighed. Sleep always proved a fine escape from stress. He'd let her retreat this time. After all, he'd caused her unhappiness.

He was so sure making Maria sail the *Honora* would nudge her mind into recalling their time aboard the boat. Instead, running aground did nothing but throw her into denial once more, erasing any desire to remember. From the look of things, retracing the accident was driving Maria deeper into herself—and further away from him.

Way to go, hotshot.

He silently pounded his open palm on the steering wheel. This entire ordeal was not working for him. He loved Elias and Maria enough to put his life on hold for yet another month to help them, but this debacle was jeopardizing his future in more ways than one.

Her accusation of gold digging insulted him right to the core. If she forced him to defend himself publicly against such slander, he'd be hard-pressed to forgive her.

Her fears battered his confidence like a hurricane descending on a rudderless ship. Maria clearly had no intention of believing his stories, or his insights.

He'd had enough.

Before the accident, she had trusted him implicitly. Not even paparazzi or reports of other women could shake her confidence in him. Yet, regardless of everything he had revealed to her since this trip began, she still held him off. Drew complete and utter blanks when trying to scrounge up an inkling of memory about him.

Relationships fell apart for many reasons. Amnesia was no different from falling out of love with someone. What hurt most about her unwillingness to believe him was that it echoed the distrust that had fueled the fight on that fatal day she seemed in such an idiotic hurry to replay.

Had Carmen poisoned Maria's love for him so completely before she died that there was no turning back?

Well, he'd undertaken this journey for a reason. He would either awaken Maria and bring her back into his life, or start a new one. He had dreams, too. He wanted a wife who loved him. Wanted a passel of kids running around his feet with their mother's eyes and his cocky attitude. He wanted to plant roots like he never had before because, damn it all, family mattered. One thing he'd learned from ten years on the ocean was that if a sailor did not have a love to come home to, he'd never come home.

He wanted with all his heart for Maria to be that love. God knew she had touched him like no woman ever could. But if their paths were meant to split, so be it. Suddenly, Brisbane loomed far more attractive than ever before.

After a while, he glanced at Maria again. Even breathing. The Bonine had done the trick. She'd sleep for at least two hours.

Watching her, he felt a hunger burn through him like a bonfire. While he felt himself steeling his gut to walk away, he still had time before giving up for good. He sent a silent prayer skyward for the wisdom to walk when, and if, the situation came to that.

In the solitude on the quiet deck, he decided to change tack with Maria. The rest of this voyage would be played *his* way. No more following the rules. Only he and Maria were on the *Honora,* now. He'd take matters into his own hands.

Right. His hands. The captain of the *Honora.* The one man Maria would damn to hell when she learned the truth.

Shaking his head, he pushed guilt far from his mind. No room for it now. The answer lay in not trying so hard. Just let the days evolve. After all, he knew Maria's fears as his own, especially because he *did* remember. When Elias asked him to do this one last favor, did he think for one stinking second that Daniel wanted to relive the boating accident once more, let alone Maria?

Hell. He felt like the mythological Icarus, craving flight, yet using feathered wings affixed with wax. He'd fly, all right—right into the sun with the *Honora* as his wings. Then truth and memory would do their dirty work. Yes, indeed, flying with no parachute. As usual.

This whole trip would end in disaster.

THE SLOW MOTION OF A furling sail edged into Maria's awareness. Low enough now, the sun slanted hot on her body beneath the bimini. She had rolled over onto her back, the trade winds tickling her senses between sleep and wakefulness.

The air smelled salty, pure, alive. She sucked a breath deep into her lungs and stretched, unwilling to open her eyes. Dregs of sleep still held her, her imagination tingling with visions of dolphins and rolling sapphire waves.

An anchor chain rattled, the tremor prodding Maria fully awake. She opened her eyes. No longer under sail, the boat swung in a lazy arc as the anchor set. The memory of running aground invaded her thoughts and she bolted upright.

Del Rio was returning from the bow.

"Easy, Princess. We made it safe and sound. How about a swim?"

He must have noticed perspiration drenched her. She glanced at their anchorage in the lee of a tiny island. Remote. Breathtaking. Incredibly romantic.

Uh-oh.

"A swim's not a bad idea." She stood.

Del Rio pointed to her bikini bottom. "Don't forget the phone."

He was already pulling off his T-shirt and heading for the stern, a flash of lean, tanned muscle, dark hair and fathomless blue eyes.

Maria swallowed hard. Maybe she'd wait for that swim.

He shot her a grin. "Last one in cooks dinner."

With an easy lunge, he dived into water so clear she

could see his broad strokes beneath the surface. The sun dappled his skin through the water. Starfish the size of shoe boxes littered the bottom. Sea creatures darted about him. He surfaced a good twenty feet from the boat and floated on his back. Neptune in his element.

"Ahh. Heaven."

Maria dropped the phone and her sarong next to the sunglasses and visor. Del Rio made the water look irresistible. Besides, a long day at sea always ended with a swim. She dived, wondering, *Where did I get that idea?*

The world beneath the surface was almost surreal. Salt water stung her eyes, but curiosity compelled her to look. Blurred, colors and shapes took form exactly as she'd paint them on canvas. The sea's purity had an almost gel-like texture against her skin. If diamonds and sapphires could be liquid, they'd feel like this.

Yes. She'd spend the night creating. The thought calmed her considerably as she kicked to the surface.

Del Rio floated nearby. "Doesn't get much better than this, Maria, my dear."

Sheer bliss suffused his face. She couldn't help but share the feeling. "This is pretty spectacular. Where are we?"

He turned on his stomach and swam toward her. "Around the north end of Grand Bahama Island. Like it?"

She treaded water as he grew closer, fighting the urge to use him as a floating device. Or was it an urge to wrap herself around his body? Ugh. She took one huge stroke backward. "Am I supposed to remember this, too?"

He circled her, but not so close as to threaten her comfort. Briefly, his gaze penetrated hers before he swam away. Over his shoulder he called, "Do you think you should?"

"Hey." She swam after him. "Are you playing games with me?"

He reached the anchor line, grabbing it. He motioned for her to hold the line above his hand. They faced each other, treading water.

"No. I'm just changing the rules."

"What do you mean?"

He pushed hair off his forehead. "I think there's just a little too much pressure going on here. Pressure for you to remember. Pressure for me to make you remember. Let's just forget it all and see what develops."

Water dripped off his straggly hair, his eyes practically the color of the sea, his straight, white teeth perfect for nibbling— *Cut it out, Maria.*

"Why?"

He shrugged. "I did some thinking while you slept. If I was caught in an objectionable situation beyond my control, I'd be pretty riled. You don't deserve this treatment, and neither do I. So I give up."

"You're playing me like some fish you'd catch."

"No." He made a silly motion with his hand. "If I was a Boy Scout, I'd swear I'm telling the truth."

Relief flooded her to have Del Rio acknowledge her position, but she knew better. He was up to something, she was sure. She swam for the ladder. As she reached the first rung, she peered at Del Rio still holding the anchor line.

"First one out doesn't have to do a damn thing tonight. My canvas calls. You can let me know when dinner is ready."

MARIA CLAIMED THE BOW for painting. This narrow point of the ship not only offered the most remote spot on the sailboat, but the smooth, teak deck was wide enough to support her easel and stool. The most comforting breeze a girl could ever imagine tugged at her sleeveless peach tunic and her bare legs, exposed to the thigh in a pair of cuffed, linen shorts already smeared with paint.

Maria was in her glory.

Below, Del Rio rattled pots and pans. The savory aroma of sautéed shallots and mushrooms blended with reggae music and filtered up through the open hatches. Already, her mouth watered. Every now and then, his voice rose with the music, imitating the island dialect perfectly.

A tinge of guilt crossed her mind for leaving him to cook, but it quickly disappeared with another brushstroke, and another, and another.

Soon, her stomach growled, pulling her back to the sounds and smells emanating from the hatch. She'd slept through lunch and hadn't realized how hungry she was. Meanwhile, Del Rio had received nothing but her cold shoulder since their swim.

She'd do dishes as penance.

While absorbed in her work earlier, she'd caught a glimpse of another sailboat dropping anchor. But when a woman's voice rose with excitement from a dinghy below, Maria nearly jumped out of her skin. Before she could even answer, Del Rio appeared on deck.

He shaded his eyes from the lowering sun. "Ahoy, sailors."

The couple looked younger than the two of them. The guy grinned through his dark beard, and lifted a Dolphins baseball cap in a wave. His mate, a tiny blonde holding a pair of binoculars, had her eyes glued on Maria.

"You're Maria Santiago. I saw you through the field glasses. I love your work!" She turned to the man. "See, Brad? She's painting. I told you."

Before the woman could gush on, Maria waved. "Hi." She managed a smile, although the last thing she wanted was to socialize with strangers. She had been shy about attention before her amnesia, and now her reticence was even more exaggerated. She didn't want to be rude, but she preferred anonymity. The worst was when a stranger would say, "Oh, it's so nice to see you again."

Did that mean she was supposed to pretend to know them? Admit she couldn't remember anything? It was even worse when people brought up the accident, or Carmen. She'd started to feel like part of a three-ring circus in public. She could hear the media now: "And in this corner, we have Maria Santiago, amnesia victim extraordinaire. Go ahead, ask her a question. Watch her struggle for the answer."

She had cloaked herself in solitude because it was safe. That's why she no longer attended gallery showings or interviews or luncheons. She couldn't bear making a fool of herself.

She slid her sunglasses back onto her face.

The woman continued. "We own one of your paintings. Bought it in the spring show at your gallery. You know, the *Sleeping Palms?* We just love it."

Del Rio answered for her. "That's one of my favorites, too. Glad you're enjoying the piece."

Maria shot him a grateful glance before closing the tops on her oils. Clearly, her solitude had been interrupted.

The woman pointed and slapped a hand over her mouth. "Oh, my God. Daniel Del Rio."

"Okay, Traci. Easy does it." He laughed at his wife's enthusiasm. "She gets a bit carried away with celebrities. I'm Brad Mitchell."

Del Rio nodded. "Nice to meet you. Where you headed?"

"As far as we can get in a week." He pointed a thumb over his shoulder. "Chartered the boat. We're celebrating our first wedding anniversary."

The easy grin on Del Rio's face broke. "Well, congratulations."

Maria wanted to dive off the other side. The last thing she needed to witness while in the company of Del Rio was wedded bliss. Not when she accused him of trying to manipulate her into his arms so he could inherit Reefside.

The woman, Traci, pointed back and forth between Maria and Del Rio. "I see you two are still an item. Who knew? It's been so long since you've been in the papers."

A bomb could have exploded in Maria's lap. She jerked back to look at the woman. Using every ounce of cool she could muster and ignoring the blast of Del Rio's gaze, she managed a laugh. "Please don't go spreading rumors."

Traci looked confused, then brightened. "Oh, I understand. Privacy is important for you."

Del Rio spoke, amusement bubbling in his voice. "We certainly appreciate your understanding."

He gestured to the set table in the cockpit. "I haven't prepared enough to offer you dinner, but you're welcome to join us later for coffee."

Brad waved him off. "Too kind of you. This is our first night out. We've dinner plans of our own."

The couple exchanged glances as only newlyweds could. Maria wanted to choke. The intimacy these two shared lay nowhere on her horizon. To her surprise, she felt a twinge of sadness.

"Well, happy anniversary," Maria said, smiling.

Traci peered past Maria to her canvas. "Ooh, that's gorgeous. What are you going to call it?"

Despite her shyness, Maria warmed to the woman's enthusiasm. She shrugged, wiping paint from her hand as she studied her underwater impression.

"Haven't decided yet."

"Well, I want to buy it."

Brad groaned. "Honey, is that before or after we put the down payment on the house?"

"We'll discuss it at dinner, dear."

Traci's dismissal held all sorts of promises.

"Only been a year, eh?" Del Rio's laughter carried over the water as they rowed away.

Traci waved her field glasses. "Wonderful meeting you, Maria."

Maria waved then turned toward her easel before she lost the last dregs of her composure. The woman's words ricocheted in her head.

You two are still an item.

Her hands shook as she wiped her brush with a cloth. Little tremors rocked her body. She stared blindly at her task, searching her mind. Each and every nerve ending strained to capture some wisp of memory.

Nothing.

She. Could. Not. Remember.

Del Rio made his way toward the bow. He was smart enough not to get too close. "You okay, Princess?"

She couldn't even lift her head. "How much did you pay for that setup?"

"Oh, Maria."

"Don't act hurt." Maria swung to her feet. "I can't remember anything, Daniel. That woman calls us an item and it's killing me because it's all black inside my mind."

Daniel slapped a hand to his chest, his eyes reflecting both hope and agony.

"What?" She swiped her nose with the back of her hand.

"You called me Daniel."

His voice was so low, she wasn't sure if she heard him or read his lips. "So what?"

"I haven't heard you say my name in a year. You don't mind if I just revel in the moment, do you?"

She rolled her eyes. "Cut the comedy. How do I find the truth, will you tell me that?"

He offered her a crooked smile. "We can try to jog your memory."

He moved closer, ever so slowly, as if loath to spook a wounded animal. He brushed his knuckles against her cheek, his warm, familiar scent mingling with the salt air.

"I can suggest two ways."

Her muscles tensed, but her blood warmed at the whisper of his touch. She jutted her chin a notch. "What are they?"

He stepped infinitesimally closer. "For one, you can let me kiss you and see if the sensation is familiar...."

Her knees practically buckled beneath her. She cleared her throat to speak. "And the other?"

He shrugged. "Call Elias."

That snapped her awake. "Great idea." She pushed past him. "Now, what did I do with that phone?"

CHAPTER EIGHT

FOR HEAVEN'S SAKE. At her age, her hands shouldn't be trembling while dialing a darned telephone.

She waited for the number to connect. On the other side of her locked cabin door, Del Rio continued to bang around the kitchen. At least he had the good grace to turn up the music so he wouldn't eavesdrop on her phone call.

Three rings...four rings...

Where was Nurse Mills? She always kept a portable phone nearby while attending Poppa.

"Reefside."

"Hello, Eduardo? Is that you?"

"*Sí*. Señorita Santiago. All is well?"

"Yes. Thank you. My father. Is he about?" If she didn't get to the point, the butler would begin rambling about the day's affairs.

"*Sí*. I believe in the study. Let me check."

The silence while on hold seemed cavernous. If she didn't hear Poppa's voice soon, she'd be lost.

"*Querida*."

Relief flooded her. "Poppa. How are you?"

He grumbled a bit. "Nothing different from yesterday or the day you left. Nice of you to worry about me."

"I'm not worried, Poppa, but I do miss you."

"You are enjoying your trip?"

She swallowed the knot in her throat. "I have questions."

Silence fell for a moment. "You sound frightened, *my daughter*. Is everything all right?"

"Poppa. Captain Del Rio and I…"

A soft chuckle rose in the phone. "So, you have become sweet on him?"

"No!"

"He's a fine man. Give him time."

"Poppa. That's not my question."

After an odd silence, he said, "No, I would assume not." He didn't sound pleased.

She lowered her voice. "Del Rio insists we were an item before my accident. Is it true?"

"What is this item?"

Poppa had an enfuriating habit of misunderstanding American idioms when he wanted to avoid answering a question. Tamping down frustration, she replied, "No, Poppa. Del Rio and I. Were we *los amantes*?"

"How come you have not asked me this question before now?"

"It never occurred to me."

"And would I let you sail away with Daniel if I thought he would mistreat you in any way?"

She grew still. "No, Poppa. You would not."

"Then I cannot answer a question when you already know the answer. Trust yourself, Maria. You are a smart woman."

"But—"

The line went dead. He hung up on her. She slapped the phone onto the bunk.

Damn. Damn. Damn.

She needed air. Though it had become quiet in the galley, opening her cabin door and facing Del Rio did not seem an option at the moment. So she climbed out the hatch.

The sun lay on the horizon in a spectacular encore to the day. Golden rays spilled against the silhouette of clouds growing deep amber against a fading sky of burnt umber and goldenrod. It always amazed her that such colors would dominate when an hour ago, azure skies filled the horizon. In the blink of an eye, one's world could change.

Yes, indeed.

Despite her disquiet, she sighed at the beauty of the sunset, letting her spirit drink in the tranquility. Okay. She couldn't remember. She'd pretended for the past year that her memory didn't matter. After all, there was nothing she could do about it. Images simply would not come. Painting proved a great channel to forget the past and forge a future. But, clearly, her escape had failed. Every time she looked at her own reflection now, she saw Carmen. It was as if she, Maria, no longer mattered. The mirror of her soul had been shattered when Carmen died. With the recent onslaught of horrible nightmares where Carmen appeared cruel and distorted, even Maria's precious memories of her twin were being violated. Sleep had become a precious commodity of which she had little.

Sighing, she retrieved her canvas and paints from the bow. Couldn't she just wake up from her amnesia? Was it too much to ask? Standing in the quiet bow of a sailboat, wrestling with her own identity, had never been part of her schedule. Yet, it sure seemed as if Dr. Hernandez thought she should be doing just that. Dr. Hernandez, Poppa and Captain—

"Del Rio?"

Silence.

She climbed across the deck to the companionway and stuck her head below. No one. Lights were on, but no Del Rio.

' She hustled her supplies into the spare cabin and propped the canvas on a shelf to continue drying.

She knocked on his cabin door. No answer. She peered inside. Tidy bunk. Shirt on the stool by the chart table. VHF on. Stereo on. Hum of AC. No Del Rio.

"Hey? Where are you?"

The cockpit was empty, but she knew that. She looked past the beautifully set table to the stern.

Del Rio was climbing into the dinghy tied to the back of the Mitchells' sailboat, his silhouette an athlete in motion.

Her blood ran hot. He said he didn't know those people. Dios mio. Had he lied once more? Was their rendezvous intended?

DANIEL KNEW THAT STANCE way too well. He suppressed a chuckle. In the past, every time she'd face him with fists on hips, they'd ended up making love. Heaven help him, he wanted to kiss that scowl right off her face, just like old times.

Even in the fading light she looked forbidding and sexy as hell with the breeze wrapping her hair around her shoulders. He'd have to use kid gloves on this encounter, because if this was about her phone call with Elias, their trip could become shorter than anticipated.

He reached to secure the dinghy. "You sure are doing a slow burn."

She pointed a finger at him. "I think you have been lying to me."

"Whoa. That sounds serious." *Uh-oh. Did Elias tell her?* He almost fell overboard with relief when she pointed to the Mitchells' sailboat.

"You said they were strangers? How much are you paying them to convince me we were lovers?"

"Maria. I've never seen those two before today."

He climbed on board, but Maria refused to budge, blocking his way on deck. She poked an angry finger into his chest. "What is going on here, Daniel?"

He stepped closer to her. This eruption had to be more than him rowing over to the *Blue Moon.* Time to level the playing field.

A grin tugged at his mouth. "You know, when we used to argue like this, we'd end up kissing."

"Stop it."

He met her gaze. "What the hell is the matter?"

"Poppa didn't answer my questions."

So here she was, more confused and steaming-mad because she'd have to trust her own judgment, or worse, him.

"It must truly suck to be you right now." He reached to light a lantern on the table. "I'm sorry for you."

"Why did you leave the boat?"

She had the good grace to cringe at her own petulance, but that oh, so familiar need to spar had her cranking. If she didn't know her own habits, Daniel surely did. He was ready. He could use a release for all his pent-up emotions.

He reached into the fridge for a beer. "For your information, Princess, despite the music, I could hear your conversation with Elias. So, I went for a row and got waved over by your favorite fan. I spent twenty minutes telling Traci fairy tales about you. You might want to thank me when art sales start increasing." He took another swig of beer.

"You're such a liar."

With lightning speed, he pulled her against him and

dropped onto the cushions, wrapping her tightly in his arms. His mouth inches from hers, he said, "I told you. I don't lie to you, Maria. I'll tolerate no more insults."

She pushed to free herself, but his grip tightened. His face inches from hers, he inhaled the sweet scent that was purely Maria and loved it. Anger pressed her lips together in a hard line, making them all the more tempting.

"Oh, no, sweet pea. You picked this fight, and I'll see it end with an apology."

"You can rot in hell."

She pummeled his chest once, but he put down the beer and locked her arms beneath his.

He licked her cheek like a big dog. "Apologize, Maria Santiago."

"Stop it, right now." She twisted her face away.

He licked her other cheek, wanting more than life itself to turn this torture into kisses. "Say you're sorry."

She arched her back, straining to escape his grip, pressing her breasts against his chest. He practically groaned at her usual reaction. This type of sparring had been so typical between them; it was as if he responded on autopilot. Chuckling, he licked the entire length of her neck from exposed collarbone to her ear, then caught her earlobe between his teeth.

She stilled.

He whispered, "Apologize."

She pushed and he released her. She fell onto the cockpit floor with an ungraceful thud. Pulling herself to her feet, she glared at him while rubbing her backside. "I will not apologize."

She headed for the companionway then turned before he could reply, fury blazing in her eyes. "And don't you ever touch me again. Do you understand?"

He held her gaze for a long moment, releasing a frustrated breath. There was no way in hell he'd follow that order. Not until he knew for sure that he'd lost her for good.

He reached for his beer. "Quit getting your thong in a twist. Let's forget you had a little tantrum and eat."

CHAPTER NINE

THIS WAS THE SECOND DAY in Hope Town Harbour and Maria hadn't uttered a word. She was too angry over how Del Rio had treated her. That, and the useless call to Poppa had her fuming, although she had been glad to hear his voice and know he was well.

She would have stayed in her cabin for the sail, but the sunlight and breeze pouring through the hatch had drawn her out. She'd also discovered that even with her sea legs, staying below deck when waves hit set her stomach off. It was either waves or nerves. She chose to think the former.

At one point, Del Rio asked her to take the helm. She was sure he expected her to object and start talking. Instead, she took the wheel in silence. In her solitude, she discovered the process of steering in open water calmed her. There were no sandbars to run aground on and the *Honora* flew under the breeze on their charted course. The exhilarating feeling of skimming over the waves had helped soothe her angry heart.

Nevertheless, she ignored Del Rio's questions. She took her meals to the bow on deck, where she finished yet another painting with the porpoises. It didn't take long for Del Rio to catch on to her intentions, and he soon seemed as comfortable with the silence as she was.

Only, Maria wasn't comfortable. Almost a week had passed and she was no more enlightened about her amnesia than before setting sail. She was, however, becoming all too familiar with how good it was having Del Rio around. Close enough for the scent of his skin to invade her senses. The strong pull she felt toward him left her even more confused about the possibility of "them." Del Rio didn't seem familiar, but he was incredibly enticing.

Damn him. This was not about them. This was about her amnesia and finding the answers she so desperately sought. She had decided to keep her silence like a cloistered nun. Carmen and Momma deserved as much.

But in her silence she became aware this particular tactic wasn't about Carmen and Momma. How could she find answers if she refused to ask questions? Keeping quiet had become a way to avoid interacting with this man who set her emotions whirring like a turbine.

No matter. She'd swallow her pride and speak with him again. She had to. She'd demand an apology for his rudeness to save face. With that behind them, she'd be very careful in further interactions with him. But truth was, they had to carry on.

She sat in the cockpit, wearing a straw hat, bikini cover-up and sandals. Her painting equipment sat in an oversize straw bag. She planned to spend the morning on the beach. Nothing like a little local color to get ideas flowing. She just needed the damn dinghy and Del Rio had yet to return from shore.

Leaving him stranded on board for a few hours seemed like decent revenge. She would speak with him, as soon as she recovered from the feel of his tongue trailing from her neck to her earlobe. And his teeth...

Thinking about it sent heat searing through her. The moment had felt divine and that's what riled her. She'd defy any woman not to react to his touch...and lie awake all night wondering what his mouth would feel like on the rest of her body.

Damn Del Rio. Damn all men.

Like radar, she spotted Del Rio emerging from the grocery store, hold the door open for a woman and a child before heading down the dock. His dark hair seemed to absorb and reflect spikes of morning sun. He wore sunglasses. His easy gait had her salivating. She shook herself. He was danger, for goodness' sake.

He climbed the ladder into the dinghy one-handed, carrying groceries in his other arm as effortlessly as he had held her.

Part of her wanted to corner him and explain herself. She wanted to explain her fears. She wanted him to free her from her nightmares. Tell her the answers Elias refused to disclose. She wanted to apologize for being suspicious, for hating him for knowing what she didn't know, and hating him for being the most seductive man she ever laid eyes on. She wanted to be friends, yet send him packing to keep her world safe. She wanted to be set free from the darkness.

But as he approached, she became tongue-tied. This was why she had enjoyed her solitude so much. She hated sounding foolish. Vulnerable. Needy.

Del Rio climbed the ladder into the cockpit. "Morning, Princess."

"Morning."

He seemed surprised that she answered. She waited until he passed before descending the ladder halfway herself. She slid her sunglasses on the bridge of her nose and reached for her supplies, Del Rio watching her.

"I take it you'll be busy this morning."

"I'm heading to the beach," she answered without meeting his gaze. Damn, dealing with this man was so difficult when her heart was pounding.

Settling herself, she realized she'd neglected to untie

the dinghy. How dumb. She stood. Del Rio watched like
Zeus from Mount Olympus, then waved her into her seat.

"I'll release you, Ice Queen."

He wagged an admonishing finger at her in utter mock-
ery. "Careful not to exert yourself rowing. You might melt."

He tossed the line into the craft, and without a second
glance, disappeared below deck.

Yeah. She deserved that. But she still wanted his apology.

HOURS MUST HAVE PASSED because the color of the daylight
had changed, and her canvas was nearly finished. She'd
discovered a perfect spot under a palm tree on the beach
near the Hope Town Harbour Lodge. Between the manta
rays riding the surf, the smattering of tourists on the sand
and the candy-colored cottages dotting the beachfront,
Maria had discovered another world to re-create. Accom-
plishment sent a wash of warmth through her. Karen, her
gallery manager, would be delighted with the new art.

Her stomach grumbled, reminding her that she'd missed
lunch. Capping her paints, she stepped up to the bar, the
smell of conch fritters mingling with the coconut smell
of suntan lotion from sunbathers by the pool. Steel drum
music and children's laughter set a carefree rhythm to her
step. The bartender offered her a toothy grin. These island-
ers seemed so content. She placed her order then twisted
open the water he'd given her, drinking half the bottle...
and felt the uncomfortable heat of a stare.

A man sat at the end of the bar. The first impression
to hit her was that this guy had been in the sun too long.
His hair, thin, unkempt and sun bleached, stuck out from
beneath a baseball cap. The cap and sunglasses hid most
of his face, yet he blatantly stared at her. An old bandage
wrapped the better part of the hand holding a French fry

before he lifted it to his mouth. His arms and upper torso looked trim, yet he sported a beer gut that would inspire a sumo wrestler.

Maria wished this guy would find someone else to look at. The hairs on her neck rose. She ignored him, growing impatient under his gaze.

Getting up, she worked her way to the other side of the bar, where the waitresses delivered their orders to the cook. A beautiful woman wearing a bright yellow top and tight jeans was pouring gummy bear candies into a glass of milk.

The action momentarily distracted Maria as she watched the woman stir the concoction. Maria felt her nose crinkle. "You going to eat…er, drink that?"

The woman laughed, her voice throaty and tropical. "It's my lunch. I love it."

Maria shook her head. "Sorry. Looks awful from here."

She held the glass out. "Try it."

"I think I'll pass. But would you mind bringing my lunch down to the beach? The guy at the end of the bar is making me nervous."

The waitress didn't even have to look. "That's Jack."

"I don't care if he's Brad Pitt."

"He's an odd one, all right."

Maria glanced that way. He still watched her. "He lives here, then."

"If you call it livin'." The woman dipped a spoon into the glass of milk and shoveled a few gummies into her mouth. She met Maria's grimace and laughed.

"Don't worry, girl. I won't put any in your beer. And I'll bring lunch down to you as soon as it's ready."

"MY MOTHER WORE A HAT like yours."

The weirdo from the bar. Jack. Oh, great.

His grating, smoke-ravaged voice was wistful like a small child's. She didn't like thinking unkindly of people, but if this guy got much closer, she might have to use her paint box and give him a head butt.

He stood in his baseball cap, sunglasses, Hawaiian shirt and shorts like a bad version of Jimmy Buffett.

She forced a smile. "Helen Kaminski."

He frowned. "I thought you were Maria Santiago."

He knows my name? The primal urge to flee shot through her like lightning. She inhaled, playing it cool. "Helen Kaminski designed my hat."

He drowned his gruff laugh with beer.

She had to ditch him. She turned her attention to her work. A few more finishing touches, then she'd leave.

He moved into her line of vision, blocking the ocean-front cottages she was replicating.

"My mother died. Heart attack. Then the hurricane hit. Ruined our house. Now they want me to move out."

She looked up. Definitely information overload, but the guy sounded miserably forlorn. Sympathy swelled unbidden. Before she could stop, the words tumbled from her mouth. "Who does?"

He gestured east. "My sister. On the mainland."

"Well, tell her you want to stay."

"She does what she wants since my mother died."

"My mother died last year."

He nodded. "I know."

Uh-oh. She didn't like the fact he knew her business, though many strangers did, since the accident had flooded the media.

He circled behind her to look at the painting, his breathing almost asthmatic. From the corner of her eye, she saw a neglected gauze bandage wrapped around his ankle and part of his foot. Maybe walking was still painful and caused the grating sound of his breathing.

Maria stopped working. She'd finish later.

"I really must get going."

"Where's your boyfriend? He's the one I want to talk to."

Time's up. She wrapped her brushes in the cloth.

He watched in silence, the only sound his annoying wheezing, while she organized her things.

His voice dropped to a whisper. "My brother and sister say I killed my mother."

Please don't start confessing a murder.

He swung the bottle in his bandaged hand as if he had a chicken by the neck. His voice rose, suddenly angry.

"They said I upset her the last time she was here. So she had a heart attack when she returned to the mainland."

Maria froze. This guy was like a wounded dog. You'd like to help, but were almost certain he'd bite if you got too close.

"You must feel awful." She meant it, but wanted away from him, immediately.

"It's their fault, you know. Ryan getting tossed in jail. All their bickering. It wasn't me."

"Well, good. Fight for what's yours." She dropped her satchel of paints into the straw bag.

He leaned closer, pointing a finger. "Not even you can stop me."

She recoiled from the acrid smell of his breath. "Well, I certainly wouldn't want to—"

"Everything okay here?"

Del Rio's voice was like the cavalry coming to the rescue. Seeing his strong body and determined face made her practically want to applaud. Suddenly her anger at him seemed meaningless, she was so grateful to see him.

She released a breath in relief and gave him a brilliant smile. "Captain. You're just in time to haul my things to the dinghy."

If Del Rio was surprised by her change in attitude, he didn't show it. Instead, he stepped dangerously close to the intruder.

"Is there something I can do for you? Miss Santiago prefers to paint in solitude."

The man pulled off his sunglasses. Maria gasped. The whites of his eyes were bloodred, like they'd been bleeding.

"Name's Jack. Jack Sheppard."

He spoke his name as if it should mean something, dropping both arms to his sides and puffing his chest as he faced Del Rio like an overblown rooster.

Much to her surprise, the name did register with Del Rio. He stepped protectively between Jack and Maria.

"What do you want?"

"Just comparing notes with Miss Santiago, here. We have a lot in common."

Del Rio cocked an eyebrow. "I can't imagine how."

Maria rose. "I'm ready to go. Thanks for being so punctual, Captain."

Daniel pointed to the empty tray. "Let's pay your tab." He hoisted Maria's gear and led her toward the bar.

Jack replaced his sunglasses as if there had been no confrontation. "You two on vacation?"

Before Maria could reply, Del Rio answered, "Yes. Our flight leaves for the mainland this afternoon. It's been a great visit."

Maria looked at Del Rio in astonishment.

Jack grasped Maria's hand, his chapped fingers chafing her skin, and kissed her knuckles. "You really do remind me of my mother."

Something about this man was so pathetic, she actually felt sympathy for him. People didn't usually become unkempt and antisocial on their own. Something in their lives turned them. Sad. She found herself appreciating the life Poppa had provided for her, even more.

Del Rio led Maria away. He held her close enough that she could feel him stiffen. As they approached the patio, Maria whispered, "I guess you know that man."

Even behind sunglasses, Maria saw his expression of disgust. "I know the family. This was an unfortunate encounter."

"Why?"

"I'll explain later. Let's get out of here."

When they arrived at the dock a thought occurred to Maria. "How did you get to shore when I had the dinghy?"

"I hitched a ride with a pretty blonde. You jealous?"

She looked down her nose at him standing in the watercraft and ignored the twist in her chest.

Not getting a response, he pointed to a ladder at the dock. "I wrapped my shirt around my hat and swam over. Do it all the time."

So much for leaving him stranded. She took his offered hand as she balanced herself and headed for the stern seat. Damn. Her fingers tingled from his touch. As Del Rio rowed toward the *Honora* with sure, easy strokes, her eyes couldn't help but rove over his muscled arms. Man, this guy could tempt a saint.

He returned her gaze as if reading her mind.

"So, it took a wacko like Jack Sheppard to get you to appreciate my finer points and talk to me again, eh?"

Odd as it seemed, she was grateful for that. She smirked. "Sometimes one prefers the devil she knows."

He nodded in slow appreciation. "I understand that sentiment."

"Is everything all right with my father?"

He looked confused. "I think so. Why?"

"You told Jack we were flying home."

"I don't want him looking for us."

She sat back. "Think he's dangerous?"

He shrugged. "I'm thinking he'd like to cause trouble, but don't worry. I won't let it happen."

"Why?"

They'd reached the boat and Del Rio held the dinghy still so Maria could climb aboard. He handed her the canvas, admiring her work first. "This is beautiful, Maria. Your talent amazes me."

For the first time, she felt he genuinely meant the compliment.

She smiled. "Thanks, Captain."

She took the work and placed it on the bench before reaching for the bag.

"So, explain Jack to me."

He climbed aboard, secured the dinghy then stood way too close to her. "Why don't I make you a margarita first? You'll need it."

CHAPTER TEN

MARIA SIPPED HER DRINK. Cool. Tart and sweet. A hint of grainy salt on her tongue. Delicious. She was seated beneath the shade of the bimini, the lime and tequila mixture the perfect antidote for her frazzled nerves. She tucked her feet beneath her and glanced across the cockpit at Del Rio. He watched her, amusement ripe in his eyes.

"What?"

"Easy, girl. That drink is potent."

She shrugged. "Look. Before we become all buddy-buddy again, we have to clear the air."

"That would be a novel idea."

She reached for a tortilla chip and dipped it unceremoniously into guacamole. "I would like an apology."

She couldn't see his eyes behind the sunglasses, but given how his face grew still, she figured he didn't appreciate the request.

He said, "I have an idea."

"Like?"

"How about you start, then I'll follow."

"What? Me? Apologize?"

He shrugged. "Evens the score. You picked the fight. I ended it. We were both wrong."

A ready excuse almost popped on the tip of her tongue. She caught herself. No way would she use her amnesia as an excuse for bad behavior. He was right. They both knew this trip would have more tense moments than not. It was time they dealt with that fact.

"Okay, Captain. I'm sorry that I started the fight and you finished it."

"Fair enough. I'm sorry I upset you, but I sure loved holding you in my lap."

She felt heat rush up her neck and into her cheeks.

He grinned. "Sorry, couldn't help myself."

Before she could respond, he held up a hand. "Truth be told, Maria, I cannot imagine how difficult it must be for you to take this journey. Whether or not my opinion means anything at all to you, I want you to know I admire your courage." He shook his head. "I'm not so sure I'd have the strength to fight the fears you must feel from not remembering."

She was stunned. "Wow. Thank you."

"You're welcome. And from now on, I'll be more conscious of how challenging this trip is for you. If I get bullheaded or say something stupid, just smack me."

She laughed. Here he was, doing it again. Tugging on her heartstrings. At least with his cooperation, it should be easier to accomplish her goals—as long as she didn't read any hidden meanings into his promise. Already, tension drained from her shoulders.

"I'm speechless."

"Now, that's one for the records."

They both laughed, until a pleasant silence fell between them.

She hesitated to break the mood, but it was time for answers. "So, tell me about our friend from the beach."

He immediately sobered. "Jack Sheppard."

"How do you know him?"

"That name doesn't ring a bell?"

Frowning, she shook her head.

KATHLEEN PICKERING   137

"Hold on to your drink, Maria. This isn't good."

"Maybe I should put it down." She folded her hands in her lap, and waited.

Del Rio looked decidedly uncomfortable. "I know you can't remember the details, Maria, but please understand this is the truth."

She was about to step over the line of her defenses and believe him. Releasing the breath she held, she said, "Okay. I'll listen."

He removed his sunglasses, letting them drop in his lap. "Jack's brother drove the thunder boat that rammed the skiff at the accident."

The protective shield inside her head slammed into place so hard she winced. She tried to breathe, but could not. Del Rio immediately stood and seated himself next to her. He cradled her hand in his.

"Hold on, Princess."

She stared at him, seeing nothing but black. Her body wanted to shut down, retreat, run for her life.

She managed to gasp. "Let go."

Del Rio's grip tightened. "No."

Struggling, she stared, the sound of fear echoing in her ears as she labored to pull air into her lungs. She could hear Del Rio's voice but saw nothing.

Blackness.

He grabbed her shoulders. "Maria. Look at me."

The brusqueness of his voice startled her. It took a few moments before she realized Del Rio had pulled her against his chest, distressed for her. She felt like an idiot for reacting so intensely, but she couldn't help herself. Jack had known what she did not, and played her for a fool. Now she understood why she had felt such fear in his presence. He harbored bad intent.

Damn her amnesia.

She let Del Rio hold her until the chill left her bones. She was aware of how gently he was trying to help her understand. She must be scaring the wits out of him. She pulled away, immediately missing the heat of his body, but managed to meet the concern in his eyes.

"I'm okay. Sorry."

He cupped her head, smoothing her hair, capturing her face with his hands. His smile, so simple, so real, warmed her heart.

"Lost your focus there for a second. I thought you were going to faint."

"Are you sure it's him?" Her voice was a whisper.

He chuckled. "Looks just like his brother. Only uglier."

She wanted to feel the warmth of his body once again. Moving closer, he wrapped his arms around her, pulling her to him. She rested her cheek against his chest. His body warmth, the salty fragrance of his skin, the strength of those arms and the press of his body offered too much of a haven to resist.

Shoot.

Another reality check. For another time. Right now, she had to hear this story.

He must have felt the same because he pulled away, meeting her gaze with concern. "I didn't want to skirt the issue. Sorry I was so direct."

"Is he following us?"

"No. His family lives somewhere on the island—or did live here. I thought they moved back to Florida after Hurricane Floyd ruined their compound. Jack must be the last holdout."

"From what he told me, his family is trying to run him off the land."

"Rumor has it his father's pretty deep in debt. The scandal from the accident destroyed the sales of his boat line."

"Why?"

Del Rio searched her face as if unsure whether or not he should continue.

She nodded. "I want to know. Please."

"Okay." He handed her the margarita. "Jack's father had just released a prototype of a new racer. His brother was pretty high on alcohol and cocaine while driving the boat. His father had to admit that not only was his son DWI on the water in his new creation but that he'd caused the death of two women. Bad press shattered the family reputation. Sales died."

She let this information sink in. Surprisingly, it didn't hurt her to hear it, but it didn't jar any memories, either. Frustration more than fear filled her head.

"I can't remember any of that day."

"Unfortunately, I remember all too clearly."

His words hit like a brick. "*You* were at Little Harbour?"

"I'm almost glad you can't recall that afternoon."

This information was mind-boggling. "Is that why he was looking for you?"

"He said that?"

"Yes. Why?"

He hesitated a bit too long before saying, "Your father and I are suing his family."

They sat for a while in silence. His explanation seemed so foreign to her, as though it belonged to someone else. The fact that her mother and sister were no longer alive proved the story was true.

Del Rio lifted his drink. "Now, don't you be worrying about Jack Sheppard, Maria darlin'. I'm sure we've seen the last of him." He used his best Irish brogue.

She shuddered. "I can't believe our bad luck running into him."

In the harbor, pelicans dived into the clear water then floated along unceremoniously as they swallowed their catch. Along the docks, laughter mingled with music from the outdoor restaurants. Though the sun was lower in the sky, the heat of the late afternoon made their spot under the shade of the bimini with the warm breeze the perfect place to be. How fabulous this moment would be if she and Del Rio were simply vacationing.

She sighed. Why did her world have to be so complicated?

Del Rio raised his glass to her. "So…"

"So what?"

"Since I rescued you from impending disaster with your nemesis, I'm thinking you can thank me by cooking dinner."

She looked at him, shocked. "I don't cook. Ever."

"I'll show you how to make a pasta Bolognese to die for."

"If you're going to show me, why don't you just cook it? After this drink, and this news, I need a nap."

"I love late-afternoon naps."

The intimacy of helping her overcome her encounter with Jack had shrunk their battlefield. She stood, for fear of melting in the sudden heat rising between them.

"Then you're going to love the hammock."

She placed the half-finished drink on the table, resisting the urge to visualize them entwined in it together.

"Thank you for enlightening me about Jack," she added. "I hope my reaction didn't upset you."

The honesty in his gaze was hotter than a come-on. "Maria, I truly care that you recover."

She held up a hand. "I'm beginning to believe you."

She headed for the companionway, needing to bolt before her mind's eye took off the last of his clothing.

Moments like these could become her undoing. She was either falling for his charm, or seeing the true man. Either way, her libido leaned toward betraying reason.

She'd have to channel these feelings by painting, for sure. By the end of this trip she'd paint him naked—create a personal collection for her eyes only. A nude of Del Rio would be the first. It would be something to keep when this whole ordeal was finished.

The notion sent a shudder through her. Creating an image of him, maybe muscled, wet and rising out of the water with sun spilling over his shoulders, would make it difficult to send the man packing.

Heading for her cabin, it didn't help to hear Del Rio call from the cockpit, "Enjoy your nap, Princess. I'll meet you in the galley in an hour."

THE BREEZE ROCKED Daniel gently, but he could have been on a rolling sea. Try as he might to nap, his conscience repeatedly nudged him awake.

He'd skirted the truth behind the accident because he still didn't feel she was ready to hear the entire story. This fact didn't help lift the weight of what needed to be said off his chest. And she'd been so grateful for the little bit he'd given her that he felt like a heel.

Some hero.

Well, he'd spared her more anguish, that's for sure. Reason enough to justify his actions. Learning who Jack was almost sent her over the edge. She didn't need another push to the dark side. Besides, their apologies for last night's conflict seemed to have created a new comfort level between them. Why jeopardize that?

For now.

He groaned inwardly at the thought of the inevitable

end to all this—losing her. It took a special kind of fool to consent to a kamikaze mission.

He calmed himself, and sleep started to take hold when his hammock rocked, nearly dumping him.

"Whoa." He pulled his hat off his face and met Maria's burning glare.

"Did he die?"

He shook his head to get his mind clear. "Who?"

"Jack's brother. Did he die, too?"

"No, he's in jail for two counts of manslaughter, and other things."

"What other things?" Concern filled her velvet brown eyes.

"Possession of narcotics, perjury and tampering with evidence."

"That's awful for Jack. His entire world has been destroyed because of his brother."

He expelled a breath. "Look, I agree, but Jack has a skewered perception of reality. He idolized his brother and he blames *us* for the family falling apart. He could find better ways to cope with this tragedy than climbing into a bottle of booze."

"Do you think he's seeking revenge?"

Did he think so? Yes. Did he want to say so? "Maria, don't worry about Jack."

The anguish in her eyes twisted his gut. "Were we responsible?"

He squeezed her hand. "Maria, Ryan Sheppard killed two people because he operated a dangerous vessel at high speed while out of his mind on drugs and alcohol, then tried to hide the truth. He deserved his sentence."

"Ryan Sheppard." She whispered the man's name as if trying to tap a memory bank, then looked up, empty. She let her fingers intertwine with his. So soft, trusting.

"I couldn't sleep. Will the nightmares ever end?"

He pulled her hand to his lips and kissed the soft skin. "Soon, Princess. You're getting stronger every day. This trip is doing more good than you know."

She pulled her hand away. "Please don't be so pleasant. I need you to be difficult."

He climbed out of the hammock and stood close to her, the scent of flowers and heaven filling his nostrils and making his chest tighten with sheer want of her.

"I am who I am. Judge me as you will."

She stepped aside to give him room. The gesture seemed reluctant. He had a sudden urge to pull her back into the hammock and kiss her blind. Instead, he gave her a playful shove toward the cockpit.

"Let's cook. I'll even trust you enough to let you handle a knife."

CHAPTER ELEVEN

"Ahoy, you two."

Maria climbed into the cockpit and shielded her eyes from the lowering sun to see who spoke. Brad Mitchell was pulling up the mooring line just behind the *Honora*. As he secured the line around the bow cleat, Traci waved.

"What a beautiful harbor," she said.

Her grin was contagious. Maria waved back. "Welcome to Hope Town."

Brad straightened. "You two have dinner plans?"

"We were just about to start a pasta dish."

Del Rio glanced at Maria and whispered, "Shall we invite them over?"

Her better judgment prevailed. Things were getting too cozy between them. Having a third party on board would help tamp down the heat. Maria shrugged. "Sure."

Del Rio called over. "Why don't you join us?"

Brad made his way to the stern of the boat. He reached into a cooler and pulled out two lobsters.

"I have a better idea. We got lucky today. Plenty here. Why don't you join us?"

Maria and Del Rio exchanged glances of agreement. Nothing tasted better than fresh-caught lobster.

Maria answered, "We'll bring dessert."

Traci clapped her hands in delight. "Great. See you in an hour."

Maria turned to Del Rio. "So, what can you whip up in an hour?"

"Me?"

With a playful tug, he pulled her down the companion-way and into the galley. "You made the dessert offer."

He retrieved a box of brownie mix and vegetable oil from the cupboard, reached into a storage bin beneath the counter and produced a bowl and a baking pan, a spatula from a drawer, two eggs from the icebox. Reading the temperature on the box, he set the oven.

"I'd leave the oven to you, but don't trust you not to blow up the cabin." Placing both hands on her shoulders, he moved her into the spot where he stood. "Here. Read the directions. I'm taking a shower."

THE SMELL OF BROWNIES filled the cabin when he emerged from the shower. He smiled to himself.

"Well, I'll be damned."

His grin faded when he entered the galley. From the sound of drawers rattling behind Maria's open cabin door, she was preparing to shower. But she'd left behind a di-saster.

Brownie batter was smeared across the countertop, and eggshells nestled within each other in their own goo. Beside them sat the dirty bowl and spatula. Hadn't she thought to use the sink? The empty box stood on a cloud of brownie dust from the mix, and the vegetable oil bottle, though capped, lay on its side.

He couldn't help himself. He checked, half expecting to see the batter poured into the oven without a pan. Nope. The brownies looked great. She'd created a masterpiece out of a war zone.

He started to clean up.

"Hey! Don't touch anything."

He stopped, eggshells in hand.

Maria stood in her cabin doorway just as messy as the galley.

"Put them down."

Brownie mix streaked across her nose, but she didn't seem to notice. The knot she'd tied her hair in had come loose, and dark tendrils fell about her face. Those eyes—man, oh man. The pleasure lighting her chocolate eyes made him feel giddy inside.

"You want me to stop?"

She indicated he move to where she stood. "Yeah. But first put those shells where they were."

He complied, wiping his hands on a paper towel and shaking his head.

She lifted the camera in her hand, her enthusiasm huge. "I want to capture my first baking moment. I may have to paint it."

A chuckle escaped him. "And here I thought you were a hopeless slob."

She looked at him in surprise. "Well, I am. But I'm proud of this mess."

He watched as she clicked away from different angles with enough energy to fill the sails, her movement itself like art in motion. He found himself more than curious to see what form her mischief would take. He waited patiently until she finished shooting.

"You think fifty shots is enough?"

"You making fun of me?"

He crossed his arms. "You bet, Princess. Now will you clean up your mess?"

She pouted, camera in hand. "I have to shower."

He headed for the companionway. "I'm sure you have plenty of time. I'm going ashore to buy a bottle of wine."

DANIEL ROWED THE DINGHY as though each stroke would take him farther away from his lust for Maria.

Everything about the woman turned him on. He loved the way her eyes lit up when she was happy, the way her body moved with the effortless grace of a dancer. Had he come upon her after her baking attempt before the accident, he would have kissed the brownie mix off her nose and made love to her right there on the galley table.

This was the problem with having her aboard. He remembered intimate moments they shared in all different areas of the *Honora*. The bow. His cabin. The cockpit. The shower. The hammock. Holding on to the anchor line while swimming. They had been very creative in their lovemaking. It killed him to remember their intimate moments, while she hadn't a clue.

Did she feel attracted to him at all?

At least she was warming up to him. Two days ago, she never would have included him in her devilry. And she wasn't protesting any longer when he called her Princess. He briefly closed his eyes to relish the moment. If he won her affections again, could he leave for Brisbane? Would he be able to tear himself away from her to recapture his passion for racing?

He'd have to cross that bridge if and when by any whim of the gods it should be built between them.

As he rowed for the dock closest to the packaged goods store, he scanned the harbor area. His blood ran cold. Jack Sheppard stood on the wharf of the Hope Town Harbour Lodge, sipping his ever-present beer and studying the *Honora*.

When Jack's gaze slid from the sailboat and clashed with Daniel's, he didn't even flinch. Just kept sipping his beer and watching. Daniel stared at the man until he finally turned and walked away.

Shit.

BOTH WOMEN SQUEALED AS Brad dropped the first lobster into the pot of boiling water.

"I heard it scream." Traci covered her ears.

Brad shook his head. "Stop it, honey. You're still going to eat it, so quit fussing."

A sheepish grin crossed her face. She poured more wine into Maria's glass, then her own. Maria considered stopping her, but didn't. She was having too much fun. Del Rio sat across from them in the cabin, beer in hand, watching Brad commit the murders.

He smacked his lips. "Need me to melt some butter?"

Brad shook his head. "Already done and warming in the oven with the corn. He pointed to the colorful bowls on the counter. Salad and rolls are waiting. We can eat in the cockpit."

Del Rio gave Maria an appreciative glance. "We have to save room for dessert. The brownies are Maria's first baking expedition."

"Really?" Envy laced Traci's voice. "How'd you get away with not cooking?"

The last thing Maria wanted to admit was that Momma never permitted her or Carmen in the kitchen. Cooking was for servants. Maria had been amazed at how much fun she'd had making brownies this afternoon. Del Rio had opened another door for her. She waved a dismissive hand. "Don't ask. The truth would bore you to tears."

Traci laughed. "Oh, sure. You artist types don't even take time to eat, let alone cook."

Maria felt the heat of a blush burn her cheeks. Thankfully, Brad pulled two lobsters from the pot, distracting them while he dumped in two more.

Maria winced. "I might stick with salad tonight."

"There's something to be said for restaurants." Del Rio laughed. "No one sees the slaughter in the kitchen."

"Why don't you two go above?" Brad suggested. "We'll bring the lobsters when they cool."

"How much time do we have?"

"About twenty minutes."

Traci checked her watch, then turned to Maria. "Have you painted anything more?"

"I've finished four pieces since we set sail."

Traci tugged Maria toward the stern. "Let's row over and take a look."

Brad motioned for them to go. "We'll call you when dinner's ready."

Traci was already descending into the dinghy. "Come on, Maria. I'll row."

"Listen for the VHF. It's already on." Del Rio was clearly enjoying the fact that Maria would chafe under Traci's praise.

She followed Traci, her nose in the air. She wouldn't give Del Rio the satisfaction of knowing he was right.

"NICE BOAT." Traci looked around in awe. The *Honora* was almost fifteen feet longer than the Mitchells' rented sailboat. Fifteen feet in the boat world made a huge difference in interior space and comfort.

Maria retrieved the paintings from the guest cabin. She perched them behind the salon sofas for support, but not before noticing that both her and Del Rio's cabin doors were open. By the look in her eyes, Traci realized immediately that the two lived in separate quarters. Thankfully, Traci said nothing. Instead, she slapped her hands to her cheeks.

"Oh, my. These paintings are spectacular. How did you blend those colors? Those dolphins look real. Look what you did to that dock…it's blooming with leaves. And that river in the sky…I love it. And look. Is that Hope Town?

On the beach? Look at this underwater scene. This is wonderful. I want them all."

Maria laughed. "You're sweet, Traci, but stop. You're making me uncomfortable with all the fuss."

Traci looked surprised. "Why? You must hear this all the time."

"No."

"What? You're deaf or something?"

"My gallery manager comes to the house, picks up the work and takes it away. I create the pieces for my own satisfaction. I don't require feedback."

"Why? I should think your publicist would demand you make appearances."

The answer caught in her throat. How could she explain? "Maybe I will when we get back."

Traci held a hand to her heart.

"I'm still stunned that I even met you, let alone am standing here looking at paintings that no one else has seen yet...except for Daniel."

His name hung between them in an awkward moment. Maria fretted that her thoughts were way too transparent as she glanced at his open cabin door.

"How long have you two been together?"

A vise closed over Maria's chest. She couldn't answer. "Are you finished looking at these?"

Without waiting, she scooped up the canvases and deposited them back into the cabin. "The lobsters are probably ready."

"Sorry, Maria. I wasn't probing. I just... Well, you're such a hot couple. Brad and I are celebrating... I thought you two—"

"It's okay, Traci. I'm not insulted. I just don't know if you're asking me a valid question."

"I don't understand."

Maria sat, deflated. What the heck. It couldn't hurt to have someone to talk to about all this.

"I have amnesia. I remember very little about what happened before the boat accident last year. Up until this sailing trip, Daniel Del Rio has been no more than a family friend my father hired as captain of his yacht. I'm just now getting to know him."

"What?" Traci stared at her in surprise. "Would you like me to tell you how I remember you two?"

"You knew us?"

"No. Of course not. Only what I read in the papers or saw on television."

Maria's back straightened. "You're kidding."

Traci frowned. "What kind of amnesia do you have?"

"Retrograde amnesia. Del Rio has been helping me jog my memory. This trip has been rather difficult."

"I can't imagine."

A sinking feeling hit. "If what you say is correct, then I owe him an apology."

Traci chuckled. "Well, making up is always fun."

Maria rubbed her forehead, feeling stretched like a rubber band. So Del Rio hadn't been lying. Then why in God's name could she not remember him? And worse, why had being around him caused such trepidation? Of everyone in her life now, only Daniel Murphy Del Rio made her anxious.

Traci watched her, her face reflecting only concern and goodwill. Maria hadn't expected this conversation to be so bonding, so easy. Had she made this admission to Carmen, her twin would have chided and teased her, making her feel like a fool.

Dismissing her discomfort, she pressed on. "So, how do you remember us?"

Traci spilled her information like a tapped water supply.

"Well, I first heard about Daniel about three years ago—you know, a handsome, blue-eyed champion sailor. The fact that he was a bachelor with Chilean parents-gone-missing made him quite the celebrity. His story gave him mystique. The tabloids love it."

"Tabloids?"

"Sure. Once, on *Good Morning America,* Daniel said he used his racing to rebuild his life."

"I'm not surprised. He took quite a hit when he lost his family."

"The media followed him like a hawk."

"Really?" Now, this was news.

"Daniel was a super eligible bachelor. Newspapers and sports magazines featured him all the time. Sailboat builders sponsored him. Debutantes mobbed him."

Maria laughed out loud. "Oh, I can see that."

Traci got all moon-eyed. "Then one night, he showed up on South Beach with you. The chemistry between you two was dynamite even in newspaper photos. I was hooked. I read every tidbit that was printed about you."

"I don't believe it."

"Oh, come on, girl. You two are local legends. The beautiful, mysterious Latina artist snags the media's latest heartthrob? It doesn't get better than that."

This explained so much. Maria grabbed Traci's hand. "*Dios mio.* He tried to tell me and I called him a liar."

Traci squeezed her hand in reassurance. "Well, you will need to apologize. You two were center stage in the magazines and tabloids for months." As an afterthought she added, "They even tried to drum up intrigue by questioning whether Daniel could tell the difference between you and your twin."

Maria's blood grew cold. "Why?"

"There were so many shots of Daniel sitting between

the two of you. No one could tell if it was you or your twin whispering in his ear. What was her name?" Traci snapped her fingers. "Carmen. That's it."

Maria jolted. Her words were a lightning strike to her heart. Had there been something between Del Rio and Carmen? The thought twisted tight in her chest. Something dark niggled at her senses. She couldn't stomach any more.

"You have to stop talking. This is too much."

Traci's eyes grew wide. "Oh, I'm sorry, Maria. I forgot your loss. Total foot in mouth."

Shaking her head, Maria stood. "No, it's okay. It's just scary to hear information like this. I—I don't even know if I can believe you."

"Why hasn't anyone told you this before? I feel so awkward." Traci chewed her lower lip. "I so apologize for upsetting you, Maria. Please forgive me."

"*Blue Moon* to the *Honora*. Lobsters are ready." Del Rio's voice crackled over the VHF in his cabin. Maria jumped, unsure if his was the sweetest or most terrifying voice she'd ever heard.

"I appreciate everything you said. I'm pretty stunned. So let's not talk about it with the guys for now. Okay?"

"I'm going to have to buy a hundred paintings to make up for this. Wait until Brad hears what I did."

Maria laughed. "No, honey. I'll paint one just for you. I appreciate your honesty. In the meantime, let's go eat lobster, but don't be surprised if I make this an early night."

CHAPTER TWELVE

DANIEL WAS ABOUT TO DROP his shorts when his cabin door slammed open. Maria stood, fists on her hips, ready for battle. Restless, aching for Maria after sitting so close to her at dinner, smelling her perfume all night, Daniel knew the last thing he needed was for her to invade his cabin unless she was asking for trouble.

"What do you want?"

Without a word she stalked toward him, her questioning, molten dark eyes speaking more than words. He'd seen that look before. This wasn't war she was waging. A look like that usually ended with them sweaty and sated and more in love than ever.

His senses electrified.

Her hair fell about her shoulders. The pale blue nightdress caressed her curves as she moved. Her scent invaded his nostrils and shot right down to his groin. He inhaled deeply. She'd been so subdued during dinner. What was she doing now? He took a step back.

"Maria…"

She rested a palm on his chest, her eyes momentarily connecting with her hand as she touched his skin, then she looked up at him again.

"How come I can't remember?"

"Remember what?"

She rose on tiptoe. "This."

She tilted her head ever so slightly and caught his lower

lip between hers. Gently, she kissed his mouth, with soft kisses, testing with tentative curiosity.

The moment her mouth met his, Daniel became rock hard. He used every ounce of willpower to fight for control. This was very wrong, but oh, so right. This boundary, should he cross it, could screw up his plans for Australia. He should back away, but God almighty, he could not ignore her touch.

The tremor rocking his body must have encouraged her. She reached for his face, molding herself against his body, his erection pressing against the flat of her stomach. A small gasp escaped her lips, as if she were awed by the power she held over him. She leaned up to kiss him once more.

The feel of her fingers splaying against his cheeks burned deep into his psyche. Oh, God, he remembered these kisses. Unable to stop, he crushed her in his arms, capturing her head with one hand, and plundered her mouth. She tasted like heaven, willing and yielding just like the old days. If this was the last chance he had to make love to her, he'd be damned before losing it. Right now, all he wanted was more.

More. More. More.

No. Damn it. He couldn't deceive her.

He broke the kiss, inhaling a desperate breath. "Maria, love. What are you doing?"

"Please don't stop me."

"Why?"

Her eyes pleaded with him. "I have to know."

He held her at arm's length. The moment of truth. His conscience prodded him. Elias wanted him to hold his tongue, but could he make love to her without revealing his terrible secret? *Tell her, old boy. Then see if she wants to make love with you.*

She watched him with appealing eyes, hot and hungry, as she had countless times before. That look alone turned him on. She brushed fingertips across his belly as her eyes pleaded. He inhaled a sharp breath.

Sexy. Seductive. Innocent. He'd never experienced such a generous lover before Maria. She'd driven him mad with her smile. Now she stood before him, naked under this flimsy nightdress and begging him to help her remember what had been so mind-blowingly amazing between them.

How could he say no? He wanted it worse than she did, because he *did* remember. He had hungered, craved and blamed himself when he'd lost her love for all these months. No, sir. If he could win her back, his conscience could go to hell. He'd figure out what to do about telling her. He'd figure out what to do about Australia. Just let him get through this one moment...and the next.

"Maria, I've missed you for so long. If you want this, I'll make sure you remember everything." His voice was thick with need.

Pain filled her eyes. "Traci said..."

He silenced her with a finger to her lips. His mind was kicking his butt from here to Brisbane for being so weak, but the magic of her touch was like a narcotic. If he tasted her again, he could be lost, forever.

Her perfume rose between them with the heated scent of her body. Her breasts rose and fell beneath the satin nightgown as her eyes searched his, fired with a desire of their own. Oh, yeah. He was going down.

"Shh, love. Don't think. Just feel."

His hand slid off her shoulder, gently traveling down, the pads of his fingers teasing the pale softness inside her arms. His fingers fanned, his touch whispered across her chest. Her nipples tightened as he pressed the flat of his palm against one breast and then the other. He bent to follow the path along the lace of her bodice with gentle, slow kisses. Maria's head fell back so he could continue the heated trail up her neck and jawline. Small, tender kisses. With each one he took a moment to savor the skin beneath his lips, sending a quiver through her.

Daniel thought he would die. She was in his arms once more. His hands caressed her shoulders, down her back, rested on her hips briefly while his mouth sought hers. Then, as he deepened the kiss, one hand captured her waist, pressing her against him while the other burrowed beneath the silk of her hair to the small of her neck, cupping her head for his kiss.

MARIA MELTED IN HIS ARMS. Good lord, his kiss left her breathless…and the feel of him swamped her with pin-pricks of pleasure across her skin. Anticipation drove her hands to seek their own pleasure as she explored the hair matting his chest, the flat plane of his stomach. She dared reach down, brushing fingertips along the length of his erection beneath the fabric of his shorts. He sighed, deep in his throat, and her hand drove him to deepen his kiss, setting her insides on fire.

She pressed her pelvis into his hardness, impatience now directing her movements. Her hands explored the warm, smooth skin of his lower back, up his sides and down his firm, muscled arms. She wrapped her arms around his neck, holding on for dear life while he took her with his kiss, driving her further out of her senses.

Why had she resisted this man for so long?

As one, they broke the kiss, gasping for air. She stared at him in wonder. He returned her gaze, his blue eyes molten, ravenous, concerned. He rested his forehead against hers, that pirate grin breaking on his face.

"I love kissing you, Maria."

Tears filled her eyes. "You feel amazing, Del Rio. But I don't remember this. Your touch. Your kisses. It all seems new to me."

He lifted her chin with a finger. "Is that okay?"

She felt sad, but hungry for more. "You feel right. I mean...there's something good about being in your arms. Like I belong here. So I guess it has to be okay."

"You're an amazing lover, Maria. There's so much I have to tell you."

She shook her head. "Later. Right now please, kiss me again."

He touched her nose. "On one condition."

"What's that?"

As he lowered his mouth to hers, he spoke against her lips. "Call me Daniel from now on."

MARIA AWOKE IN Daniel's bed. Naked. Alone. Her first reaction was to flee, yet she froze in panic under the sheet.

What in heaven's name had she done last night?

Where was he now?

Had she romanticized Traci's story? Had he twisted the opportunity to his advantage? Was he above deck strutting around like a proud rooster, uncaring how earth-shattering their lovemaking had been for her?

She fell back against the pillows, sighing. Daniel had touched her like she'd never before been touched. Magic. All night long. She might be aching in delicious places, but making love hadn't jarred her memory. If a bond existed between her and Daniel, if indeed, they truly had been lovers, then why hadn't this mind-blowing sex awakened her memories?

Last night only served to leave her in awe of what two bodies could do together. Was she doomed never to recover?

Dios. Had she made a mistake giving herself to him?

She sat up, ready to bolt, as Daniel appeared in the doorway. Naked. He balanced two cups in his hands. One had a buttered roll on top, the other roll was caught in his mouth.

His hair was mussed, his eyes alive, his bronze body moving with the ease of an athlete. He smiled behind the roll and murmured something incomprehensible. He was so damned sexy. He handed her the cup with the roll, taking his own from his mouth.

"Thought we could use a bit of sustenance. Did I wake you with my noise?"

She shook her head, feeling awful and awkward for her unkind musings. "Actually, I didn't hear a thing. I thought you'd ravished then abandoned me without a second thought."

His grin faded. "Really?"

"Guess old fears die hard."

He chewed the bite he'd taken, swallowing hard. "Maria, love. There are plenty of things you can hate me for, but loving you is not one of them. I never took your love lightly and never will."

There. The words lay between them. He sounded sincere. Solemn. She wanted to absorb every word deep into her being. But their lovemaking had not shaken her amnesia. If Traci hadn't revealed what the rest of the world knew about her and Daniel as lovers, and she had given herself to him under other circumstances, she might still consider him a liar...with motives.

"Sorry. I keep thinking, opportunist."

He seemed disappointed. "Where did you get that idea? Don't you know how much money I have?"

"Really?"

"Remind me to show you one of my bank accounts when we get home."

He said the word *home* with such ease, as if to him Reefside *was* home. She'd think about that later. "So, Traci told the truth about your racing and sponsors and all the notoriety?"

"Did *you* seduce *me* for my money?"

She laughed, feeling her stress peel away. "For heaven's sake, no." She hesitated. "I've had this attraction to you that I couldn't understand. While it was almost impossible to ignore on this trip, it seemed wrong. Traci's news set me free."

"Wow. I should send over a bottle of champagne. Without her, last night might never have happened."

Maria felt herself blush. "She was pretty convincing."

He waited until she met his gaze once more. "Do you regret last night?"

She shrugged. "I feel a bit awkward."

"Don't, love. I knew we were lovers. I was just hoping you'd catch on."

He watched as she chewed, and she knew her questions and uncertainty were written on her face.

"What do you want to ask, Maria?"

She touched two fingers to his lips, tracing the lower one. "Were we in love?"

He kissed her palm. "The truth?"

She nodded, the knot in her stomach slowly yielding to butterflies and warm, liquid desire.

"You and I sailed here to meet your family a year ago to celebrate our engagement."

Her jaw dropped. "Why didn't you or Poppa tell me?"

He looked away. "When you regained consciousness, I upset you on sight. To try and convince you about our relationship seemed useless. You actually screamed the first time you saw me in the hospital."

She closed her eyes. "I remember."

"Can you tell me why?"

She felt embarrassed. "No. I can't. I thought you...could hurt me or something. Silly, eh?"

He watched her a long moment, his gaze hooded with thoughts he would not express.

"Well, we believed it prudent to give you time. But you just holed up in your studio and started painting like a raging storm. I stopped racing because I wanted to be with you when your memory returned. A year had passed before we realized you weren't planning on resurfacing anytime soon."

She entwined her fingers with his. "Did we announce our engagement?"

"The accident occurred the day we arrived. So, no, we never did."

To Maria's surprise, calm filled her. No shock. No terror. Something in Daniel's eyes gave her the strength to believe this information was safe. After last night's tenderness, she had to trust him. Maybe this was what Poppa meant when he said she had to find out for herself.

She shook her head. "For the life of me, I can't recall any of this."

"Yeah. I could be lying and reeling you in to inherit all your money."

She took a swipe at him and splashed her coffee. "Hey. You're hitting a raw nerve."

He laughed, took the cup from her, the devilment in his eyes incredibly angelic.

"What are you doing?"

Daniel placed his cup next to hers on the shelf above the bunk. He lay full against her with only the sheet between their naked bodies. He smoothed a strand of hair from her cheek, devouring her with his gaze. A small sheen of perspiration gleamed on his forehead, and she knew the heat rising from him was caused by more than just the morning sun. The scent of their bodies mingled with the warm breeze from the overhead hatch, intoxicating them like fine wine.

The hardness of his thighs, the press of his stomach and chest against Maria's body promised heaven. Daniel Del Rio felt perfect. She laid a hand on his face in encouragement, wanting more of the love he'd taught her last night.

"You are incredibly handsome," she whispered.

"And you are a siren luring me to shipwreck."

Oh, she wanted him. She wanted his hands all over her until she lost all thought and nothing would satisfy except feeling him deep inside her. She wanted to lose herself in the magic he wove so the darkness filling her mind would explode in the light of his love.

Daniel's hands teased through the sheet, arousing sensations along her stomach, breasts, her bare shoulders, neck. He stole kisses, gentle yet insistent, while his hands spread their magic downward, caressing her thighs, teasing the hidden place between her legs.

He raised himself on one elbow, his eyes simmering with intent, all the while his hands caressing. "I hope you're not in a hurry, love. I have a lot of ground to cover with you this morning."

She nipped along his jaw. "You're going to be the death of me, Captain."

HER WORDS THREATENED to shatter the thin veneer shielding his memory from images of unnecessary deaths, but he pushed away the dread, focusing instead on desire. Here. The heat. The touch. Now. The sheer need.

The moment had arrived, as he had dared to hope for so many months, days, weeks, hours. This instant was their second chance at life. They had both escaped death, when others had not. Feeling the softness of her body, the scent of her skin, Daniel vowed to celebrate life—celebrate Maria, every waking moment from this one forward, no matter how their story ended. Lying in his arms, every inch of her vibrant and wanting, this woman made him want to live. Each nerve in his body pulsed with the urgency to make her his. Again.

He captured her lips in a desperate kiss, his hands doing wild things along the length of her body, to her breasts, making her nipples harden and her back arch for more.

He slid the sheet away, taking her mouth once more, their tongues mating in a dance promising the sweet agony of ecstasy. She wrapped her arms around him, entwining their legs, her body begging him to explore further, make her completely his.

Daniel broke the kiss and met the love shimmering in her velvet brown eyes. He'd done it. He'd reached her. He'd take as long as necessary to teach her all over again the love they'd shared. Who knew how much time he'd have before she learned the truth?

He cupped her face with his hand before losing his mind, body and soul to her as he'd done countless times before, and whispered, "Welcome to paradise, sweetheart."

CHAPTER THIRTEEN

BANGING ON THE TRANSOM woke them. Brad's voice filtered down to the cabin. "Want to go snorkeling?"

Daniel checked his watch. Noon.

"Stay put. I'll handle this." He tugged on a pair of shorts and disappeared. Moments later, he returned.

"Gave Brad something to look forward to in the waning years of his marriage."

"Oh, no. What did you say?"

"I said you kept me up all night and we're just now surfacing. He got flustered and said they'd see us later."

"No." She slapped a hand over her mouth, giggling. "Well, won't Traci be glad to hear the news."

"You really don't mind if I said that?"

"Why not? It's true, isn't it?"

"Well then, I wish I had."

"What *did* you say?"

"They should go ahead and we'd catch up. I want to set sail anyway."

"Really? I like it here."

"Yeah. Me, too. But I spotted Jack snooping around the docks last night. I don't want to invite any more of his attention."

She visibly paled, and that distressed him.

"Don't worry, Princess. My guess is he stays pretty lit with booze. I don't think he's capable of much."

"I won't think about it." She held his gaze, as if drinking in his confidence. Mischief lit her eyes.

"What are you thinking?"

Maria slid off the bunk, letting the sheet drop. She stood before him naked, her bronze skin glowing, her hair spilling on her shoulders in dark disarray, her lips pouty from his kisses. She inhaled a deep cleansing breath, which did beautiful things for her breasts. Flashing her most daring smile, she beckoned him with her eyes. His body tightened in response. She was so relaxed in her own nakedness, it made her sexy as hell.

A slow whistle escaped his lips. "I could pay homage to your body all day long, Maria, my dear."

She crooked a finger at him. "Then join me in the shower, Captain. We'll take turns admiring each other."

She caught on quick.

THE EXTRA FIFTEEN FEET of waterline had the *Honora* reaching the Mitchells' sloop within an hour. Daniel loosened the sails to meet the *Blue Moon*'s hull speed so they could arrive at the reef together. With the late start, they'd get in a leisurely swim before heading to an anchorage for sunset.

Maria stared at the amazing reef below the surface of the water, wondering if her jitters were from something buried in her amnesia or merely the thought of trying something new. Daniel had handed her snorkeling gear that looked perfect for her—and had been used before.

She held up the mask, snorkel and fins. "Tell me these are mine."

"You always chose yellow. Carmen demanded red."

He looked up, worry filling his eyes as he realized what he'd told her.

Did she hear bitterness in the way he said her twin's name? She latched onto one word. *"Demanded?"*

He shrugged. "You know how she was."

Yes, she knew how Carmen was. Flirty. Vivacious. Fun. The complete opposite of Maria. And possibly a paramour of Daniel's. Damn. She had forgotten that one concern in her frenzy to seduce him. Would Daniel have found Carmen more enticing than her? Maria's throat tightened, choking her. She reached for a bottle of water, gulping down the hot lump that made it hard to breathe.

"You okay?"

She met his gaze. "I've never heard you mention Carmen's name."

"Until recently, we rarely had occasion to talk, let alone bring up your sister." His voice teased, but there was an undercurrent of tension in his words.

"Did you and Carmen not get along, Daniel?"

He dug his own gear from the diving bag. "Let's just say, your twin was nothing like you."

"Hey, you two ready yet?" Brad waved from their boat moored several feet away.

Traci perched on the side rails. "This is supposed to be one of the best reefs in the area."

Gear in hand, she jumped and swam to the float Brad had tied to the boat. Holding on, she donned her mask and fins.

Daniel held out a hand to Maria. "You're going to love the view, honey. I'm curious to know what you think."

The subject of Carmen had been dropped. Well, she wouldn't forget to ask about her later. She might have amnesia, but the here and now was crystal clear. Maria moved past him to the ladder.

"Have I done this before?"

Daniel laughed, his cheerful self once again. "Oh yeah.

I always dragged you out of the water way after your fingers wrinkled like prunes."

"If only I could remember."

He swept his hand toward the transom. "Well. Jump in. See if anything clicks."

The reef was nothing short of spectacular. She must have known how to snorkel because using the equipment came easily. Any moment now, Maria expected to see a mermaid hiding within the forest of giant staghorn coral or popping up behind a brain coral the size of a weather balloon. And the fish. Countless schools in myriad colors, all busy among the coral while magenta sea fans and tubular anemone swayed in the current to a tune only the fish seemed to hear.

Maria almost gasped on salt water when she spied a line of manta rays swimming in formation along the sandy bottom beside the reef. They moved as if flying through the water, effortless, working together as they scavenged for food.

Daniel swam beside her, rollicking around her like a seal one moment, diving down to investigate a nook or cranny in the next. Thankfully, he was always aware of her, offering reassurance should she require it. But this teeming, undersea metropolis seemed docile, beckoning. Snorkeling was like second nature to her, so she felt confident.

Brad and Traci swam nearby. Traci's voice carried through the water as she tried to talk through her snorkel, pointing out one interest then the next. Her exuberance matched the brilliant colors of the reef changing like a kaleidoscope beneath the sunlit water.

Maria would paint this moment, and give the work to Traci as a gift for her kindness. She'd call it *The Metropolis.* Maybe the two women would keep in touch once they returned to the mainland. Maria liked the idea of a new friend—a friend that she had made on her own and not introduced by her sister or mother.

As she floated peacefully along the surface of the sea, the sun warm on her back, everything seemed right in the world. She couldn't help but wonder if the lull of the sea and the sound of one's own breathing recalled the tranquility of resting in a mother's womb.

Everyone needed to snorkel, she decided. The world would be a better place.

Daniel tapped her arm and pointed.

A long silver fish, big, with intimidating teeth, floated beneath them. It watched them with a wary eye. She might not remember the fish, but its stare spoke volumes. She raised her head up from the water.

Daniel removed his snorkel. "Barracuda. He won't strike, but give him a wide berth."

She nodded and returned to swimming, giving the fish a small wave as she moved on. Nothing was going to harm her today.

MARIA FELT A TUG OF affection pull her heartstrings. She'd been painting on the bow since sunrise and no one had disturbed her beneath the makeshift canopy Daniel had rigged the night before.

As she came to her senses, as she called it, the sounds around her came alive. Water lapped at the hull, rocking the boat ever so gently. Seabirds called and dived nearby, sending splashes skyward. The breeze off the island carried scents of scrub pines and sea creatures on the briny air. Despite the shade, a diffused disc of sun blotted the canopy heating up the morning.

Behind her, Daniel rocked quietly in the hammock beneath another canopy, reading a book. She hadn't even heard him come above deck. Quite a feat since her radar always sensed him near.

As danger.

Had her fear of him vanished since she'd become his lover? If last night was any indication, it had. The freedom she found in loving Daniel unleashed a power in her she'd never known. *Padre Sanctificado.* If she wasn't careful, she'd tumble helplessly in love with the man. Had that been his intention, all along?

Glancing over at the *Blue Moon* anchored nearby, she saw Traci lying in the cockpit, her head in Brad's lap, the two talking quietly. The remains of breakfast littered the small cockpit table. Brad looked up to see her watching and waved.

She waved back, surprised at the surge of warmth that filled her. Brad was a wonderful guy. Traci had been so very easy to know, so generous with her affection. Maria hadn't felt camaraderie like this since... Well, since Carmen was alive. She and her twin enjoyed an unspoken bond of understanding, despite their different personalities.

Carmen may have been bossy, but she always knew when Maria needed solitude or when she needed to be reeled back to reality. Her sister may have seemed self-serving to others, but no one had understood Maria better, or indulged her more.

Maria always believed Carmen's loss would be irreparable. Now she began to understand that life would not let her remain alone. All she had to do was reach out.

Daniel waited for her, that she knew. But his reaction to mention of Carmen yesterday raised the hairs on her neck. He most certainly harbored a definite opinion about her twin. She'd have to ask him about it, especially if they were working on building trust.

"Morning, Princess." Daniel's voice was a caress.

She turned to meet his gaze. *Dios,* the love in his eyes. She pushed her suspicion to a far corner of her mind to tackle later. A grin spread across her face.

"You really must stop calling me that."

He smiled in return. "Sorry. I like it."

She bit the end of her paintbrush. "I can't believe you three managed to stay so quiet. I didn't even know you were there."

He laid his book on his stomach. "Well, why don't you come over here and reward me for good behavior?"

She stood and stretched, feeling wanton as Daniel's expression registered she was naked beneath the full-length, turquoise sheath.

"How about I'll cook breakfast?"

Incredulity filled his eyes. "Excuse me?"

She shrugged. "I make a mean cinnamon toast."

He laughed, reaching for her as she moved closer.

"It's almost noon. I ate breakfast hours ago."

"Oh, then *you* can make cinnamon toast."

She bent over him, her neckline falling open. Daniel used a finger to push the fabric wider, exposing the soft mounds of her breasts to his probing eyes.

She offered him her lips, letting him kiss her soundly. He tasted good. Sea. Sunshine. Pure man.

Daniel groaned. "You sure know how to make a guy forget what he's thinking."

She chuckled, covering his face with tiny kisses. "Food. One of us is hungry. Remember?"

He grabbed her about the waist, pulling her into the hammock. They laughed, struggling to keep from toppling over.

"Forget the food."

Maria glanced over her shoulder to the *Blue Moon.* "We have an audience."

He continued kissing her neck. "They ate already, too."

She pushed away, climbing out of the hammock. "Irresistible as you may be, sweet Daniel. I am famished."

He grabbed her hand, the intensity of his grip surprising her.

"What?"

"You called me sweet."

She smiled shyly. "Yes. It felt good to say it, too."

His eyes hardened beneath the shadow of the baseball cap he'd slid onto his head.

"Do me a favor. Remember this little moment. Okay?" The mercurial change in his emotions came from nowhere and it unsettled her.

"Is something wrong?"

Like a wind shift, the troubled gaze vanished. He shrugged. "Guess I'm still gun-shy at your change of heart toward me."

"I understand."

She headed below, suddenly aware of how acutely Daniel had suffered from her disdain. She'd have to focus on rebuilding the trust between them.

"Hey, Maria." Traci waved before diving into the water for a swim.

Maybe she'd join her friend before eating. As she disappeared into the coolness of the cabin salon, a little voice niggled at Maria. Daniel might have chafed at her treatment of him, but he *was* keeping a secret from her. She would trust him to tell her in his own good time. She knew he would.

WHILE MARIA SWAM, Daniel took the opportunity to make a phone call. He paced the small salon while dialing.

"Reefside."

"Eduardo. Good morning. It's Daniel."

"Senor Del Rio. *Hola! Como te vas?*"

"*Bien. Gracias, amigo.* All is well. How is Elias?"

The butler remained silent for a moment. "He naps more now since the house is quiet."

"Is there anything we should know?"

"No, *señor.* I would be sure to contact you."

Daniel nodded, uneasy leaving Elias for so long. "We're only an hour away by plane, if you need us."

"*Claro, señor. Claro.*"

"So, is Elias there? I'd like to speak with him."

"*Sí. Momento.* I will bring the phone to him."

The soft clicking of Eduardo's heels echoed in the receiver, each step heightening Daniel's dismay. Elias wasn't going to like this conversation.

"Daniel."

"Elias. Hello. How are you?"

"All is well, my son. Tell me…Maria? The *Honora?*"

Daniel nodded as he spoke. "Except for a slight run-in with a sandbar, all is well. But you'd be pleased to know Maria manned the helm."

Elias emitted a low whistle. "You are making progress."

"Yes."

"But…"

"We ran into Jack Sheppard."

"*Dios.* Did he cause trouble?"

"Not this time. I'm thinking we'll need a restraining order. He has shown up twice."

"I will contact Arroyo."

"Can he make the order stick in the Abacos?"

"I'll make sure he does."

Daniel changed the subject. "I took her to the reef, Elias. She loved it."

"She swam?"

"Like a fish. Only she couldn't remember a thing."

Elias's silence indicated his surprise. After a moment he said, "Daniel, she will remember. You know this."

"Yes, I know. Please, take care of the restraining order. I'll take care of Maria. I'm glad you are well, old man. I look forward to seeing you when this is over."

Daniel tossed the phone on the couch, willing himself calm. Elias was miles away. If he took care of the legal side of protecting them, Daniel would take care of the emotional side. He was going to handle Maria his way.

He headed for the companionway. He needed a swim.

CHAPTER FOURTEEN

MARIA AND DANIEL AWAITED THE Mitchells for a late lunch on the *Honora*. As Daniel loaded tuna sandwiches on a platter, Maria watched him. She waited for him to say something. He'd been sullen since their swim and spoken very little. Not even the calypso music on the iPod dock brightened the atmosphere.

She leaned across the counter, turning her face into his. "Barracuda got your tongue?"

"Sandwiches take concentration."

"And so did washing the deck and polishing the starboard side of the boat. What's eating you, Daniel?"

"I'm in love and it's killing me."

"Oh."

"Yeah. Oh."

She reached for napkins instead of smoothing back the errant curls across his forehead. "So you think love is terminal?"

He slanted a questioning glance. "Do you?"

"I'm starting to think it's pretty amazing."

She was surprised at how much his grin warmed her. "That makes me happy."

He pulled a container of iced tea from the refrigerator and poured two glasses lined with mint leaves. Maria's chest tightened at the sight of Momma's favorite drink. Would the pain of loss ever ease? Maybe. Just maybe.

Daniel had begun showing her how. She reached for his hand.

"It's nice of you to make our iced tea with mint leaves. Reminds me of my mother."

"Yep. She was quite a woman."

The sarcasm in his voice stopped her. "What does that mean?"

"Absolutely nothing."

"I don't get you, Daniel. I've been trying to ignore your cutting comments about Carmen at the reef. Now you're mocking Momma. Don't you like my family?"

"Elias means the world to me. And you're not so bad yourself."

His humor missed the mark and her earlier suspicions kicked in. Was this about Carmen? Was he falling in love with her and feeling guilty that he'd messed around with Carmen? She inhaled a deep breath. "Okay, but…"

He stepped back from the counter. Leaning against the stove, he crossed his arms. "What do you want me to say, Maria?"

"Tell me the truth."

"Okay. Ask a question."

Her conversation with Traci circled inside her head. Tabloids could be cruel. They fostered lies. Did she want to believe the suspicion planted in gossip rags?

"Did you like Carmen?"

He held her gaze. "You have good memories of your sister. I don't want to trash her."

"Did she hurt you?"

"Let's just say I don't think we'd be trying to dodge Jack if it weren't for your mother's and Carmen's antics."

That answer, she didn't expect. "What do you mean?"

He watched her face as if making a decision. "Forget it. It doesn't matter."

"Yes, Daniel, it does. Are you telling me Carmen was flirting with him?"

He ran a hand through his hair. "No. Ryan Sheppard. But never mind. I called the mainland to make sure Jack Sheppard stays out of our way. It's on my mind and I'm just angry we have to deal with him."

She saw his point. Jack Sheppard could ruin anyone's good mood. On the other hand, she didn't like that Carmen had been flirting with his brother. "I didn't know Carmen knew Ryan."

He shook his head. "Me neither."

This was not good news. But truthfully, Carmen was a consummate flirt. This information didn't bother Maria. "Listen, Daniel. Let's just enjoy ourselves. Okay?"

He sighed. "I'm trying. Sometimes it's not that simple."

"Well, it is for me. I've been way too serious." *And too damned happy to have your affections sour on me now.* She stepped on tiptoes to kiss his cheek. "Besides, you promised we'd turn this trip into an adventure. Don't renege on me."

MARIA EMERGED FROM the salon as Brad was securing the dinghy. She sent a small prayer skyward for the diversion these enjoyable people offered. Traci handed up a chilled six-pack of Red Stripe beer.

"Brad will only eat tuna washed down with beer."

"Welcome aboard, you two. Just in time." *In more ways than one.*

Daniel stepped out, balancing a tray with condiments, iced tea and the chips. "I'm with Brad. I'll take one of those beers."

He deposited the tray and disappeared below once more, only to reappear with a navigation chart. "Brad, how much longer till you head back?"

"One more day. Two tops." He handed Daniel a beer then bit into his sandwich.

Daniel took a swig. Not sure if the invitation was a good idea or not, he asked, "Thought we'd head over to Little Harbour this afternoon. Care to join us?"

Traci's head shot up in concern. "Why go there?"

Their new friend probably knew that Little Harbour was the site of the fateful boat accident. "It's important to Maria."

He glanced at Maria. Her smile had disappeared.

Brad stuffed the end of the sandwich into his mouth, chewing between words. "Heard about Little Harbour. It's an art colony, right?"

The touchy subject escaped Brad's awareness. Good. The less attention, the better. Daniel smiled. "I'd like Maria to get reacquainted with Kevin's Pub and the Foundry."

Gratefully, her face lit up. "Oh, yes. I forgot." When Daniel glanced at her, she held his gaze and mouthed the words, "I'll be okay."

He sure would like to know that was the truth. He took a long pull on his beer before turning his attention back to Brad and Tracy. "Kevin at the Foundry follows his dad's tradition in casting bronze sculptures. His work is known worldwide. You might enjoy seeing it."

"But, Daniel…" Traci's voice trailed off. Frowning, she glanced from Maria to Daniel.

Maria reached across the table. "I know what you're thinking, Traci. Please, don't worry. I insisted on this trip specifically so I could return there."

Traci's gaze shot to Daniel as if this was not a good idea. He gave her what he hoped was a reassuring smile. "You don't have to come, if you are uncomfortable."

Brad looked confused. "Is there a problem I should know about?"

Daniel waved away his concern. "The entrance to the harbor is tricky. Lots of shallow water and a narrow channel. We'll want to go at high tide."

He glanced at Maria. She listened with interest, but no recognition seemed to register on her face.

"I'd like to see this place if Traci wants to," Brad said.

Traci glanced at him warily. "Sure, honey. Let's go."

Daniel traced the markings on the chart for Brad to see. "The channel is seven feet deep at high tide, which should be in about two hours. That's plenty of water for the *Honora*."

"The *Blue Moon* needs five," Brad said.

Daniel took another half sandwich, and bit into it as if he were chewing the last meal of his life. "We'll weigh anchor after lunch."

THE ONLY SURPRISE IN negotiating the entrance to Little Harbour was Maria's delight in the beauty of the sheer cliffs lining the narrow passage into the anchorage. Only she wasn't fooling Daniel.

She was nervous. Her face had paled, her eyes tensed, but she covered her distress by climbing all over the deck taking pictures and commenting on the way light spilled on the cliffs and surrounding beach.

Daniel followed her lead, smiling, while every muscle tensed with each move Maria made. At any moment he expected her to stop cold and crumble once her memory hit. But no. She remained as enchanted by the harbor and village as if it was their first visit.

Finally, as they moved farther into the harbor she returned to his side, clicked one photo of him at the helm then reached for his arm. "I don't remember this at all, Daniel."

He expelled a breath, gave himself a little shake to release the tension and adjusted the baseball cap on his head. He pulled her close if only to feel the heat of her body, and was rewarded when she snaked her arms around his waist.

"Are you okay, then?"

She shrugged. "So far. I'm nervous."

He chuckled. "No kidding."

"It feels strange how this just looks like a very beautiful place when I know there's more."

He shook his head. "I can't imagine what you must be feeling."

She looked up at him. "Do they know us here?"

"Kevin. His wife. Want me to give them a heads-up to treat you lightly?"

"Reintroduce us. I'll be fine after that."

He kissed her temple, lingering to smell the citrus scent from her shampoo. "Okay, then, sweetheart. Just ask if you have any questions."

He waved to Brad, following behind the *Honora,* and pointed to two open moorings over by the quay. Who knew? With any luck their visit might prove to be an enjoyable stay.

This time.

But try as he might, while mooring and securing the boat, Daniel could not relax. It was like holding a ticking bomb with no hint of detonation time.

Every minute of that fateful afternoon here had been fraught with tension. Daniel had brought the women to Kevin's Pub from the reef to escape Ryan Sheppard. Carmen was drunk, irascible. Rosalinda flirted with everyone. Maria had watched the two women as if seeing them for the first time. The look on her face had been devastating.

That afternoon had been one angry argument after another. Daniel *could* remember that day and the memories were disturbing enough to twist his gut in a knot. He was amazed nothing had surfaced yet for Maria.

If and when her memory returned, what then? Would they live happily ever after? Chances were Maria would remember more than she should. Then she'd refuse to believe him, let alone forgive him.

He closed his eyes for a moment to escape the possibilities. Bottom line, when all of this was over, he was headed for Australia. It would be nice if Elias and Maria were still options in his life. But if not, he wanted to get on with things.

In the meantime, this stop was the reason they'd set sail in the first place. He'd get Maria through this ordeal the best he could. He planned to keep her close until they departed this harbor. Damn. He'd be glad if he never saw it again.

Next hurdle was to bring Maria ashore. He hoped the Mitchells had the backbone to handle whatever went down next.

MUCH TO MARIA'S disappointment, the Foundry was closed since it was after five, but laughter from Kevin's Pub meant the lively spot was still open for business. The watering hole, true to remote island style, stood open-air, its roof a tad off center, the facade covered with boating paraphernalia, signs, buoys and even a traffic light. Almost embarrassed that she felt nothing unusual except curiosity for this wonderful place, she reached for Daniel's hand as they approached the bar. He took it, kissing her fingertips in reassurance. His action elicited a smile from Traci.

"I am so happy to see you two back together," she said, under her breath.

"The good captain has been very persuasive."

"It's about time."

"Well, if it wasn't for you, I'd still be resisting."

"Resisting what?" Brad and Daniel asked, simultaneously.

Traci laughed. "You two like that word, eh?"

Daniel grinned. "I like a challenge."

Maria tugged him toward the pub. "Well, we won't resist a cool drink."

When they entered the bar, Daniel didn't miss the surprise on the bartender's face. Kevin clearly remembered all too well. Daniel led Maria to a table facing the beach.

"We'll get the drinks. The breeze is great over here."

Once the women were seated, Brad sidled up to Daniel at the bar. "Traci told me on the sail over. I'm sorry I didn't realize your concern before we left."

Daniel wanted to make light of the situation, but as soon as Kevin came over, the topic would arise.

"No worries, Brad. It's tricky right now. I'm thinking it might be a blessing if she doesn't remember."

He looked from Brad to the approaching bartender, who had a smile wider than the Atlantic and a hand ready for shaking.

"Kevin. Great to see you, again."

Kevin tapped his heart with a fist. "The shock of seeing you two almost stopped the ol' ticker." He looked toward Maria. "So, she decided to keep you after all, eh?"

Daniel leaned across the bar. "Kevin, listen. Maria has amnesia from the accident. She doesn't remember anything."

Kevin grew still. "You're kidding."

"That's why we're here. She probably won't remember you. So don't be disappointed. Okay?"

"You brought her here to make her remember?"

"Her idea. Believe me. It's been a helluva year."

Kevin slapped Daniel's shoulder. "Sailing in shallow waters, aren't you, buddy?"

"Feels more like walking the edge of a razor blade. But listen. I want to give you a heads-up. I don't know if you remember the Sheppards?"

"Of course I do."

"I've had a restraining order issued against the younger brother, Jack."

"Trouble?"

"Not sure. Just being careful. If he shows up here, give me a warning. Okay?"

"I know the guy. Got it. Wow. Hey, here's Janice."

Kevin gestured to his wife, a pretty blonde entering the pub in a sundress and flip-lops.

"Well then, why wait for reintroductions," Daniel said. "Can you two join us for drinks?"

The bartender grinned. "Come sit over here by the bar. That way I can serve everyone while we get reacquainted."

MORNING WARMED BENEATH the rising sun as Maria finished *The Metropolis*. On its heels, she began another painting. She'd start another after that, and another. While she couldn't remember anything since they'd arrived at Little Harbour, disquiet prodded her darkened memories. Somewhere in this small harbor, her sister and mother had died. The more she tried to corral the unsettling feelings, the louder the alarm bells sounded, making her turn to her easel for escape.

She'd awakened early, again, leaving Daniel's bunk as the predawn beckoned. She could never resist the lure of sunrise. Now morning's lemon light spilled on the cliffs, the houses, the water, changing hues right before her eyes in glorious abandon.

She tugged her straw hat lower on her forehead and reached for her water glass. The harbor had been cooler in dawn's first light, but as the sun's heat intensified, her energy began to fade. Maybe the heat was causing her to feel unsettled. Everything else about this place charmed her.

Last night at Kevin's Pub had been wonderful. Kevin and his wife were excellent hosts. Maria had been captivated by Kevin's talk about the Foundry and the art techniques they used. He may have told her all of this information once before, but he explained each detail with the enthusiasm he held for his craft. The bond she forged with this kindred artist warmed her heart.

It wasn't until Kevin said how glad he was to see her doing so well since the accident that a chill raised goose bumps on her skin, making her aware of the uneasiness she'd chosen to ignore since they arrived.

Why couldn't she recall the first time she'd met Kevin or Janice? Why couldn't she remember Little Harbour or its colorful inhabitants? She rested her palette in her lap. She knew the accident occurred here, although she hadn't asked where, and that distressed her. She hadn't remembered Hope Town, or the reef, but that hadn't upset her as much as her inability to remember this place. Was it because Carmen and Momma haunted her here? Was the possibility of Carmen and Daniel invading her peace of mind?

She turned her face into the rising breeze, and inhaled the salty air. A smattering of high clouds caressed the pale, sapphire sky. Why couldn't life be as carefree as the world before her?

She picked up her palette. The best she could do was relax and see if any memories returned as their visit progressed. She added another brushstroke, shading with indigo below the cliffs where the *Honora* and the *Blue Moon* rested in miniature on the canvas. She stopped painting, her concentration lost.

Her throat tightened. She needed peace for her turbulent soul. For a woman who required serenity, she'd lived at the mercy of her amnesia for too long. She swallowed the lump in her throat as seabirds circled low, waiting to catch an unsuspecting fish near the surface. Capping her paints, she sighed, feeling very much like one of the fish hiding in the shadows. She headed below. She needed Daniel. He was rapidly becoming as much of an addiction as painting.

Surprisingly, he still slept. She smiled to herself as she watched his quiet form beneath the sheets. She'd paint him, soon. He was too beautiful for words.

She peeled off her caftan and crawled next to him. She'd worn him out last night. Heaven knows, after making love with him she had slept soundly and dreamlessly, too.

Gracias a Dios. For that one blessing alone, she was grateful to Daniel. She hadn't had a nightmare since he took her to his bed.

Half-asleep, he turned to reach for her, tucking her against his warm, hard body. Burying her face in his neck, she inhaled the appealing spice of his scent. His fragrance, purely Daniel, urged her on, setting her hands wandering across his chest, down his stomach, her fingertips tingling as she brushed the matted, soft hair. She explored lower still, the silk of him making her pulse race.

"Ah," she breathed into his ear as she caressed the slope of his buttocks, his lower back and the muscles along his shoulder blades. His body responded as he stretched against her, cradling her in his arms.

"Maria," he whispered, sleepy. Dreaming.

She feathered his lips with small kisses. Still lost in sleep, he murmured something incoherent as she worked a trail across his jaw, down his neck, to his shoulder, chest. She moved over him, her kisses taking a leisurely path, her tongue teasing a nipple.

Slowly, Daniel awakened, the low moan in his throat spurring her on. Sure, she wanted to ask him questions. Sure, she needed sanctuary from the fears that being in Little Harbour had elicited. But for now, she'd let her mouth, hands and body do the questioning over every masculine inch of this man who was bringing her back to life.

For now, getting lost in Daniel seemed a far better solution than chasing ghosts.

CHAPTER FIFTEEN

TRACI SAT IN THE COCKPIT of the *Honora*, holding *The Metropolis* at arm's length.

"This is for me? Oh, and you signed it."

"I promised you a painting. Only it hasn't completely dried. Lay the canvas in the sun for a while, and be careful not to touch the paint."

Traci admired the underwater reef scene.

"Look, you made me a mermaid. This is probably worth a fortune. You have to let me pay for it."

"Absolutely not. It's my thanks to you for your kindness."

She looked confused. "What are you talking about? I'm your biggest fan. I can't believe you let us follow you two around the islands."

Maria laughed. "Oh, come on, Traci. I can't tell you how good you've been for me. It's been such a long time since I've had a friend. I hope we see each other on the mainland."

"I'm sad Brad and I have to turn back already."

Maria sipped her coffee. She'd invited Traci over for one last visit before the *Blue Moon* set sail for home, the port of Boca Raton, a little north of Maria's home in Fort Lauderdale. Daniel was over on the Mitchells' boat helping Brad plot GPS points for their journey back.

"You have great wind for sailing," Maria mused, watching the palm trees sway beneath the trade winds' gentle hands.

A sleek ocean racer entered the harbor motoring way too fast. The craft cast a large wake that would disrupt the moored boats. She shook her head at the skipper's poor driving and returned her gaze to Traci.

"We have one more night, but Brad has some incredibly romantic spot he wants to show me before we deliver the boat." Traci leaned in conspiratorially. "We're trying for a baby."

"A baby! Oh, Traci. How wonderful."

Traci laughed. "Brad wants twins so we can have an instant family."

Twins. Maria thought of Carmen and felt a pang of loss. "Maybe someday I'll have a baby, and our children can be friends."

"Then you're feeling better about Daniel?"

She smiled. "Oh, yes. Thanks to you helping me take the first step back. You and Brad have been an inspiration."

"Time heals all wounds, Maria. Daniel Del Rio is good for you. He always has been."

As the wake rocked the *Honora*, Maria decided to voice her next concern.

"Do you promise to come see me at Reefside when I get back?"

"Of course, silly. Invite me. Watch how fast I show up."

Maria laughed. "Traci, will you do me one last favor?"

"Of course."

"Please don't tell anyone about what Daniel and I have been going through."

Traci frowned. "Maria, I'll keep it in strictest confidence. Your friendship means the world to me." She placed her own cup down, now that the rocking had passed. "Sweetie, just trust your instincts with Daniel. You two will come out of this better than you started. I can just feel it."

MARIA AND DANIEL WAVED goodbye as the *Blue Moon* sailed out of the harbor. The two stood in the cockpit, side by side. Maria laughed as she saw Traci snap a photo of them with her camera's telephoto lens.

"I'm going to want a copy of that one," Daniel mused.

Maria didn't miss the sadness in his voice. "Worried about being alone with me?"

His sky-blue gaze had her body temperature rising to a slow, molten heat. "Honey, I could spend the rest of my life alone with you and not miss a thing."

That did it. When had she decided his smooth talk was genuine? She melted against his side, wrapping herself beneath his arm. "I would like that very much."

He searched her face, as if at any moment she'd vanish into thin air. "Ah. Another one for the memory banks."

"Another what?"

"One of those moments when you fill me so completely I could die and go to heaven a happy man. I don't want to forget the love in your eyes right now."

Her transparent emotions made her squirm. Reining in the affection might be the only fair thing to do until she cleared the air between them.

"Then be my slave and row me to shore. Kevin promised a tour of his foundry."

He turned, cupping her face in his hands. Slowly, he descended on her lips, his eyes devouring them as if he were starved. He whispered, "Sure, but ferry service will cost you a kiss."

Two hours later, lips swollen from many kisses, muscles she didn't even know existed sore but satisfied, Maria let Daniel help her into the dinghy.

Santa Maria, that man knew how to make love to her. His passion obliterated any suspicions she held, despite the small voice in her head pleading caution. Her traitorous body refused to listen. Daniel Del Rio was enchantment. In his arms, the constant yearning to remember fell away like some unimportant garment. The heat of his hands, his promises spoken so close to her lips, dragged her into the here and now with keen assurance. The past and her lost memories seemed unimportant. Now she and this man could build something new and so very beautiful.

She couldn't resist brushing her body against his as he guided her into the tiny craft.

"You are something else, Ms. Santiago. Give me some time to regain my strength then I'm all yours."

She snatched a quick kiss before settling on the bench. "I never knew sailing could be so much fun."

The mischief in her eyes was intoxicating. Daniel made goofy faces as Maria snapped photos of him rowing toward the wharf, yet all the while his heart tattooed warning at the change in her. It seemed as if some cosmic hand had flicked a switch and the woman who once loved him had returned.

The mere whisper of her sighs in his ear stole his heart. The passion she offered through her body defied time and trauma. Like a wind shift, a year had vanished and they were the very same couple as before the accident—deeply in love, with the future holding so much promise.

He was scared shitless.

As long as they stayed anchored in Little Harbour, their world could topple with the blink of an eye. Not until they set sail without incident could he feel confident enough to take an easy breath. Maria grew quiet now, looking around, but she hadn't asked any questions.

So, for now, he counted his blessings and kept jesting as they made their way across the harbor. All he wanted to do was keep his precious Maria distracted until they weighed anchor in the morning.

Daniel jolted when he noticed the ocean racer tied at the dock along with the string of pleasure boats. He'd recognize that boat design anywhere, damn it all. A Sheppard. No one was aboard or within sight. Maria hadn't noticed.

He led her toward the Foundry. For all he knew, someone other than a Sheppard family member owned the racer. The line had been one of the hottest commodities on the water before the accident. He'd already warned Kevin, so if Jack was here, he'd find out quickly. He shrugged away a shudder. No sense looking for trouble if it didn't exist.

Kevin and his son were pouring a bronze when they arrived. Maria became immediately absorbed in the process, keeping a safe distance from the operation while snapping pictures. Daniel watched, intrigued by the intensity of the heat needed to create such impressive art. Maria came over and squeezed his hand as the men released a careful, steady stream of hot-orange liquid metal into the casting shell.

Maria sighed, as if watching the birth of a child. Daniel wanted to pull her into his arms all over again. Her curiosity, so genuine and innocent, tugged at his heart like nothing else in this world.

She chatted with Kevin's other son as he explained the casting process and different chemicals used for the bronze patina. Her exotic eyes, dark, warm and intelligent, were intensely focused as she absorbed every fact. Each time she smiled, the air seemed to brighten. Daniel had no doubt the young man was meticulous in his explanations just to keep Maria's attention for as long as possible.

Maria did that to a man. Her straightforward, friendly demeanor only enhanced her beauty. She was too darned gorgeous for her own good. With those long legs and perfect curves, even in Bermuda shorts and a tank top, her hair twisted into mahogany braids falling over her shoulders like Pocahontas, she looked like every man's fantasy in the flesh.

Could he possibly convince Maria to marry him before their trip was over?

While the men removed their protective gear after the pour was completed, Maria and Daniel explored the art studio and the sculptures in the garden around the building.

"Look at that monkey."

Maria clapped her hands as she circled the pedestal holding the tiny, bronze animal hanging in a branch. "Looks like Sylvester."

"Sylvester?"

Maria met the amusement in his eyes. "One of the little imps outside my studio. Sylvester is the only one who will eat from my hand." She turned to Kevin as he approached. "This one's mine. Can you ship it?"

His eyes lit with laughter. "Don't you want to haggle about the price? It's not cheap."

"A girl knows when to make a purchase."

He appraised Maria, shaking his head in wonder. "You know, I never cast monkeys. Didn't know what possessed me to carve this mold in the first place. Now I remember why."

"Why?"

"Because last year when you were here, you told me

about the monkeys in the trees at your home. After the...
Well, I guess I hadn't forgotten your story."

"I don't remember telling that story. I'm honored."

Kevin shot a sad glance at Daniel before answering
Maria. "Sometimes a man sees things he never forgets.
You were not easy to forget."

Kevin's words were more than mere flattery. As she
opened her mouth to ask, Daniel took her hand.

"I want to show you something."

He led her to the jewelry display. He pointed to a ring
with two dolphins swimming together on a band of gold.

"Let's see how this looks on your hand."

Kevin placed the ring in Maria's palm. She tested it
on her ring finger. Too big. The band slid snugly on her
middle finger, the fine chunk of gold a warm contrast
against her tanned skin.

She loved it, immediately.

"I don't usually wear rings, but this is beautiful."

Daniel smiled. "It's my gift to you."

COULD SHE ACCEPT SUCH an expensive gift? Rings were
tokens of love. She and Daniel still had unfinished business between them before they could start buying each
other gifts.

The two dolphins could very easily be her and Daniel
rollicking in the water. Surely, he intended this token to
represent their journey on the *Honora,* but deep inside her
that little voice whispered, *Can you trust him*?

Kevin had stepped away to help another customer. She
returned her gaze to Daniel's. He stood there in a pirate's
stance, arms crossed at his chest, casual, yet imposing.
His head tilted as he watched her, dark, sun-bleached curls
falling on his forehead, sunglasses hooked into his shirt
collar. Only his eyes gave him away. Those sky-blue eyes

questioned her, hoping, no, pleading, as if her next words determined whether he lived or died.

She expelled a breath. When had it become impossible to resist this man? He was mystery and goodness rolled into one. And, single-handedly, he had pried her from a seclusion that had bound her not only physically but emotionally, as well.

"I love it, Daniel. Thank you." She stood on tiptoe to brush a kiss on his lips, meaning every word.

The joy in his face nearly melted her. "Think of me when you look at it."

Again, an odd statement with finality written all over it.

She shook her head, questioning. "Why do you speak as if you're never going to see me again?"

He swallowed hard before shrugging. "Guess I'm still expecting the big kiss-off. You know, adventures always end."

She chuckled. "Maybe you can consider my ranting before I slept with you as verbal foreplay."

"Oh, yeah, you certainly had me turned on."

She patted his butt. "Well, if you want to stick around, Reefside can always use another gardener."

He gave her a dangerously sexy glance. "Or something."

They finished their transactions. It would be a while before the sculpture was transported to her home, but Maria couldn't wait to put *Sylvester* by the windows in her studio. She kissed Kevin on the cheek, said goodbye and followed Daniel the few steps to the pub next door.

"Shopping always makes me hungry," she said.

"Kevin told me they caught fresh dolphin this morning."

"Yum."

Maria rubbed her stomach, making Daniel want to follow suit. "Here, let me do that for you."

She laughed, grabbing his hand. "Stop, silly." She pulled his face close to hers. "My ring is the sweetest gesture." She kissed him soundly on the lips, drawing a hoot from Kevin inside the foundry.

After lunch, they took a leisurely walk on the beach and visited the lighthouse. Escaping the heat, they found themselves back at the pub for a drink. No sooner had they stepped from the glaring sunlight into the shade of the bar when Maria felt the hair rise on her neck. The only other time she'd felt this sensation was in Hope Town. She reached for Daniel's hand.

"I'm not getting a good feeling."

He didn't answer. She followed his gaze.

Jack Sheppard. By his stance at the bar, he'd been drinking all morning, but his inebriation did little to lessen the intent in his eyes.

"Coming back to gloat, are you?" Jack's voice rasped with too much beer and cigarettes.

Daniel's hand tightened around Maria's. Kevin hadn't had a chance to alert him to Jack's arrival; he and the boys were still in the foundry. "Let's go back to the *Honora*."

The look of helpless outrage on Daniel's face confused her. "What does he mean?"

"I don't want to hang around to find out."

Daniel waved goodbye to the bartender, then led her from the pub.

Silence lay between them on the row back to the boat, Daniel's anger evident in the hard line of his jaw.

"You don't think it's a coincidence, do you?"

Daniel inhaled a deep breath. "I'm not sure what to think. I don't want to be anywhere near a Sheppard. They're a crazy bunch."

"So let's leave, Daniel." She checked the waterline on the beach. "The tide is still high. We can make it through the channel."

He nodded. "If you don't mind, I think that's the wisest choice. I don't trust Jack to remain civil."

The *Honora* was always ready to sail at a moment's notice. While Daniel usually loved powering the boat by sail, this time he took prudent measures and fired the engine before releasing the mooring. Maria brought iced tea to the cockpit as the sailboat eased into the channel.

Daniel gave her a devilish grin. "I know this great spot. Nice and quiet. It'll take about an hour to get there."

Maria seated herself on the cushions facing Daniel as he steered. The Foundry, studio and pub on shore, slowly fell away in the boat's wake. The thought of being in a secluded cove alone with Daniel shot a shiver of desire through her.

She nipped at a mint leaf in her glass. "Maybe running into Jack wasn't so bad after all."

He laughed. "Let's forget about him."

THE LOW, THROATY THUNDER of a high-performance engine rose from the dock behind them. Daniel glanced back, dreading the worst, his expectations met in spades.

Jack was untying the lines to the Sheppard racer. No doubt he'd been waiting for their departure, and would have waited for however long it took.

Daniel had suspected Jack had followed them to Little Harbour to cause trouble. Now that he was hot on their trail, he had no doubt. The enormity of the damage he was about to inflict was not lost on Daniel. His blood chilled in his veins. He might not be able to stop the bastard, but this time he wouldn't be distracted.

The roar of the racer rose behind them as they entered

the narrow channel by the cliffs. Daniel knew the *Honora* wasn't fast enough to outrun him. He watched Maria's eyes grow wide as Jack gunned the boat and headed directly for the stern of the *Honora*—precisely at the point by the channel marker where Maria's mother and sister lost their lives.

Daniel's gaze riveted on Maria.

"God, no."

The groan left his lips as he watched awareness awaken in her eyes. She knew. The truth exploded in her face. Her eyes darted from the cliffs to the oncoming boat, then back to the cliffs. Her fingers gripped the boat's lifeline as if that thin, white cable might keep her safe. Her mouth dropped open in silent shock as the long, cigarette-shaped racer grew nearer, engines blasting.

It seemed that history was about to repeat itself. Daniel was helpless to do anything but turn the boat toward the cliffs and run hard aground, which he did, as the Sheppard craft came within inches of the *Honora,* midship. At the last second, the boat turned abruptly, its gleaming red hull looming, ready to crash into the cockpit just as another Sheppard boat had done to the rented powerboat one year ago.

A scream of terror rose from Maria's throat, and Daniel died a thousand deaths as he watched the agony rack her face.

A mere flick of Jack's wrist on the steering wheel and the racer veered away, swamping them completely. A wave of water drenched the deck, slapping their faces like shards of salty glass. The roar of the engine pierced their ears. The fuel exhaust stung their throats as the *Honora* pounded the bottom mercilessly in the shallows from the wake's onslaught. The iced teas tumbled from their hold-ers. Dishes crashed in the galley. The halyards clanged in outrage.

Daniel groped for balance, trying to reach Maria as she dropped into a dead faint.

CHAPTER SIXTEEN

MARIA FELT AS IF SHE STRUGGLED beneath a tremendous weight. Daniel's voice, concerned and edged with fear, called quietly to her from what seemed like far, far away. The buzzing in her ears grew softer. She inhaled a warm draft of salty air and felt the press of Daniel's palms cradling her face.

He was whispering, "It's okay, honey. Wake up."

She didn't want to. Drifting in this dark place took no effort. Opening her eyes would require energy and thought and— Oh, my God.

Her eyes shot open.

Daniel hovered over her, salt water and perspiration— and relief—drenching his face. When her eyes focused on his, he managed a smile.

"That was a close one."

The press of tears blinded her. "Daniel."

She struggled to climb into his arms, but her muscles felt like jelly. He gently pushed her down. She realized her clothes were sopping wet.

"You fainted, darlin'. Don't move so fast."

She sucked in a ragged breath. "He almost killed us."

"He was trying to scare us. That's all. I'm going below to get you some water and a cold compress. Will you be okay till I get back?"

She managed a mute nod, closing her eyes to regain her strength.

KATHLEEN PICKERING   199

As Daniel emerged from the cabin seconds later, Kevin and his son pulled up to the boat. "You two all right?"

"We're fine."

Kevin's concern was laced with outrage as they secured the boat. "I'm going to break that clown in half the next time he comes around here."

Daniel sat by Maria, pressing the compress on her forehead. She listened listlessly as Daniel spoke.

"He's nursing a grudge."

Kevin was glaring at the speck in the distance that was Jack's boat. "I saw him leave the pub and follow you, so I grabbed my camera and taped his chase. You should press charges."

Daniel nodded, his eyes roaming over Maria. He laid a hand on her cheek. She wanted to smile, but could not, closing her eyes instead. His hand felt dry against her damp skin.

She opened her eyes as Daniel shot his friend an angry glance. "I'd like to do more than press charges."

Kevin's son Jesse climbed aboard and began cleaning up the mess on the cockpit floor.

"From the dock it looked like he hit you."

"He missed by a matter of inches. He's a sick man."

The fog in Maria's head started to clear. She clutched Daniel's arm.

"This is the place. Isn't it, Daniel?"

He could only nod in reply.

"Momma and Carmen? Here?" Her voice dropped to a whisper.

It took a moment for Daniel to find his voice. "Jack decided to rub our noses in that cruel fact."

Her gaze drifted from Daniel to the sky, and for a moment she waited to see if she could sense Momma. Carmen.

Nothing.

A press of tears filled her eyes. Her stomach roiled. She swallowed, refusing to indulge the urge to vomit.

Sucking air deep into her lungs she forced herself to concentrate. The smell of gas fumes from the racer still lingered, triggering dull thoughts. Laughter. Sunshine. A white center console skiff moving at top speed. Carmen screaming in outrage. Maria wishing she was anywhere but within sound of her sister's wrath. But why?

She jammed her eyes shut, tears squeezing from the corners, as these vague memories returned. The roar of Ryan Sheppard's thunder boat rose deep inside her head like an oncoming freight train. She remembered seeing the sandy-haired man in the cockpit. Another man with him. Anger in both their faces as Ryan bore down on them with terrifying speed. There had been that moment of stunned silence before the collision when Momma screamed, as if knowing her life was over. Then, the earsplitting crunch and splintering of impact.

Like a crashing wave, her mind slammed black. Again. That damned nothingness. She could practically smell its oily slickness suffocating her thoughts. Inside her mind she screamed, *Show me! I don't want to lie here terrified, coming all this way, fighting you off day after day only for darkness to slam down on me, one more time. Show me everything.*

Her eyes flew open. Daniel hovered over her, watching, his eyes fraught with distress. The *Honora* continued to pound the bottom in the current, and he didn't care. She could tell by the way he focused on her face.

Did she really want to keep revisiting this horror? Momma and Carmen were gone. The accident was over. She now knew how and where their deaths occurred. Did she really need to know any more? It was the past.

Daniel visibly suffered as he watched her reliving this torment. Knowing what she would discover, he had willingly brought her here. Because he cared for her. Wanted to honor her wishes. Knowing it could destroy her.

No wonder he had given her such a hard time from the start. He knew. He had been trying to forget the past and move forward. He'd spent a year at Reefside mired in the horrific memories hoping that she would come out of her hole and start living again. That was why he had finally decided to leave for Australia. He hadn't been able to reach her. He had given up.

Jack had given them an awful reminder of what mattered in this world. Did she want pain and strife and anger in her life any longer when Daniel had so effectively awakened her to love? Did she really need to know any more?

She was vaguely aware of Kevin tying a line to the *Honora* and Jesse cleaning up. They were going to pull the yacht out of the sand.

Lifting her hand, still weak, she reached for Daniel's cheek. "You look like hell."

A bark of laughter erupted from his throat. "You don't look much better yourself."

KEVIN AND JESSE GREW QUIET, watching Daniel. He could feel the heat of Kevin's gaze on his back. They, too, had witnessed the crash last year. Now they might witness the moment of truth when his relationship with Maria finally ended.

Color was returning to her face, her breathing was back to normal. She had been silent way too long for his liking. Yet she hadn't started screaming, or condemning. Yet.

His insides burned like acid. It was time. He might as well kick the box from under his feet now and meet his fate. He laid a hand on Maria's stomach.

"Maria, honey, do you remember?"

She pulled the compress over her eyes for a moment and inhaled deeply. She looked so vulnerable lying there, her hand trembling against the compress, her lower lip fighting valiantly to keep her from outright crying while silent tears spilled into the hair at her temples.

He moved a strand from her cheek and waited, the moments ticking by.

Arranging the cloth back on her forehead, she slowly met his gaze, those dark eyes clouded with confusion.

"Bits and pieces. The racer coming at us. Momma laughing. Carmen screaming. I'm not sure, but I think she was driving. I was sitting in the bow, but what boat were we in?"

"A rental." Daniel's voice was a whisper.

She nodded, letting the information register. She frowned as she concentrated, staring at him in frustration. "I can't remember anything else."

Daniel's pulse pounded like a jackhammer. He watched her, amazed at the questions rather than condemnation in her eyes. She reached for his hand. "What am I not remembering?"

Oh, Lord. How much? How much more did she need to hear? He shot a glance at Kevin. A quick frown and small shake of his head confirmed his own thoughts. Small doses. She didn't need any more shock.

"Carmen and Rosalinda died instantly. You were unconscious in the water. I fished you out."

Her voice broke in despair. "I don't think I want to know any more, Daniel."

He expelled a held breath. There was a God, after all. He'd be more than happy to forget that damned day. "Your wish is my command, Princess. We ll only talk about it if, and when, you choose."

Kevin spoke quietly. "We should pull your boat back
into deep water before the tide drops any farther."

Daniel rested a palm on Maria's face. "Will you be okay
while we get to work here?"

Maria tried to sit. "It's hot. I think I'll go below. Do you
mind?"

Daniel lifted her into his arms and practically groaned
with gratitude when she laid her head against his chest.

"I'll take you to your cabin."

Her smile was weary. "You can't get down the companionway carrying me. I'm okay to walk."

Reluctantly, he lowered her to her feet.

"Okay, I'll help you get settled." He lifted her chin to
look into her eyes, facing the inevitable. "Do you want to
go home, Maria?"

Maria watched him, silent for a moment. It was so clear
that fainting had left her weak. "The truth? Yes. I'd love
to run home, lock myself in my studio, forget all of this."
She waved a listless hand toward the cliffs. "But I won't.
I'd just like to rest for now."

THE *HONORA* ROCKED QUIETLY on the mooring inside Little
Harbour, the sun setting with a flourish as if no trauma
had hit their world today. Daniel thought Maria slept,
but now heard her moving around the cabin. He sat in
the cockpit, frozen in thought. She'd given him a reason
never to utter another word about the accident. Relief and
guilt warred inside him, stinging his senses like army ants
swarming a tethered animal. There really was no choice.
He had to tell her.

He gazed blindly at the channel marker where one year
ago the two powerboats had crashed, left intertwined,
splintered, one partially sunken as the engine on their
rented smaller boat continued pushing the mangled crafts

in a slow circle. The sound of impact still haunted him, the broken and bleeding bodies of the women crushed under the thunder boat, Maria facedown in water slick with leaking gasoline, the debris. Daniel blindly swimming to reach Maria. Ryan Sheppard screaming for help. Rescuers coming from the docks. People shouting. The taste of pure rage and the smell of horror. How long would this memory taunt him?

He had so much to answer for...still.

"Daniel?"

She watched him from the companionway, her hands resting on the frame of the entry as though wondering if it was safe to come out. The dolphin ring glinted on her finger.

He held out a hand to her. "Sit with me. Sunset is almost as beautiful as you."

She stepped out. She had showered and was wearing that fluttering, turquoise caftan with enough opacity to both shadow her figure and capture his attention. Her mahogany hair hung wet and loose down her back. Dark smudges stained beneath her eyes.

He reached for her and she nestled her back against his chest. He encircled her with his arms, inhaling her sweet, citrusy scent, never wanting to let her go. "You okay, sweetheart?"

"I will be. I'm hungry."

He chuckled. "That's my girl. Shall we go ashore?"

She turned in his arms. Her breasts pressed against his chest beneath the thin fabric. He adjusted her against him. Her gaze rested on his lips.

"Not for food, you foolish man."

DESPITE THE LATE HOUR, Maria could not sleep. She moved around the main salon, blowing out candles, fidgeting in the galley. She'd left Daniel dozing in his cabin. The heat of his body still lingered in her thoughts and against her skin as she padded through the cabin, making her smile.

Daniel had made love to her with a sure and gentle fire until her fears had burned to cinders, filling her with security and balance when she teetered on that edge caused by her amnesia. She needed to feel normal. For both of them to feel normal. Like any other couple in the world. So she let herself find sanctuary in his arms, and had come to the realization that she wanted to be a part of his life, and have him as a part of hers, forever, if possible.

This awareness thrummed through her with an excitement and satisfaction she'd never before known. Had she felt this attraction for him previously? Had she experienced such peace in her heart? She hadn't been aware of peace in a long time. She felt it now, and had Daniel to thank for the small blessing, especially after this afternoon.

She climbed into the cockpit and settled on the cushions. Waning moonlight cast an ethereal glow on the cliffs across the harbor while a wash of stars burned the inky night. Fragmented memories of last year's accident swirled around her head, causing pressure along her brow. She wished the pieces would fit together, so she could have closure, but once again, the cost seemed too great, too painful.

This afternoon, Daniel had seemed tortured by her distress. His concern touched her to the core. She was grateful for his gentle treatment, and his willingness to answer her questions, despite how uncomfortable recounting the memories seemed to make him. Afterward, she'd rested on her bunk, dozing, slowly regaining her energy, when yet another thought would intrude in her mind, questioning that awful day, nudging her into discomfort once more.

Why couldn't she remember the entire incident?

The question exhausted her. Right now she didn't want to know any more. Today's onslaught of remembering was more than she could handle. She wasn't as strong as she'd believed, and sadness washed through her once again.

There was wisdom in accepting the accident was over, a tragedy of the past. Her mother and sister were buried and would be forever remembered. Time would heal all hurts. She just had to give herself that gift.

In the meantime, she had Daniel. Her chest tightened at the thought of his tenderness. How could she have mistaken his intentions? Then again, why, out of everyone she loved, had he been the one person she could not remember?

More questions. The matter of Carmen still existed, but at this point, Maria was too damned exhausted to consider the possibility. The question lingered, but *did the answer really matter?*

Living for the moment seemed the only solution. Their narrow encounter with disaster this afternoon accentuated that fact. One never knew what the next hour would bring. Right now she had life. She had love.

What more did she need?

"Maria?"

Daniel stepped into the cockpit. "What are you doing out here, honey? It's late."

Santa Maria, would the sight of this man always make her pulse race? Her throat grew dry, but she managed to speak. "I guess I'm dealing with aftershocks from this afternoon."

He slid next to her, wrapping an arm around her shoulder. His body tensed as he watched her, as if testing her resolve. "You took quite a blow to the memory banks today."

She pressed two fingers against his lips, drinking in the

love, and concern, in his gaze. "I still can't believe you brought me here knowing what I would unearth."

He captured her hand, kissed the palm, then pressed it against his heart. "I promised myself to be ground zero for you when your memory returned." His eyes softened. "We have all the time in the world to figure out what to do next."

She rested her head against his chest, lulled by the sound of his heart thrumming in his chest. He felt so strong. So capable. So sure of their world. A wave of security wrapped around her like a soft blanket. Stars above glistened like tiny diamonds of hope. She wrapped her arms tighter around him, a yawn tugging at her mouth. "How about we just go back to bed?"

He had drifted off into his own thoughts, staring into the night, his face a study of profound sorrow. Then, as if her suggestion just registered, relief in his eyes transformed into a sensual gaze. "Now, Princess, are you hitting on me again?"

She pressed her lips against his, reveling in the sensation, determined to live in the now, if only for tonight. "Someone has to, Captain."

WHILE DANIEL PREPARED THE SHIP for departure the next morning, Kevin hailed him from his dinghy.

"Permission to board?"

Daniel waved. "Granted." He secured the dinghy with the line Kevin tossed. "Coffee?"

"No thanks. Just wanted to give you this copy of the video. I emailed it to you, as well."

Daniel accepted the file and shook the man's hand. "Thank you, Kevin. I'm going to nail that SOB as soon as we land at Hope Town."

He nodded in agreement. "How is Maria doing?"

She climbed up from below deck. "Hello, Kevin. I'm better today. Thanks."

He tapped his heart. "Listen darling, I'd certainly appreciate it if in the future, you'd give this old ticker a better reason to thump."

She laughed. "You and I both." She laid a hand on his arm. "Thank you for all you've done for us."

"No worries. You two are family."

Worry creased her brow. "Did I hear you say you caught Jack swamping us on video?"

He nodded. "It's a good idea for you to press charges."

A chill coursed through her body. She shot Daniel a concerned look. "Can't we just go home and forget all of this, Daniel? Really, I don't want any more trouble."

He had moved to the cabin top, tending the mainsail. He shook his head. "Sorry, honey. No can do. I don't trust this guy. We might not put him in jail, but I certainly want him to know we mean business."

Kevin agreed. "You have an entire pub of witnesses to back your accusation. I say report him to the authorities."

THEY HEADED BACK TO Hope Town, the issue of pressing charges heavy between them. Daniel needed the registration numbers of the Sheppard racer, but a little research would handle that hurdle. Maria, no longer willing to discuss the matter, took her favorite perch on the bow, letting the breaking waves soothe her thoughts. Daniel was right. She had to let him register the complaint.

They arrived in port by midafternoon. Typical of the islands, the constable's office was empty. The vacant building did little to dispel Daniel's anger.

Maria tugged at his arm. "Let's get some conch fritters. We'll come back later."

"Wait a minute."

He pulled a piece of paper from the bulletin board on the wall by the door and scribbled a note with the pen from the backpack on his shoulder.

"I'll have them radio me when they get in."

Maria shook her head. "Let me guess. You brought the handheld radio."

He patted the backpack. "I'm more than just good looks, Princess."

Desperate to lighten his mood, she said, "I've been meaning to remind you. Never call me Princess."

He laughed, and it tickled her to know she had that power to dispel his bad mood. She let him wrap an arm around her and lead her to a dockside restaurant.

No sooner had their meals been served when the familiar sound of an ocean racer rumbled over the water. They both turned in the direction of the port entrance.

In motored Jack, seated low in the craft, baseball cap and sunglasses shielding his face. They watched as he eyed the *Honora,* slowing the throttle as he passed. His gaze circled the harbor and spotted their dinghy at the dock. He headed in the opposite direction toward the wharf at Hope Town Harbour Lodge, but his intentions were clear.

Maria shook her head in disbelief. "*Dios mio,* he's stalking us."

Daniel already had pen and paper in hand, scribbling down the boat's registration numbers. "How convenient for us."

"Should we leave?"

Incredulity lit his face. "Hell, no. Not until I blacken those bloodshot eyes of his."

"You're not going to look for him, Daniel. Please."

He studied her face. "Okay, honey. We'll take these numbers to the constable. We'll let him handle Jack."

"Thank you." That answer sat much better with her.

She so wanted to end this trip and head back home. Elias had been left alone for long enough.

"I want to warn you, however. If we run into the guy, I'm not going to back away."

Her gaze drifted to the boat disappearing down a narrow waterway. "Hopefully, we'll never see his face again."

CHAPTER SEVENTEEN

DANIEL INSISTED HE TAKE MARIA back to the *Honora* while he looked for the constable, but she refused.

"You might need my help."

He laughed. "What? You think I can't explain what happened to the man?"

"No, I'm going to make sure you don't sneak off looking for your target." Her stomach roiled over the lump that was lunch. "When do you want to head back to Reefside?"

"We can leave tonight if you're in a hurry. But we could use a good night's sleep. Can you wait until dawn?"

The urge to take off now nudged unmercifully. She had had enough of this sojourn. She wanted to go home. To Poppa. To her studio. But she understood what Daniel meant. A solid night of sleep would do them both a world of good.

"Dawn will be perfect. I'm ready when you are."

He toyed with the string of her bikini top peeking out from beneath her sundress.

"Well then, how about we drop these numbers off at the constable's office then go for a swim at the beach behind the Hope Town Lodge?"

An hour later, they strolled hand in hand along the path past the lodge's pool, headed for the stairs to the beach.

Daniel squeezed her hand, his gaze riveted to the poolside bar. Jack. They'd taken him by surprise and his jaw tightened and his back straightened. His rumpled clothes were the same he'd worn yesterday. He must have slept in them.

Daniel charged toward him.

Maria grabbed his arm. "Daniel, wait."

He pulled away. Jack already had his back to the bar, anticipating Daniel. An odd, smug satisfaction filled his face. He shook his bandaged hand at Daniel.

"I'm a real problem for you, aren't I?"

Daniel throttled him, practically lifting him off the ground. Jack sputtered, grasping at Daniel's arm.

"Hey, no fights in my bar."

The bartender with the toothy grin wasn't smiling now. His gaze shot back and forth between the two men.

He leaned across the bar to speak just for their hearing. "Now, I know old Jack here probably deserves a clobbering." His cheerful, island accent made the threat sound like a reward. He gestured to the people swimming in the pool and seated under umbrellas, some gaping in shock. "This is a family spot. You'll take your disagreement away from here."

Daniel slapped a twenty on the bar, "Would you call the constable? Tell them I'll be on Back Street heading to the station."

He dragged Jack with him down the side path. Maria followed, her heart in her throat. No matter how much the creep deserved a clobbering, as the bartender called it, she hated violence.

Jack took a swing at Daniel and missed when Daniel sidestepped him. Jack's face grew crimson.

"You can't treat me like this."

Daniel grabbed a fistful of the other man's shirt, and spoke through clenched teeth. "I'm pressing charges, buddy. You could have killed us driving drunk like that.

I'm going to see you bunking with your brother as soon as possible."

"You can't prove anything." Spittle mixed with Jack's words.

Daniel slammed him against the wall of a house close to the sidewalk, pinning him with a glare. "Kevin's bartender already agreed to testify to the ten beers you drank in two hours. He also supplied a video of you swamping us with the racer. You're screwed, pal."

Jack's eyes grew wide. He reverted into a pouty juvenile. "Why do you keep ruining everyone's life?"

"What are you talking about? You could have killed us."

Jack slumped against the wall, staring at him like an errant child. "I just want things to go back to the way they were. My life isn't the same. Everything is gone."

Maria's breath caught in her throat. She'd had that same wish over and over again. She recognized a kindred misery in Jack's eyes, but she wasn't trying to kill someone.

Fists clenched, she stood next to Daniel, facing this wretched man. "We've all had a difficult time since the accident, Jack. It doesn't mean you can risk other people's lives."

"At least you have someone." Anger blistered his words. "I'm alone. Momma's dead. My sister won't talk to me and Ryan is in jail...all because of him!" He pointed at Daniel.

Maria felt pinpricks of alarm. "What do you mean?"

"Shut up, Jack." Daniel's voice boomed down the narrow street. He pulled the man off the wall and headed for the constable's station. "I'm itching to knock you out, so keep your mouth closed."

Jack chuckled, near hysteria. "Go ahead and hit me. Then I can put you in jail where *you* belong, not Ryan."

He flailed his arms as Daniel half ran, dragging him. Unperturbed by the treatment, Jack craned his neck to make sure Maria listened.

"I don't know how you can stand being with Romeo here when that crash is his fault."

Maria stopped dead in her tracks. "What?"

"That's enough, Jack." Daniel's voice sounded deadly.

With a tug of strength neither Maria nor Daniel expected, Jack wrenched himself free from Daniel's grip. He poked a finger at Daniel.

"You're lucky I didn't kill you yesterday. You put my brother in jail to cover your tracks."

Maria stalked over to Jack. "What are you saying?"

Gratification spread across his face as he realized Maria didn't know. He gestured to Daniel, all the more belligerent. "Ask him."

Color drained from Daniel's face. His eyes held hers, already begging for forgiveness. Something was truly wrong here.

"Ask you what, Daniel?"

Jack clapped his hands. "Go ahead, Romeo, tell her."

Both Maria and Daniel turned on him at the same time. "Shut up, Jack," they said in unison.

"Tell her how my brother was right on course and you swerved into his path. You killed them. Tell her."

"What is all the yelling about?"

The constable came around the corner, his crisp white uniform and cool confidence a welcome sight as panic ripped through Maria's gut. Someone had to stop the madness she was hearing.

Daniel motioned to Jack. "This is the man I reported. I want to press charges for reckless driving of a vessel while intoxicated."

The constable clucked his tongue, recognizing Daniel's

captive. "In trouble again, Jack Sheppard. What will your father say?"

"He'd wish I'd killed the son of a bitch." Jack tried to swing at Daniel one more time, but lost his balance.

The constable caught him by the arm. "Well, that's one sorry admission, my friend. I think you had better come with me." Looking over his shoulder, he added to Daniel, "You might want to fill out a report."

Daniel nodded. "We'll follow in a moment."

Maria's knees threatened to buckle.

"Daniel?" Questions tightened her chest and she felt as if she were watching Jack's boat bear down on them again and feeling helpless to outrun it.

Guilt pooled in Daniel's eyes. "He's telling the truth, Maria. Carmen was not driving the boat when Ryan Sheppard hit us. I was."

His admission was the last thing she'd expected.

Daniel had been in the boat.

Why did she think he had been at the pub and Carmen was driving the skiff? Okay. But why wouldn't he have told her previously that Carmen was not driving? "Daniel, you're a professional. How could you have caused the accident?"

He closed his eyes. "I was arguing with Carmen."

Maria stepped back as if she'd been punched. Had the horror of witnessing Daniel cause the accident blocked him out of her mind? Carmen had been screaming at someone. Did the recklessness of their anger cause the deaths?

Her words escaped as a whisper. "Then...the tabloids. It's true about Carmen, Daniel?"

Daniel closed his eyes, as if evading the accusation in her own. "Can we talk about this later, Princess?"

"No! Tell me, now."

He held open his palms. "Not like this in the middle of a street."

Her hand flew to her throat as she realized Daniel wasn't going to deny there was something between him and Carmen. Suddenly, she couldn't breathe. "I said, tell me. Now."

Daniel took a stance as if readying for a blow. He ran a hand through his hair, not taking his hot, blue gaze from Maria's, as if she was his last lifeline.

He expelled a tortured breath. "Yes, damn it all. Carmen and Rosalinda died because of me. I will admit that, but Carmen is not worth discussing. The lies she spewed were ugly and untrue."

Maria felt the darkness blotting out the memory of that awful day rip away like a scab from a wound. The rush of remembering practically floored her. Carmen's voice rose in her head…screaming at Daniel as he drove the skiff away from the dock at Little Harbour, Ryan's ocean racer eating up their wake. Carmen had punched Daniel's arm, her words now as clear as the moment she screamed them. *"You're making me leave him because you are jealous."*

Maria stood there, staring blindly at Daniel, hands over her mouth, the event replaying in her mind. Why Ryan chased them still made no sense, but she remembered her sister screaming as the ocean racer gained ground on them, her mother laughing because Carmen's outrage amused her.

Carmen continued accosting Daniel, crying, "Turn around, damn you. Or I'll tell Maria about us."

Daniel's retort had been hoarse with emotion. "Shut up, Carmen. I have had enough of you."

Her sister had continued taunting Daniel. "You never

get enough, Daniel. That's your problem. Now turn this damn boat around."

Maria choked as the memory of the horror she had felt at Carmen's words hit home. Her heart had twisted, unable to bear the angry emotions sparking between her lover and Carmen. At that moment all the rumors she'd heard suddenly rang true. A surge of hate had filled her like she'd never known. Carmen. Daniel. Cheating on her, while her mother applauded her favorite daughter's triumph.

Maria remembered screaming, while registering her sister's satisfaction at her rage. "Stop it! Daniel? You and Carmen? And everyone knows? You two make me sick. Oh, God, I hate you, Daniel. I will always hate you. I hate you all!"

It was then, with Maria screaming at Daniel, his eyes burning with rage, that the ocean racer thundered nearer and Carmen screamed, "Take me back."

Then the skiff swerved with a jerk, her mother's scream caught in her throat, and the world ended.

She dropped her hands from her eyes and stood face-to-face with Daniel, steeling herself against the onslaught of emotions tearing her insides raw.

She tried to breathe but her throat closed. Her lungs burned. Here stood the one man she had not been able to remember from the start. The one man who had plundered her world, pulling her from seclusion, slowly and seductively bringing her back to life, and then captured her heart, one more time. Now, rack her brain as she tried, she couldn't dredge up one single memory to exonerate him.

Her outrage rose. He'd killed her mother and sister. And over a lover's quarrel.

Her gaze raked this pirate who had rattled her world, who stood waiting now as she prepared her verdict, and all the while she vehemently wished something other than

Carmen's screams and the heat and anger in Daniel's eyes filled the small space between them on this narrow, dusty path. She winced as her trust in Daniel snapped like a twig.

She slapped his face. "How dare you?" Her voice trembled with rage.

Daniel's face jolted with the impact, but he did not move. Guilt and sadness filled his eyes.

She slapped him again.

He grabbed her wrist. "That's enough, Maria."

She jerked her hand from his grasp. "When were you going to tell me?" She spat the words, gaining small satisfaction from the welt rising on his cheek.

He closed his eyes briefly before answering. "I tried. God knows, I just knew that no matter what I said, you would not believe me. I knew I'd have to bear the condemnation I see on your face right now."

Her compassion hardened with a thud. She wasn't going to be moved by his misery, not while her own despair shredded her insides. The truth was all too clear. Daniel had manipulated her from the moment she'd stepped foot on the *Honora*. He'd never planned to tell her. And if he did, he would have twisted the truth. The liar. She'd suspected he'd hidden something from the start and ignored her better judgment because she couldn't keep her goddamn hands off his goddamn body.

She felt sick at her own weakness.

She'd fallen for him. Hook, line and sinker. Now Daniel had the audacity to twist stories to gain her sympathy. He'd killed her sister and mother. Accidents were forgivable, but not when duplicity caused them. She choked back bile rising in her throat. How could she have been so stupid to fall for him a second time?

Damn her amnesia.

Her words caught in her throat. "I hate you, Daniel Del Rio."

She swiped at him again, but his hand, lightning quick, intercepted her mark. "Maria, please. Let me explain."

Dios. How could he look like an avenging angel when he was the devil incarnate? She hoped he registered the loathing in her eyes.

"Let go of me."

"Not until you listen."

She wrenched her hand from his. "Listen? You lie."

His voice broke with regret. "You think I wanted to keep this from you? I had to win you back, Maria. Then I was going to tell you."

"I don't believe you."

She turned to leave, and then swung around, needing to vent her rage. "You knew I'd fall in love with you, but you didn't figure how completely I'd hate you for betraying me."

Her throat tightened at the thought of Daniel making love to Carmen. Maria knew Carmen took lovers and suspected the same about her mother, but they were her family. Neither of them would trespass on her boyfriend. Would they?

She struggled for one simple breath. God help her. Her sister and mother were dead. That's all that mattered. She'd see this through to the end. For their sake. And for hers.

She met the rising anger in Daniel's eyes and didn't care. "Is everything else false, too, Daniel?"

"What do you mean?"

She wrapped her arms around her middle, feeling too small to fight this battle, but unwilling to surrender. "Did you fake loving me when all along you wanted my sister?"

"God, no. Maria, you have this all wrong."

He reached for her, but she pulled out of his grasp once

more. She held out a hand, keeping him at arm's length. The dolphins dancing on the ring on her middle finger glinted in the sun, but she ignored it. She only saw Daniel Del Rio. The gorgeous pirate who pillaged her heart. The moment of truth had arrived. She might as well ask him, and kill her soul, as well. After all, they'd been damned from the start.

"So, tell me, Captain. Was I not enough for you? Did you require my twin for a lover, as well?"

His head shot back as if she'd slapped him again. She could swear he searched her face for the reason she'd asked so he could calculate his response. The answer rose in his eyes before he even spoke.

He wasn't going to tell her.

"If I tell you the truth now, you won't believe me, Maria. You have already condemned me."

Her breath seared her lungs. She pointed a finger at him, her voice dripping with betrayal.

"You slept with her."

He stepped toward her. "No! Never, Maria. I will explain, if you will let me."

"You lie."

She had to get out of here before she collapsed. Repulsed by the memories assaulting her mind, she used every ounce of strength to make her feet move her as far from this man as she could get.

She ran as if the devil himself chased after her.

CHAPTER EIGHTEEN

DANIEL TOOK ANOTHER HIT OF RUM. The *Honora* rocked quietly at the mooring and felt as empty as he did. The peaceful harbor taunted his turbulent mind.

He sat in the cockpit facing the lighthouse, mentally calculating the next flash of light. The mindless distraction didn't help. The only guiding light for him had holed up in the Hope Town Harbour Lodge and would probably stay there.

Too bad Jack wasn't around. He'd love to bloody the bastard's nose. Grudgingly, he had to admit that if it hadn't been Jack, someone else, even Elias, would have told his story. Truth sooner or later found its mark. Always did.

The only satisfaction gained from this afternoon was filing the charges against Jack. That should keep him confined for a while.

He swallowed another shot, letting it burn down his throat. How could he have been so stupid? If he had just told Maria from the start, she might have rejected him, but at least he would have kept his integrity for telling the truth. He could have moved on.

But no. Because of his own stupid fears, because of his foolish pride and inability to admit guilt for killing two people to the woman he cherished more than his own life, the fragile trust he had built with Maria toppled before his eyes like a house of cards.

He could have sworn he heard her heart break on that

path. Elias's prediction knocked him flat on his ass, as promised. He should have listened to the old man.

Yeah, but the old man hadn't seen the torment filling his daughter's eyes every time she came close to regaining her memory. Would Elias have told her, as he expected Daniel to do, if he was here living her fears right alongside her?

He thought not.

A sigh escaped his lips. This afternoon's confrontation was such a train wreck. Instead of admitting the truth to Maria when he had the chance, he ended up accused and humiliated, watching the love he craved to see in her eyes gasp its last breath on that narrow street.

And a goddamn Sheppard dealt the final blow.

God help him.

Jack provided the facts, all right. Daniel's boat did swerve into Ryan's path. But, given the speed at which the man drove and his inebriated state, the court found favor with Daniel.

But to what end? Maria's twin and mother were dead because Daniel let Carmen goad him into anger. Because he couldn't manage Carmen, Maria had almost died and now suffered from amnesia. He was a professional, for heaven's sake. How could he have mishandled a center console speedboat—with such catastrophic results?

Shame had eaten at him every single day. Who could love a man like him?

He could no longer defend his actions with excuses and finger-pointing, especially now. No matter how ironclad his explanation, Maria wouldn't believe him. Carmen saw to that. Her angry words had been calculated to hit Maria directly in the heart.

That Maria would remember Carmen's anger was precisely what he had feared from the beginning. He practically choked as the noose he'd avoided for over a year jerked tight around his neck. His chest still hurt from not being able to breathe.

He hadn't wanted to expose Maria to the raw underbelly of events leading up to the accident. Maria and Carmen may have been identical twins, but their souls were light-years apart. Anyone looking closely would have seen the black hole in Carmen's.

Maria, always caught up in her art, had been blissfully unaware of Carmen's seething jealousy. It ripped his heart just thinking about the trouble Carmen had caused, especially once Maria had gained such rave reviews for her art.

Since Carmen had no talent other than her body to create a sensation, Daniel had become her next target. And because of her deceit, now, even dead, the woman was poison.

Lies. He hated them. Lies and political intrigue under Pinochet's dictatorship had caused his parents' disappearance. Lies had caused the death of two women.

Now a lie just destroyed his future.

When he and Maria were deeply in love he had received the first phone call from a reporter. He discovered Carmen had been feeding lies about him to the tabloids, intent on dragging him into her sordid fantasies. When he had confronted her, he learned that Rosalinda approved of Carmen's games. Carmen's genuine belief that he would prefer her over Maria made him want to puke. After that, he had dodged both women like a disease. Carmen, however, always managed to show up.

She continued weaving tales about her and Daniel, notifying reporters where to find them. Daniel had to constantly defend himself. He finally told Maria of Carmen's tricks, but Carmen had beat him to the punch.

Shedding tears to outshine any actress, Carmen had

gone to Maria declaring she'd just read the awful tabloids
and the reporters were lying. She gushed about how perfect a couple Daniel and Maria were and that the media
conjured lies to produce fodder for gossip.

Maria had asked Daniel to just let the entire issue drop.
She had been in the middle of a huge painting commission
and had been startled by the drama of it all. She'd already
felt alienated enough by her mother and sister excluding
her from their secrets. He didn't need to compound her
hurt by exposing Carmen's envy over everything that was
Maria's, including him. Besides, they loved each other.
What did they care about Carmen's childish antics?

After the accident, Daniel had been shocked that Maria
had forgotten the incident. She had continued to cherish
what happy ties she'd had with Carmen and Rosalinda.
He had kept the facts to himself because Maria seemed to
need those fragile good memories. After all, the women
had perished. Maria and Daniel had been left to pick up
the pieces of their lives. Daniel had just indulged one last
hope that Maria might stay included in his.

None of it mattered now. He had made the wrong choice
to withhold the facts, and Carmen's mischief was done.

In one last effort this evening, he'd packed a bag with
her toiletries and her clothes, all smelling sweet like
Maria, and had taken them up to the lodge.

He searched the premises, hoping to find her around,
but no luck. She'd left orders at the front desk not to be
disturbed. He'd left her things, feeling even more the fool
under the manager's knowing gaze.

The breeze teased the rigging overhead. The rhythm
sounded like a hammer nailing his loneliness firmly in
his chest. His eyes roamed the fan of stars overhead. He
shook his head, adrift like he'd never felt before. His fear
of losing Maria had become a self-fulfilled prophecy. Elias

had said she'd understand, but Daniel had thought he'd known better. How could a man who was a professional failure, the person who had killed her family members, confess guilt to his lover and expect her to love him in return when all the facts were littered with lies?

He drained the rum from his glass in one acid gulp.

Hell. He reached for the bottle. Who needed a glass?

MARIA STOOD AT THE DOOR of the oceanfront bungalow watching the moon reflect off the water. A hot shower had done nothing to ease her anger. She still seethed. She refused to admit she'd chosen this very accessible location instead of a room in the lodge hoping Daniel would show up at her door. She wanted to pound on his chest until her fists ached, or until he wrestled her into submission, kissing her into believing him again.

Nombre de Dios. What was wrong with her?

She plopped into the deck chair on the narrow porch, the facts tormenting her. The man had deceived her. Seduced her. Then lied about betraying her, yet she wanted him to come kiss her senseless? *Wrong.*

She sighed. If only she could turn back time to yesterday. Jack was the villain then. Daniel was the man who'd opened her eyes to life once more. Before Jack spewed those awful words, she had felt so righteously wronged by that awful man. Then with one sentence, he shot her whole world to hell.

Her throat tightened. Carmen. Momma. Nothing would bring them back. She could understand Daniel's guilt over causing the accident. She could have accepted his trepidation over telling her the truth. The burden must have been overwhelming. Part of her wanted to soothe his pain, but her compassion died when she reminded herself the whole event happened because of his ties with Carmen.

Maria must have blocked Daniel from her memory because of her twin. She'd suspected their liaison before the accident, but her mind mercifully had erased the memory. She didn't want to accept it then. Now she had no choice.

The sultry breeze off the ocean caressed her face. How could she stop her body from wanting Daniel while her logic condemned him? He was a murderer. A cheat. A liar. No woman, once aware, would hunger for his lips any longer…for the heat of his hand on her skin…for…

She bolted from the chair, leaned against the porch railing, turning her face into the thin light of the moon. She inhaled warm sea air deep into her lungs. The enormity of Daniel's deception burrowed into her heart. She could never forgive him.

She pressed her hands against the knot in her chest. Why had she insisted on hunting down these awful memories? Did Poppa know Daniel had caused the accident? She sighed. Of course he did. Clearly, he had expected her to fall in love with Daniel again, or he wouldn't have agreed to her plan.

Poppa wouldn't know about Carmen and Daniel. He would have only seen the love between Maria and Daniel. And from what she'd learned on this voyage, Daniel's love could turn a woman around, and make her feel like the only star in the sky. Surely their love for each other was all Elias saw. Poppa had been wrong. Daniel Murphy Del Rio was a heartbreaker.

Damn his eyes.

Damn his body.

Damn his lies.

There was nothing else left to do. All she had left was Poppa. And Reefside. She was going home.

DANIEL ROSE AT DAWN, showered, and now rowed to shore for another attempt to reach Maria. His jaw practically hit the floor of the dinghy when he saw her standing on the ferry dock.

She wore shorts and a T-shirt. Her hair was pulled into a ponytail. A baseball cap shadowed her eyes. Any observer would think she was dressed for a day of fun.

In his wildest dreams, she stood there to meet him. To make peace. The ice in her eyes said otherwise. She held her body in a stance that gave no quarter. She slid her sunglasses onto her face and looked away.

The duffel bag at her feet explained everything. He checked his watch. Five minutes before the ferry arrived. He'd have to talk fast.

She ignored him as he tied the dinghy a few feet away. She turned her back on him and faced the harbor as he climbed onto the dock. Anger poured from her body like molten lava.

He felt like a schoolboy saying the wrong things. "You're leaving without your paintings or supplies?"

She remained silent.

"Maria?"

"I have supplies at home."

"Your paintings?"

"Keep them. Sell them. I don't care."

She still hadn't looked at him and studied the harbor entrance as if willing the ferry to arrive.

"Maria, we have to talk. You don't know the whole story."

"And you're going to tell me?" She looked at him, disgust filling her voice.

"Yes."

She shook her head. "Please. Just don't speak."

He reached for her arm.

Her eyes darted to his hand as if it were lethal. "Remove your hand."

"Elias knows the truth."

"I intend to ask him."

The ferry entered the harbor and motored toward the dock. They watched as it tied up, the cockpit filled with passengers, boxes, suitcases. Each passing second was another moment closer to losing her.

He stepped into her line of vision. "Maria, come back with me. We'll set sail for home right away."

She looked at him, stunned, as people streamed past them. A ferry worker took Maria's bag aboard.

"You don't get it, do you?"

He opened his palms. "You were not the only one affected by this accident. Your memory may have returned, but what you're remembering isn't the truth. Maria. Give me a chance."

She met his gaze, revulsion tugging her lip. "Too late, lover boy."

He grabbed her hand. "I never betrayed you. You are dead wrong about Carmen and me."

She shook her head, holding her hand out as if warding off a bad dream. "I can't listen to this."

"Maria. She's dead. Don't let her rip us apart again. I love you."

She inhaled as if the atmosphere had disappeared. Reaching into her pocket, she pulled out an object and dropped it into his palm. The dolphin ring felt warm from being close to her body. He tightened his fist around it, trying to read her eyes behind the sunglasses.

She held herself rigid, shaking her head with what looked like regret. "Lose those words as fast as you can, Daniel. This little game is over."

She stepped onto the ferry and moved into the shadows of the forward cabin.

He watched the boat leave the dock. An empty, sick

feeling rocked his insides. He had to let her go. She'd never believe him. He'd known from day one this was how the story would end.

The ferry disappeared from the harbor. Not once did Maria look back. He stuck her ring on his pinkie and climbed into the dinghy, the sun burning through his shirt in the still air.

He rowed like a man condemned, and rightfully so. His lack of judgment had killed two people. Withholding the truth cost him Maria's trust. Someone else's lies cost him her love. His stubborn, foolish fears destroyed any chance of winning her back.

His course was now set. He'd leave for Brisbane as soon as he could get his act together. He'd deal with a broken heart. Time would eventually heal the wound. What he couldn't abide, however, was that this relationship had been destroyed by lies. Before he left for the other side of the world, he was going to make sure Maria understood the truth. She didn't have to love him anymore. She just needed to know that he wasn't a liar.

A surge of pride filled his chest. He'd done everything in his power to make the world right at Reefside. Now the ocean called. He could hear the wind filling his sails, the bow of the *Honora* gliding over the waves. He was, once more, a man cast away without a home, or a woman to love.

And he had been so close.

EDUARDO TOOK THE BAGS FROM Maria's hands.

"Bienvenidos, señorita! Qué sorpresa."

Bone weary, she had no energy to explain herself. "Yes, I thought I'd surprise you. Where is Poppa?"

The smile faded from his lips. "Still in his room."

"What?" She checked her watch. Two hours since lunch. "He's sleeping?"

Eduardo shook his head. "No, *señorita*. He took lunch in bed and decided to read for a while."

"That doesn't sound like Poppa."

Eduardo shrugged, his eyes speaking what his mouth wouldn't say.

She took the marble stairs two at a time.

He answered her knock immediately. "*Que*, Eduardo?" She stuck her head around the door. "It's me, Poppa."

Her father lounged in his huge, four-poster bed, the mosquito netting pulled back, the ceiling fan turning lazily overhead. The balcony doors stood wide open to the beautiful day.

"*Querida, mia. Bienvenidos!*"

She climbed into the circle of his large, welcoming arms. Outside, the hushed pulse of the ocean rose on the breeze.

"It's good to be home, Poppa."

"You have returned so soon?"

She inhaled and released an endless sigh, suddenly aware that Poppa's eyes held the bloodshot look of painkillers. Not good.

She pulled at the gray silk collar at his neck. "You're still in pajamas, Poppa. You're getting lazy in your dotage."

He chuckled. "Just a little tired today, *querida*." He tapped his book. "Ernest Hemingway and I decided to spend the morning with the Old Man and the Sea."

She sat up. "You've been worried about me and the stress made you ill."

He pulled her to his chest, nestling her head under his chin and patting her back. "No, my daughter. I'm an old man. Sometimes my illness catches up with me."

"You're taking your insulin?"

He nodded. "Nurse Mills lurks around here some-where."

"How are your feet?"

"Hmm. Not good. I see the doctor in the morning."

"That's why you're in bed."

She didn't have to ask. The degeneration of his ankle joints caused him anguish. His excess weight had led to nerve damage and sometimes cut off circulation in his feet. He always had to guard against gangrene and sores. Days he couldn't withstand the discomfort, he stayed in bed with pain medication and pillows propped beneath his knees, just as they were now. With the summer blanket over his legs, she couldn't see if his skin was bruised. She wouldn't upset him by asking him to show her. Nurse Mills would have insisted he go to the hospital if his condition was serious.

"Don't be concerned, *querida*. I will be fine in a day or so."

She laid a hand on his cheek. His skin was cool, yet perspiration broke on his brow. Once more, not good.

Worry began niggling at her. "I'm glad I came home."

He leaned away to catch her gaze. "And where is my ship's captain?"

She tried to speak but the words caught in her throat as a sob. Damn, her emotions were so raw. She chewed her bottom lip, valiantly trying to stay calm, but it didn't help. Tears fell.

He lifted her chin with a finger. "Maria?"

She shook her head, swiping at the tears, which only made things worse. Unable to stop, she buried her face in his chest and cried.

"My, my. So terrible?" A tremor rocked her father's voice.

"I…know…what happened." She interjected the words between sobs.

He smoothed her hair against her head. "Cry, my little one. I'm sure it was terrible to hear."

"Oh, Poppa."

Sadness filled his voice. "My heart breaks once more to see my only living daughter weep." He waited until Maria calmed, the dampness of her tears staining his pajama shirt. He reached for tissues from the nightstand. "Here, blow."

She took the tissue, searched his gaze. "Poppa, do I make you happy?"

He tightened his hold on her shoulder, as if wishing to drive a point home. "Maria, my sweet. You are the gentle angel who brightens my day. You make me very happy."

She closed her eyes, wanting ever so much to believe his words as they buffeted her aching heart.

"Now, what have you done with my boat captain?"

"Why didn't you tell me Daniel killed Momma and Carmen?"

"Maria, it was an accident. An awful, deadly accident. Don't you know how Daniel grieves to this day? Why do you think I agreed to send you away with him? Daniel needs your forgiveness."

She straightened. "Not the way I heard it."

"What did Daniel tell you?"

Her gaze dropped to the wad of tissues in her hand. "He didn't. We ran into Jack Sheppard."

Elias closed his eyes. "*Dios, mio.* I had little faith in a court order."

"The man's a pig." She spat her words with venom.

"*Sí.* The Sheppards are unsavory people."

"No. I mean Daniel. He lied, Poppa. He betrayed me."

Elias's chest heaved. "Some things once learned are better off forgotten. Can you not forgive him, Maria?"

"With Carmen?" She practically shrieked.

He blinked in surprise. "What are you telling me?"

"Daniel crashed our boat into Ryan Sheppard's racer because he was having a lover's quarrel with Carmen. Momma was laughing at them."

Her heart wrenched saying the words out loud. The accusation sounded so foreign. So ugly. She didn't want to hurt Poppa with the truth. One should never talk about family in such a way.

Elias's voice hardened. "Who told you of this affair between Daniel and Carmen?"

She hesitated. "No one. I remembered that day. I know you loved Carmen best, but Poppa..."

Shock filled his face. *"Querida."*

She held up a hand. "No, Poppa. I'm sure you didn't know about Carmen. But I wish you had stopped me from going on this trip. Knowing what I do, I would have preferred to forget about the past."

After a long moment, he met her gaze. "Daughter, you must listen while I explain something."

"What is it?"

"My beautiful Rosalinda was a complicated woman, and I suspect she may have influenced your sister." Understanding filled his eyes. "I knew Rosalinda took lovers, but I am to blame for her misguided attentions."

"Poppa, what are you saying?"

He shook his head. "I neglected your *madre.* Too much work. Too much travel. And the truth? Rosalinda was not my heart's love. I could not give her the passion she needed so I enjoyed her charms and let her keep her secrets. Now I fear she taught them to Carmen."

"Oh, Poppa." She jumped from the bed. "Even if this

is true, they should never have turned their attention to Daniel. I am *family*. I will never forgive Daniel. Never. Please do not permit him at Reefside, ever again."

Elias shook his head, agitation flushing his already perspiring face. "This is all wrong, *Maria*. I cannot believe Daniel would betray you. I must speak with him."

She reacted as if he struck her. She wrapped her arms around herself, staring at him. Her father had become a monster. She whispered, "You would side with Daniel against me?"

Elias held out a hand, looking helpless since he could not reach her. "Tell me what you remember. Please. I will help you sort out the truth."

She shook her head, tears falling unchecked down her face. "I can't. It hurts too much. I have to go."

Nurse Mills knocked and entered, oblivious to Maria's distress. "Welcome home, Miss Santiago."

Maria bolted from the room.

CHAPTER NINETEEN

MARIA HAD SLEPT FITFULLY, spending most of the night in the dark on her balcony, once again letting the silence and the gently breaking surf bathe her battered spirit.

She had expected Poppa to be outraged when hearing about Daniel and Carmen. She wanted him to rise to her defense like a raging lion and rip Del Rio to shreds. Instead, he chose to reserve opinion until speaking with his captain.

Did he have so little faith in her?

Some truths a daughter had to bear. Elias was too ill for her scorn. Besides, her love for him knew no bounds. She'd have to live with the knowledge that she mattered less in his eyes than her mother and sister. No pity there. Elias loved Maria—she'd never doubted that fact. But she'd always known the vivacious Rosalinda and the charming Carmen claimed the family spotlight. Maria had been the quiet one. While she believed Elias indulged her social shortcomings in favor of her art, he'd never stopped loving her. This she knew. The love he offered would have to be enough.

This morning, the thought of dressing seemed tedious, but she'd promised Eduardo to accompany Poppa to his doctor's appointment this morning. She wore a peach sundress Poppa loved and flat sandals, her hair loose on her shoulders. She had made her way to the front foyer and

now waited on the antique Spanish bench by the elevator
for Nurse Mills to descend with Poppa in his wheelchair.

The front doorbell chimed. Hurried footsteps from the
kitchen sounded down the hall.

She stood. "I'll get it, Eduardo." Maria opened the door,
shaking her head in confusion. *"Buenos dias,* Doctor Hernandez. We are on our way to see you."

The balding, older gentleman dressed in a starched,
Cuban shirt and crisp, black pants, nodded in greeting. He
looked more like a relative than the doctor who'd treated
her family since before she was born. His medical bag was
the only clue to his identity.

The faraway wail of an ambulance rose in the distance.
Dr. Hernandez offered his most comforting bedside smile.

"Ah, a phone call from Nurse Mills advised me that she
has called an ambulance. Elias seems to be in distress."

Maria's gaze shot up the stairs. "What's wrong?"

He stepped inside the foyer as she closed the door
behind him. "Perhaps if you take me to our patient, we
can both find out."

Eduardo appeared around the corner. *"Ah, el doctor."*
The butler ushered him toward the elevator. "I will take
you to him, *señor.*"

The doctor headed for the stairs. "Let's walk, Eduardo.
It'll be faster."

Despite the cool air-conditioning, they found Elias perspiring profusely. Nurse Mills stood by his bed, pressing
compresses to his forehead, his silver hair drenched with
sweat. He seemed to be dozing, unaware that the others
had entered. The sickly sweet smell of illness and the sting
of fear filled the room.

Nurse Mills spoke in a soft, insistent voice. "Chest
pains. Erratic heartbeats."

Doctor Hernandez listened to Elias's heart, read his blood pressure. He shook his head, frowning.

"Blood pressure is too high. His heart cannot withstand much more of this." He reached into his bag for a serum and needle.

Elias roused from his slumber. "I need rest. That's all. You fuss over little."

The ambulance siren grew louder then stopped abruptly. The medics would be swarming the room in a matter of seconds. Poppa's usually tanned face looked sallow. He seemed confused as he watched Dr. Hernandez administer to him.

Maria took his hand. "Poppa?"

He turned his head at the sound of her voice. His eyes were bloodshot, watery, heated. He squeezed her hand with tremulous fingers, his voice shallow. *"Ah, mi querida. Mi corazón. Yo te amo mucho."*

My dear one. My heart. I love you so much.

Tears broke in her eyes. "I love you, too, Poppa. You're going to be all right. Dr. Hernandez knows what to do."

His effort to smile seemed pained. "My chest. I cannot breathe."

The medics pressed into the room. Dr. Hernandez spoke one word: "Oxygen."

A mask was placed over Elias's face. The head medic listened as Dr. Hernandez relayed Elias's statistics and explained his diabetic condition. It took three men to maneuver her father's big frame onto the gurney. In minutes, they were out the door and lifting him into the ambulance.

"I'm going with Poppa," Maria said.

The leader stopped her from climbing into the rear. "You'll have to ride up front. We'll be assisting Dr. Hernandez back here and there's not enough room."

The ambulance siren pierced the air as the vehicle

darted down the drive. Nurse Mills and Eduardo would follow in separate cars. Maria stared blindly out the windowshield, wishing the medic would drive faster.

DANIEL SCRAMBLED FOR THE satellite phone in the chart table. When the number at Reefside appeared on the screen, his heart thundered in his chest. He shot a gaze skyward begging for a merciful call.

Inhaling, he flipped the phone open. "Del Rio."

Eduardo's voice broke with fear. "Señor Daniel. Hurry. The ambulance takes *El Elias* to the hospital."

Daniel's blood ran cold. He checked his watch. "I'll catch the next plane."

A rented Jaguar waited at the airport. Daniel didn't trust a taxi to drive fast enough for his liking. As he sped down I-95, the sun setting over his left shoulder, he prayed he wasn't too late. He slapped the radio off. Memories flooded his mind.

He'd never had the chance to say goodbye to his parents. They'd actually been missing a week before he even learned of their disappearance. Searching for them, and coming up empty, had left a hole in Daniel he still couldn't fill. Losing Elias without saying goodbye would shatter his world. This couldn't happen to him twice. Daniel loved the man too much not to have the chance to tell him.

Pulling up to the hospital, he threw the keys to a valet and bolted through the door. Eduardo had secured a pass for him, which he obtained immediately.

Daniel's mouth grew dry when the elevator opened. The antiseptic smells, fluorescent lighting and dull blue paint on the walls sucked the vitality right out of him. Only the lively voices of the nurses buoyed him down the hall.

He followed the arrow and room numbers indicated on a tiny plaque by the nurse's station. His boat shoes made no sound on the floor, but his breathing echoed against the walls, betraying his panic.

What would he say to Elias?

To Maria?

Oh, God. Let Elias live another one hundred years. Heal the old man so I can give him a piece of my mind about Maria.

Nurse Mills sat beside Elias's bed and looked up as Daniel entered. "Mr. Del Rio. Elias has been asking for you."

No one else was in the room. Elias dozed amid all the wires and machines.

"How is he?"

She shook her head. "Resting. There's a clot in the aorta. They're concerned about operating."

A monitor beat a steady monotone in rhythm with Elias's heart. He lay propped on pillows, his barrel chest rising and falling slowly as he breathed. Oxygen tubes fed into his nose. An intravenous line led from his arm, already black-and-blue where the needle entered his skin. His feet were wrapped like Frankenstein boots and jutted from beneath the thin covers.

Elias's hands lay on top of his blanket, vein-covered yet strong, capable of speaking for the man instead of words. Their immobility at this moment stated everything Daniel needed to know about the older man's condition.

A pang of guilt racked him. He met the nurse's gaze. "He worried too much about us. Didn't he?"

She smiled, despite the concern in her eyes. "If he did, he spoke little of it. He had a chart of the Bahamas on the poolside table, though, plotting what he assumed was your daily course. So, yes, I'd say you two were on his mind."

He nodded, the pressure of tears building at the back of his eyes. "And Maria?"

The nurse's gaze drifted across Elias's bed to the door. "She went to the cafeteria for coffee. She should be back any minute."

Daniel felt his back stiffen. "I'm not leaving."

"Spoken like a true Chilean." Elias's voice was hoarse, almost inaudible.

"Elias."

Daniel pulled a chair up to the bed. He molded the older man's hand to his own, the parched skin fragile against his palm. Elias still did not open his eyes.

"You old bastard. What are you doing in this bed?"

A weary smile crossed his lips. He inhaled a slow, difficult breath. "Diabetes is an awful disease. It erodes your insides."

Daniel's chest knotted. "They'll fix your heart, Elias. Keep fighting."

Elias opened his eyes, slowly working his watery gaze to find Daniel's. "Is it true about Carmen?"

The fact that Elias even asked cut bone deep. Daniel shook his head, staring at a small vein jumping in his friend's hand. This was one torment he would set straight with the old man before he died. He met his mentor's gaze.

"Never, Elias. I love Maria. You know how Carmen was."

Elias closed his eyes, as if not to see the truth. "So now?" His voice seemed stronger, as if he were determined to fight against this plan gone wrong.

Daniel shrugged. "I pray for the right moment to explain."

Elias laughed and the sound became lost in a cough.

Daniel laid a hand on the man's chest. "Take it easy."

Elias took a moment to breathe and lifted Daniel's hand with his own. "There…is no time left."

Daniel fell silent, the heart monitor marking the beats

Daniel laced Elias's fingers in his own. "I love you as a father, old man."

Elias grunted, satisfied. His eyes closed again. "Did you know I was madly in love with your mother?"

"What?"

Nurse Mills shifted slightly toward the door, but Daniel barely noticed. Elias commanded his full attention.

A hint of mischief lighted the fatigue in his eyes. "Your Irish rogue of a father stole her from me."

Daniel straightened. "What are you saying, Elias?"

He waved a gentle hand. "Thomas never knew my feelings. Nina captured my heart when we were children, but I could not hold hers." His breathing was labored. "The one time I asked her to marry me, she teased we were too much friends." He sighed in disappointment. "An angel such as Nina would never love a frog like me."

"Don't speak like that, Elias."

His gaze grew distant. "She was too beautiful for words. I met Thomas in Spain and brought him to Chile. Nina fell in love with him the day they met." He chuckled softly. "Thomas had that effect on women."

Daniel smiled at a memory of his father swinging his laughing mother in a circle before kissing her. "Dad was a charmer."

"Not even the enticing Rosalinda could erase Nina from my heart. Only in death did Nina give me something to cherish—you as a son."

A gasp from the doorway filled the air.

"Maria." Daniel stood to face her.

She stormed into the room, cutting a wide swath around Daniel. "Poppa, please don't distress yourself with such stories. We don't need to hear them."

Elias coughed, waving a hand like a fool caught in confession. "Quiet, *querida*. I am purging my heart. No matter what you hear, you know how I've loved you and Carmen."He sighed, a sad smile creasing his mouth. "And I loved my Rosalinda. Only her appetites required more men than me."

"Poppa."

Elias wheezed out his answer. "No, Maria. I do not blame Rosalinda."

As if her father's confession was Daniel's fault, she glared at him across the bed.

"What are you doing here?"

"You have to ask?"

She pointed to the door. "Get out."

He met the fury in her eyes, his neck straining with indignation. "No."

Nurse Mills stood. "I won't have you two upsetting Señor Santiago. If you're going to argue, one of you will have to leave."

The two met her fearsome glare.

She crossed her arms. "Now, please."

Maria stood, unwavering.

Daniel sat back down in his chair. "I'm not leaving."

Elias spoke, his voice broken, uneven. "I won't listen to you two butting heads like goats. Both of you. Go. Let an old man rest."

He closed his eyes as if the energy it took to speak had drained him. Nurse Mills proved formidable in ushering the couple to the door.

Through a haze of anger, Maria spared a last glance at her father. She lifted her cell phone from her pocket.

"I'll be in the lounge. Call me if anything changes."

MARIA WAS OBLIVIOUS TO THE direction she took. Red-hot emotions blinded her. How dare Daniel follow her as if he had a right to step foot into this hospital? She made a big deal of putting her cell phone in her purse to prevent herself from running from him.

She would not cave.

In the hospital room, her focus was on Poppa, but all she could feel was Daniel, feel his heat and inhale the incense of him. How, in her anger, could she possibly notice the cuffs of his white shirt rolled up on his forearms, his jeans fitting so fine, his sun-kissed hair begging for her fingers to run through it. Dear God, she could barely resuscitate her own heart because of him.

And now her father declared love for Daniel's mother? The devil surely played Elias and Maria Santiago for fools.

It irked her that she noticed exhaustion lines creasing Daniel's eyes. She didn't want to acknowledge his misery. Maybe he'd been wrestling demons of his own.

Served him right. Hopefully, they were winning.

He reached for her before entering the lounge. "Maria, we have to talk."

Her entire body stilled at his touch. She lifted his hand from her arm, her skin aching from the warmth his fingers spread.

"We have nothing to say to each other."

He stepped in front of her, those baby-blues flashing dangerously. "Oh, yes, we do."

Maria pushed past him into the lounge. A middle-aged woman and her daughter watched the television with disinterest. Their expressions revealed they'd been sitting there too long, and would more than welcome the diversion Maria and Daniel offered.

An exit led to a rooftop deck. Maria headed for it. She could use the fresh air and the anonymity of the night. She pushed past the door, a cloud of humid air caressing her face. The thud of Daniel's hand on the tempered glass announced he'd followed.

She swung around to face the heat in his eyes. "What do you want?"

Desire seemed to infuse every cell in his body. "You. Plain and simple. But if I can't have you, I need to be assured that you understand the truth before I leave."

She might as well be standing in the middle of a cyclone. She inhaled a steadying breath.

"Please leave, now. I can't think about us, Daniel."

He shook his head as if he had all the time in the world. "I'm not moving until you hear me out."

"I've heard enough."

"Jury's still out on that one."

"Not for me, Daniel. Go away."

He pulled himself to his full height, forcing her to look up. Maria had the impression of a bear rising on its haunches to intimidate. She braced herself, hands on hips. She'd handle anything he delivered.

He started to reach for her, but dropped his arms to his sides. His shirt, open at the neck, revealed that V of tanned skin and dark hair. She swallowed hard, forcing her gaze back to his eyes. Their intensity nearly flattened her.

"What I am about to say is the truth, and always was the truth."

She wanted to slap his face. Did he think she was so gullible?

"I never slept with Carmen. I never made advances toward her, or invited her attention." He enunciated the next words very slowly. "Carmen meant nothing to me. She *was not you*."

"And I'm supposed to believe you."

"She was using me to hurt you."

That one stung. She had finally come to terms with the fact that the bond she and Carmen shared as young girls stretched to breaking as they grew up. The only time she and Carmen shared heartfelt moments was when they were alone, when Carmen didn't feel the need to impress anyone around them. Maria had cherished these hours and chose to remember them.

She could never understand Carmen's insecurities and dismissed them as foolish. Carmen was the prettier twin. She was the more sought after by the boys. She made the friends. Maria knew to give Carmen the spotlight when they were with others. Why would Carmen hurt her on purpose?

She narrowed her gaze. "So, I should take your word against what I saw with my own eyes, or against what the tabloids blasted month after month?"

He expelled a breath, his frustration clear. "Your sister manipulated every situation to make it look like we were an item. She was jealous of you, Maria."

As much as she hated to hear those words, her logic started to waver. All of Carmen's teasing, all those barbs couched in jokes, were they real? Had Carmen wanted to hurt her?

Daniel pointed to the door through which they'd both come. "Didn't you hear what Elias said? Your mother and sister were shameless flirts. You know this."

She searched his eyes, wanting desperately to believe this was not another ruse. Even more, she searched her own mind, looking for a kernel of evidence to justify his allegations. Carmen teased her, yes. She interrupted Maria's conversations, yes. She excluded Maria from some of her outings with Momma or her friends, yes. And she bragged to Maria of the many men she left in her wake. But Carmen was always quick with hugs and a heartfelt *I love you* every chance she had.

Had Maria been too absorbed in her studio to care— or even consider jealousy? And for goodness' sake, Carmen had so very much. Why would she consider Maria a threat?

Daniel stepped closer, shaking his head. "I am guilty of omitting information. I apologize for that, but I have never lied to you."

She held her ground against his advance, poking him in the chest with her cell phone. "Who were you to play God with my emotions on the *Honora?*"

He grew still, his voice dropping low. "What would you have done if the situation was reversed, Maria?"

Her answer caught in her throat. What *would* she have done in his place?

She stepped back.

He stepped closer, bringing his face inches from hers, those blue eyes bearing down like fighter planes, the heat of his body engulfing her.

"Answer me. How would you handle me, if I had amnesia, and you knew, as surely as you breathe, that I needed your help to reclaim my life? What would you have done if you loved me more than life itself, and knew that once I learned the truth I would reject you? Tell me. What would you do?"

Her thoughts began to short-circuit. She had to think. Lord, she wanted to run. She turned from him, glancing out at the city lights coloring the night. Yellows. Whites. Glowing neons.

Another painting.

She ached for the quiet of her studio where all of this turmoil would disappear. Where no one would demand she answer such daunting questions and she could escape into swirling color.

"Daniel, I don't know what I'd do." Her voice dropped to a whisper.

"Then give me one more chance to run through the

events with you. If you just give me one week, maybe two, I can find facts or even witnesses to prove I'm telling you the truth about Carmen."

He would postpone Brisbane again? Jeopardize his one chance to plant himself firmly in the sailing arena to prove his innocence with her? A liar would not go to such lengths, especially when their romance had ended.

"You would do that?"

A surge of hope reflected in his eyes. He shook his head, as if unsure of himself. "If you are willing to give me the chance, I'll make damn sure I find answers."

Her phone rang. She glanced at the number on the screen. *Oh, no.*

She hit the button. "Yes?"

As she listened to the brief words, her gaze shot to Daniel's. She pushed past him for the door.

"Okay. I'm coming."

"What, Maria?"

She didn't look back. "Poppa. We're losing him."

CHAPTER TWENTY

ELIAS HAD DIED IN HER ARMS. Now, seated in a deck chair on her balcony, Maria still felt the jolt of loss when Poppa had released his last breath. Was it just last night? What time was it now?

Her gaze searched the fading stars as she inhaled searing breaths, wondering if she'd ever feel whole again. Her spirit ached for assurance that she'd be able to make it through another day. Morning complied by whispering its first hint of gold along the horizon, edging the clouds in the softest pink.

She must have held her breath while the sun broke free, rising from a single point where sea met sky, because the fire scalding her lungs reminded her she was still alive.

She exhaled, watching fingers of light splay across the ocean, reaching toward her as the sun rose higher. She prayed this glorious sunrise was Elias's message that he'd arrived safely into the arms of the woman he loved.

Heaven knew, now that Poppa was gone, no arms awaited her in this world. She felt empty. Heavy-limbed. And so very alone.

Momma. Carmen. Poppa.

She'd have to paint this sunrise in their honor. She'd call it, *Traveling*. She just wished she wasn't so weary. Her body felt like lead as she crossed the small space to her nightstand to retrieve her camera.

As she snapped pictures, a sob caught in her throat. She

was going to live, after all. The obsession to paint gripped her again. This time, as if Elias were present. Her mind would not allow her to accept that he had departed.

Not just yet.

She zoomed close for a shot of the sun, now a red-rimmed disc of what...life? *Click.* She reversed the zoom for the entire blaze across the horizon. *Click.* Next, the ripples of rainbow light on the water, heading straight for her. *Click.* The still-shadowed clouds, backlit by sunlight with the pinkest blush. *Click.* Pastels slowly changing the night sky from velvet to the palest silk. *Click. Click.*

A sigh of exhaustion escaped her lips. She dropped the camera onto her bed. Now, if she could only sleep. Every time she started to doze, that awful, spiraling nightmare she'd had since the accident haunted her. So she sat up all night, waiting for dawn to free her. It had. Now, feeling as drained as she did, she wondered how could she possibly handle all the responsibility awaiting her today.

The funeral arrangements.

The phone calls.

The legal matters.

She vaguely remembered Daniel driving her home from the hospital. Everything from the moment Elias died until now had become a blur. At the hospital, she had crawled into Poppa's bed, wrapping her arms around his neck while that damned heart monitor tortured them with erratic and slowing heartbeats.

He was unconscious, struggling for breath, but she dared not stop speaking to him while he still lived. That beautiful ear beneath the silver wisp of hair would not be there much longer. Elias might not have heard her, but she prayed he did. A man should never die without knowing the love he spread in his world.

Daniel had stood at the foot of the bed, guarding her

while she helped her father leave this life, making sure the two were protected until the end.

She would be grateful to him for that kindness, forever. It was probably why she allowed him to drive her back to Reefside. He was somewhere on the property now. But she knew his presence was short-lived. No matter what they'd discussed before Poppa died, Daniel still had to pay for his sins. He might supply her with facts to justify his actions, but too much had fallen between them. He would have to leave.

Just another chore in the hellish day ahead.

She swallowed her misery and stood, headed for the bathroom. The tub beckoned. She'd take a long, hot bath, since her legs couldn't support her in a shower.

She peeled off yesterday's sundress knowing she'd never be able to wear the garment again. She turned on the tub's faucet hard and hot, inhaling the lavender scent of the salts she poured into the water. Behind her, sunlight flooded the studio through the balcony doors.

Poppa was gone, and life was demanding she carry on.

DANIEL HUNG UP THE PHONE in Elias's study and ticked off another name from the list before him. Funeral home. Church. Flowers. Hospital. Insurance company. Attorney.

Relatives and friends, he'd leave for Maria. He checked his watch. Not even close to lunchtime.

He couldn't eat if he wanted to. He reached for the coffee Eduardo had brought earlier, only to find it cold. Elbows on desk, he buried his face in his hands.

Elias was gone.

His absence, like cannon shot through the middle of Daniel's chest, had made it impossible to breathe all morning. Elias's aftershave and his boundless energy still lingered in the room. The wheelchair still waited by the door.

Daniel had already asked Eduardo to remove it so they wouldn't have to see it vacant.

He sighed, a gut-wrenching sound. He wanted to make this trauma as easy as possible for Maria. If he had ever loved Maria before, she had stolen his heart last night while whispering loving words to Elias as he slipped away. No doubt, she'd never give Daniel the chance to tell her that.

He picked up the phone. The only way to deal with the devastation was to take action. Elias had given him this list of contacts months ago. God knew, the last thing Maria needed right now was to handle the tedium of burying the dead. It gave Daniel small satisfaction to distract himself by attending to these chores for her.

He looked up at a motion by the door.

"Get out of Poppa's chair. Right now."

Maria stood in the doorway, eyes still raw from tears, hands on hips in that infuriatingly wonderful stance she took every time she declared war. But this morning was different. She looked small and lost in a pale green cami-sole and gypsy skirt, her hair loose on her shoulders, her feet bare. She was too fragile for sparring. He wasn't going to argue.

He stood, holding the chair open for her.

"I made calls. Funeral arrangements are set." He held up the list. "Crossed off everyone contacted. Thought you might want to phone your relatives."

MARIA STARED AT DANIEL, mortified. Here she was snip-ing at him when he had shared her burden of responsibil-ity. Grief stole what shreds of composure she had left, but his actions made her think, for a moment, that she wasn't alone. An unbidden spurt of relief nudged her gratitude then quickly evaporated. She'd remain cordial, but the sooner she handled Daniel, the better.

She waved a weary hand. "I apologize, Daniel. My nerves are shot. Somewhere in my mind, I'd hoped to see Poppa sitting there." She managed a weak smile. "Thanks for your help. I dreaded making those calls."

She moved past him to Poppa's chair, a pain stabbing her insides at his absence. All she had left was the living. The twin scents of Daniel's soap and warm skin reminded her the two of them were both very much alive.

Standing so close to him, Daniel felt strong, and so damn magnetic. Her body swayed toward him before she caught herself and sat. Would she ever be able to control herself around this man?

He'd neglected his hair and hadn't shaved. His disheveled appearance tugged at her heartstrings. No doubt, Daniel grieved. She often envied the bond he'd shared with Poppa. Was that why she'd reacted so uncivilly at the sight of him in her father's chair? She mentally shook herself. No. Finding Daniel in Elias's chair seemed like a taunt, daring her to include him in her life once more.

"You have to go, Daniel."

He shook his head. "I'll give you plenty of space, Maria. But the attorney advised me to stay around until after the funeral. Matters of estate."

Her head snapped to attention. "If Elias's will has been tampered with in any way, I'll fight to the death."

He held out a hand. "Hold on, Princess. Our fathers were business partners, remember? I'm sure it has something to do with settling my share of the company."

She hadn't thought of that. Her cheeks heated in embarrassment. "Apologies. Guess I'm a little jumpy."

"I understand. Believe me." He hunkered down and

turned the desk chair on its wheels so she'd face him. "Did you sleep at all last night?"

She shook her head. "No."

He pointed to the list. "This can wait. Why don't you climb into the hammock? Morning breeze is still cool under the bohio."

Stop being so thoughtful, damn you. She slanted him an icy look. "No. Thanks."

"Breakfast?"

"Eduardo brought me juice. Toast. I managed to get it down."

He took her hands in his, but she jerked them away.

"Don't, Daniel. There's nothing left to say."

He scrubbed his face with a hand. "I wish I knew how to reach you, Maria."

Her words felt as empty as they sounded. "Forget it. You've already done a fine job."

Heat rose in his eyes, but his voice held a finality that left her cold.

"I told you last night. I deceived you by omitting facts, Maria. Not lying. I drove that damn boat, and I'll find the proof I promised you. But if you want to know what really happened with Carmen, either find out for yourself, or come to me on your own and be willing to listen."

He stood and left the library, anger spilling like debris in his wake.

Ground zero be damned.

IMMEDIATELY AFTER THE funeral, Daniel returned to Hope Town. Maria hadn't seen him until the church. Traci and Brad had sat to her right during the service, oblivious to the distress between her and Daniel. Traci promised to come see her as promised. Daniel had stood by Maria's side, silently and stoically, even at the grave site. As usual, his presence jolted her senses into awareness. Yet he had said nothing except for assuring her that she was holding up, then departed with the last of the well-wishers.

At the disbursement of Elias's estate she had learned that Elias and Daniel had merged their shares of the import/export business with another company in Chile then sold the business. Daniel had signed all the documents the day before, so had left her alone to discover the proceeds were obscenely huge.

Had she known this information before setting sail with Daniel, she would have seen how absurd her accusation of gold digging was. And he had wealth he'd earned on his own. A surge of embarrassment had humbled her a bit more.

Maria spent most of the time with Mr. Arroyo discussing charities for which she'd set up funding. One would be for amnesia research, for sure. Perhaps another for abandoned children. She'd give that more thought at another time.

Meanwhile, she needed to remove the image of Daniel's jean-clad body, the timbre of his voice and smell of his skin from her world. Knowing Eduardo had taken him to the airport offered no small satisfaction.

Time to move on. Live in the now. She had paintings to finish. A gallery to fill. Just knowing Daniel was somewhere else other than on the property set her in motion. Haunted by the memory of his touch, she climbed the stairs to her studio and bolted the door.

MORNINGS EBBED AND FLOWED as did the passing days. Anxious to finish yet another canvas, Maria stopped only long enough to sip tea or eat a small meal brought by Eduardo. Traci had come by almost every day as promised for a glass of wine on the patio at sunset, but Maria kept the conversation light, unwilling to tell her that she and Daniel had parted ways.

This morning, her easel pulled her from bed. The tug was welcome. Otherwise she may not have risen at all. Her paintbrush offered life for emotions that otherwise would leave her raw. She was loath to admit that painting induced a different type of amnesia, one she welcomed.

Immersed in a world of her own creation, she was safe. Safe from the loss of loved ones. Safe from the moment she'd laid eyes on Daniel. Safe from his unspoken questions, which had been haunting her for the past two weeks.

The canvas became a repository for her raving imagination, making her craft more addictive than heroin. When painting, Maria needed no one except that quiet, amiable companion: seclusion.

Sometime after noon a knock at her door jolted her from concentration. She cleared her throat to speak.

"Who is it?"

The doorknob rattled. "The door is locked. Can I come in?"

"Traci." Maria put down her brush and palette, hurrying to unlatch the bolt.

"I wasn't expecting you until later." She pulled the woman into a hug. Oh, Lord, her new friendship felt so good. Traci offered a sisterhood that felt stronger than her bond with Carmen had been. Traci had no agenda, no secrets, only a sincere affection that became more apparent every time she came by. After all, only a friend would make sure you were doing well practically every day.

Traci linked her hands with Maria's when they stepped apart. "You have yet to invite me into your studio. I persuaded Eduardo to let me up."

Maria pulled her inside. "Well, for goodness' sake, why didn't you ask? Come in. Pay no attention to the clutter."

Traci's eyes darted around the studio. "I don't see clutter. Wow. This place is amaz— Hey, what's that noise?" She hesitated before walking to the windows that opened onto the trees outside. "Look! The monkeys. I've heard them, but they've always managed to hide from view."

Maria joined her. "They're squirrel monkeys."

"Tame?"

"Almost. I don't let them past the windowsill. They'd wreak havoc in here."

She opened the screen, handing a peanut to the monkey on the branch closest to the window. "This little imp is Sylvester."

As the monkey's fingers touched her own, a grin broke on Maria's lips. The sensation surprised her. It had been weeks since she'd enjoyed such a simple, frivolous moment. She'd been so absorbed in painting that she'd stopped hearing the animals' antics. Now Sylvester and his siblings watched Traci with interest, chattering away as she handed them peanuts.

Maria brushed back her hair, realizing she must look a mess in her paint-stained T-shirt and shorts. She hadn't even showered yet today. Well, at least she'd changed out of her pajamas.

"I'm so glad you're here, Traci. It was a quiet weekend."

Traci closed the screen, giving Maria her full attention. "How are you, honey?"

Maria gestured to the easel as if it would explain everything. "Painting."

Traci gasped in admiration as she crossed the studio to the first of a string of paintings drying in a line.

"Oh, will you look at this."

Color printouts of the sunrise taped onto the easel paled against the magic Maria had caught with her oils.

She shrugged. "I'm not selling that one."

Traci shook her head. "I don't blame you. I've never seen so much emotion in a sunrise before."

Maria pressed a hand over her mouth to suppress her own emotions. Tears had run unchecked down her face while she'd painted this one. She had let them flow. To heal. Her tears had been the only release against the vise closing around her throat. As much as tears threatened again, she didn't want to cry in front of Traci—not this wonderful sprite who brought such joy into her life.

Traci saw her distress. She laced an arm through Maria's. "It's been unbearable, hasn't it?"

A long, slow sigh escaped her lips. "Yes."

The two stood and studied the canvas. "What are you naming this one?"

The word left Maria's lips in a whisper. *"Traveler."*

"It's for your father."

Maria reached for a tissue and wiped her nose. "And Momma. And Carmen."

"What a beautiful tribute."

Another knock sounded at the studio door. Eduardo's voice was apologetic.

"Permiso, señorita. Something has arrived."

"Sí. Come in, Eduardo."

The servant escorted a man wheeling a crate on a dolly. The stamp of Johnston's Foundry on the planks had Maria clapping her hands.

"Oh, Traci. The monkey!"

"Another one? In that box?"

Maria laughed. "Not a real monkey. I bought this at the Foundry in Little Harbour after you left."

She wanted to add, *and Daniel bought me a precious ring,* but the sentiment died on her tongue when she glanced at her naked finger.

She removed the crock holding peanuts from the table near the window.

"Can you put the sculpture here, please?"

They watched as the man unpacked the bronze and placed it on its perch. Memories of that day with Daniel flooded Maria's mind, making her eyes ache with unshed tears. She just couldn't think of him now.

Traci obviously felt otherwise.

"That reminds me." She reached into her purse and pulled out a flat parcel covered in wrapping paper with tropical designs and a sweet, yellow bow.

"What is this?"

Traci grinned. "Open it."

The framed photo floored her. It was the last shot Traci had taken with the telephoto lens as they departed Little Harbour. In the picture, Maria stood with Daniel's arm around her on the *Honora,* the two of them waving at the camera as one, their suntanned faces reflecting sheer contentment.

They looked perfect together. She could feel his heat flowing straight into her heart.

His words echoed in her mind. *"...you'll have to come to me on your own and be willing to listen."*

Right now, given her loneliness, she would give anything to resolve the questions between her and Daniel.

"Oh, Traci. I could cry. This is beautiful."

"And Daniel? He mentioned returning to Hope Town at the funeral. Has he left?"

She waved away the question. "Don't ask."

"Is he here?"

Maria shook her head. "My guess is he's back in Hope Town on the *Honora.*" She couldn't bring herself to say, *For good.* Her insides felt hollow just thinking the words.

"You'll meet him to sail back?"

Traci needed to know. "Not this time, my friend. He should be heading to Australia soon. We're no longer together."

"Those words make me very sad."

"Me, too."

"No offense, Maria, but they say people make rash decisions when faced with trauma—like a parent's death."

Maria's laugh was self-deprecating. "You think?"

She reached for a rag to wipe her brush. If satisfaction existed in victory, surely dispelling enough of her amnesia to remember what mattered shouldn't have left a knot in her stomach. There would be no way to avoid the truth with Traci. Not with her tenacity. She might as well swallow her pride and come clean, once and for all.

She plastered on what she hoped was a smile.

"I haven't eaten yet. Want some lunch?"

CHAPTER TWENTY-ONE

Two HOURS LATER, MARIA STOOD in her studio staring at the bronze of Sylvester. The whimsical primate hanging from his branch refused to lighten her spirits.

Earlier, on the pool deck, she'd unburdened her conflict about Daniel with Traci. Talking with her friend helped ease the pain, but Traci couldn't give Maria answers. She only knew what the media printed. She could neither confirm nor deny whether any liaison existed between Carmen and Daniel.

Maria's hopes were dashed once again. She wanted concrete proof that she could believe Daniel. But none existed, and all the tabloids said otherwise.

Traci had left with a promise to stop by tomorrow.

Now all that remained was Reefside. The massive, silent home Maria wished was enough. Sighing, she headed for the easel, feeling the tug of her imagination override her loneliness. Time to add the finishing touches.

Two hours after midnight, only the gentle hush of surf rolling on the beach echoed through the balcony doors. Taking a final look at her work in the moonlight over her shoulder, Maria closed her paints, stretched and headed for her closet to slip into a nightgown.

Sleep eluded her. Her restless mind engaged once more the minute she rose from the stool.

She padded from her room to stalk the corridors of the dark house, feeling like a ghost in the silence. The marble floors cooled her bare feet, reminding her, indeed, she was no specter, but a living, breathing woman, with desires she could not ignore.

Downstairs, moonlight cast smoky light across the floor, on the furnishings, windowpanes and drapes. Ceiling fans whispered quietly overhead. Maria wandered into the great room, sat on the piano bench. Her paint-stained fingers pounded scales up and down the keyboard on the baby grand, the clear notes like thunder in the still, sea air.

The musical exercise offered no peace. Her thoughts broke through. Some memory, some clue about Daniel, Carmen and the accident continued to elude her. The nebulous answer made her insides ache with frustration. She slapped the piano keys with both palms, sending her annoyance spilling into the night in discordant notes. Where was the truth to be found?

The answer jolted her to her feet.

Carmen's room. She hadn't stepped foot into her twin's bedroom since recovering from the accident. She couldn't bear the pain of familiarity when she knew she would never see Carmen again. Then the nightmares had made her terrified to enter Carmen's inner sanctum. Maria's fears only compounded when she considered her sister's treachery.

Now she ran, tripping on her nightgown. She lifted the white cotton hem, her hair flying behind her as she took the stairs two at a time to the second landing.

Breathless, she pushed open the door to her sister's quarters. Her rooms, located on the south side of the house, offered the identical east-west views of Intracoastal and ocean from the windows as Maria's did in the north wing.

Where Maria had an art studio, Carmen had a luxurious closet, with an upholstered chaise, carved wood cabinets built into the walls, an island for shoes and accessories, a sitting area leading to the balcony where French doors had remained closed these endless months.

Maria unlatched the doors, letting night air invade the room, dispelling the scent of old Christian Dior perfume. She lit the bedside lamp, spreading a small cone of light on the table and floor.

Beneath the lamp stood photos of Carmen and Maria as small girls building sand castles on the beach, at college graduation, birthday celebrations, the twins like bookends kissing Poppa's cheeks.

Maria's emotions rushed in like floodwaters. The warmth, the smells, the laughter. Gone, forever. Wrapping her arms around her middle, she sat on the bed, staring at the pictures, waiting for the hurt to cease. She and Carmen had shared such dreams. Was that the curse of being a twin? Losing half of oneself?

But once Daniel had awakened her, he revealed that her sister had been toxic to her, to their relationship, Maria felt a deeper sorrow. Had their sibling love been one-sided? Carmen was a wild child, but would she have actively acted against Maria for her own gain? Maria had chosen to reject Daniel instead of believing that.

Had she accepted lies? The possibility was like a physical ache. Something wasn't right. So much so that she would not sleep until the explanation surfaced. She needed to get to the bottom of this mess. Either Daniel was a liar, or Maria had made a huge mistake in trusting her sister. Instinct told her the answer lay in Carmen's room. Her twin. Her other half. Maria had to know the truth, no matter what she discovered. Daniel deserved that much.

She pulled open the drawer of the nightstand. Romance novels. Lotions. A nail file. A pair of sunglasses. Pens.

A small address book. Maria checked the address book. Nothing unusual.

She tore open dresser drawers, shoe drawers, vanity drawers. The feel of Carmen's clothes, the powdery scent of her sachet suddenly immersed Maria into her sister's world. The sight of a pair of baby-blue stilettos catapulted Maria back to a night when Carmen dragged Maria to South Beach.

Carmen had dressed in a blue top with a white mini-skirt, her dark hair spilling off her shoulders. One of those sexy baby-blue shoes dangled precariously from her foot while she chatted with a prospective lover at the bar. She had winked at Maria before hitting on the guy, promising he'd be putty in her hands. Maria had watched her sister sashay over in rhythm to the pulsing music, leaving Maria to watch her make the conquest.

That night, the pale blue stiletto dangling from Carmen's foot had said it all. Her sister flirted outrageously, and loved every minute. Maria had always laughed at her sister's audacious nature, envying her charm, but could not imagine herself in Carmen's shoes.

Maria reached for a St. John's jacket hanging nearby. She held the fabric to her nose, inhaling the memory of her sister. She ran her hand through the necklaces in the jewelry stand, remembering the last time she'd seen Carmen wearing them.

"Oh, Carmen. Why?"

There was no reply. Of course. She retraced her steps, securing the balcony doors and turning off the lights. She closed her sister's bedroom door with a soft click, as if regretting that she'd disturbed the dead. She'd found nothing.

NEXT EVENING, MARIA returned from a walk on the beach to find Traci waving to her from the patio.

Traci grinned. "I don't see any paint on that fabulous bikini. Didn't you work today?"

Maria slipped a sarong around her waist. "Actually, no. My easel had no attraction for me today."

"Oh, my. What's up?"

Eduardo arrived with a tray carrying a chilled bottle of wine, two glasses, a plate of shrimp cocktail and nachos. He set their usual places at the table under the umbrella, poured the wine and returned the bottle to the cooler. "Ladies, please let me know if I can bring you anything more."

Maria thanked him and led Traci to the table. "How is Brad?"

"He's fine, Maria. Don't stray from the subject." She took her favorite seat, offering a view of the beach, next to Maria. "Tell me what's on your mind."

The two women toasted their glasses before taking a sip. "It's almost impossible to put into words."

Traci popped a nacho chip into her mouth. "For you to stop painting, it's important, no matter how foolish you may think it is."

Maria hesitated. Traci understood her so well. "What if what I believed was true is not?"

"How do you mean?"

"Something Daniel said keeps coming back to me. He said he was guilty of omitting facts, not lying."

"Okay. That's understandable, given the circumstances at the time."

"Daniel insists that Carmen lied. He says Carmen made advances to him that he repelled...constantly. He said Carmen fed stories to the media. Carmen said she hadn't. But what if it was true?"

Traci squeezed her friend's hand. "I hate to say this, but that would be music to my ears. I have so much trouble believing that Daniel would betray you. Brad says the same. Daniel loves you, way too much."

Maria sipped her wine. "I searched Carmen's room last night. Looking for something to prove she lied."

Traci put her drink down. "What did you find?"

"Nothing." She took another sip. "Now that the air has cleared, my instinct tells me I may have been on emotional overload. The twenty days I spent with Daniel on the *Honora* were the finest moments in my life. He was so warm, attentive and loving. If I had to choose who I trusted most—the man I fell in love with on the ship or my sister—I would pick Daniel hands down."

Traci stood. "Then there's only one thing to do."

"What's that?"

"Search her room again." She held out her hand. "Let's go."

MARIA OPENED THE BALCONY doors, one more time. The memory of her nightmares instantly filled her head, but she refused to back away. She threw the doors open wide. Despite the air-conditioning and the clean decor, Carmen's rooms felt oppressive.

Traci had the good grace not to gawk at Carmen's things. She merely stood by the empty bed tapping a finger to her chin. "You checked the drawers. The closet?"

Maria nodded. "I thought she might have kept a diary, or travel receipts, or something." She shrugged. "What does one look for?"

Traci snapped her fingers. "Love letters. Correspondence."

"I can't imagine either Daniel or Carmen would be so foolish as to keep love letters."

"You're right and wrong, Maria."

She turned to face her friend. "How?"

Traci wagged a finger. "Daniel certainly would not leave evidence. But if Carmen wanted to hurt you, she'd stack up as many letters as possible and leave them to be found."

"Okay, let's look."

Maria reached for a box on a shelf inside Carmen's closet and stopped short. The hair on her neck bristled as she turned toward her sister's desk in the shadows by the window. Of course. She hadn't thought of it because she never used her own.

"The laptop. How could I have forgotten? She always had her nose in it."

Traci was already opening the computer, firing it up. "You may have hit pay dirt."

Maria pulled over a chair and sat next to Traci at the desk.

"You okay doing this?"

"I have no choice. Besides, who's left to get mad at me?"

Traci chuckled. "That's my girl."

In seconds, icons crowded the left-hand side of the screen. Traci hit the email icon, and was prompted for a password.

Maria shrugged. "I have no idea."

"Okay, we'll search the files."

Traci opened the documents folder, scrolled past files for bills, friends, investments. She hesitated at a file labeled, *Media,* then clicked it open. Addresses, phone numbers and names of reporters from local newspapers, magazines, radio and television stations appeared on the screen. Many of the reporters were listed by first name only.

"Well, look here. Carmen wa⌐ ⌐ight with the media."

Maria shook her head. "That could be circumstantial

evidence. We've attracted media attention since we were kids. I wouldn't be surprised if most of those reporters are Chilean."

"Okay, but almost all of these names are locals. Don't forget, Maria. Daniel believed Carmen was feeding stories to the tabloids."

She briefly closed her eyes. "I remember." Inside, she wished she didn't. It stung to be searching her sister's personal documents. But at this point, she had no choice.

Traci scanned the remaining files, shaking her head. "Nothing."

"So we're finished."

"Let's go back to the emails."

"We need a password."

Traci pulled up the screen. Carmen's ID automatically populated, but the password box remained blank.

"Okay, they say not to use birth dates or your own name. Usually people use names of someone close and numbers."

"Okay, Carmen was pretty simple. Try, Rosalinda123."

"No. Doesn't work. Give me another idea."

"Maria123."

No luck. Traci typed *Elias. Reefside.*

"None of those. Here, let's get crazy."

She typed in letters. Maria watched the asterisks fill the password space, then Traci hit Return. The file opened.

Both women stared at each other, wide-eyed. "What did you type?"

Traci shook her head. "You won't believe it. DelRio123."

"God, no," she whispered.

With a note of finality, Traci clicked the in-box file open then scrolled slowly down the page.

Maria pointed to an email, halfway down. It was dated over a year ago.

"That one. I believe that is Sandra's email. Those two shared conquests.

Traci clicked on the file.

The reply to Carmen's email read,

He is so hot. Go for it. Who would know?

"Who would know what?" Traci said.

"Scroll down. See if the sent email is attached."

Traci moved the cursor and the file rolled upward, revealing Carmen's original message. Maria sucked in a breath.

"Oh, my God." Traci whispered.

Carmen's message read,

Meeting Maria and Daniel at South Beach tonight. Daniel is celebrating yesterday's win. What do you think? A leak to Hank at The Review should rile Maria enough to walk out on Daniel. That should leave him for me. After all, he doesn't know what he's missing staying with her. I'd be doing us both a favor.

Maria's stomach lurched. "I remember that night. Carmen always made sure she was on one side of Daniel. She kept grabbing his arm, kissing him on the cheek. A reporter snapped pictures, but they'd been around for a couple of days because Daniel won the race, so I never thought anything about it."

"So you didn't get angry and spoiled her plan to get Daniel alone for the evening." Traci shook her head. "That probably goaded her to try harder."

Traci clicked into the sent messages file. She checked

down a few months before the accident. Another email to Sandra popped up. Traci opened it.

Was it dumb luck that he laid eyes on Maria before me? Dios, mio. We are identical twins. If he had seen me first, I'd be the one with the weak knees when he looked at me.

Wait a minute. I am the one with weak knees when he looks at me. I've had my sights on him since the day he arrived. How that quiet little mouse of a sister persuaded Daniel to take her sailing, I'll never know. Now he's in love with her. Is there no justice?

Maria's eyes riveted to the screen as her sister's words seared her mind. She bolted to her feet. "No."

She needed air. She raced to the balcony, her fingers gripping the railing to keep her legs from crumbling.

"That evil witch."

Traci shut down the computer, closed the top. She joined Maria on the balcony. "I think you have your proof."

Maria met her friend's gaze. "I'll tell you what I think of this proof."

She stormed the few paces and tore her sister's computer from the desk. Walking to the balcony she flung the laptop into the air, sending it crashing onto the patio pavers below. "That's what I think of her calling me a little mouse."

Was her love for Carmen so blind that she failed to recognize her twin's craving for male attention as an obsession? A sickness?

Traci spoke quietly. "So the questions remain."

Maria met her gaze, and swallowed. "Did she succeed in seducing my fiancé?"

Traci pointed to the shattered computer on the ground. "You could probably find the answer in there."

Maria laughed. "Oh, I know where to find the answer."

CHAPTER TWENTY-TWO

DANIEL STOWED ANOTHER CRATE of canned goods into the galley cabinets. He couldn't set sail for the Caribbean soon enough.

His iPod played at an earsplitting level. He turned it down. Blaring music wasn't going to lighten his mood. Damn it all, he'd waited for three weeks, hoping Maria would materialize. He held this fantasy that she'd come to her senses and call him on the satellite phone. If she did, he'd point the *Honora* back to Reefside in a heartbeat.

But three weeks had passed with nothing. Yesterday, he finally settled the Jack issue. Instead of pressing charges, Jack would voluntarily enter a rehabilitation facility on the mainland until he cleaned up his act. Now all the circles were closed. Except for his broken heart.

There was still time to make it to Brisbane, if he set off today.

Daniel had woken up deciding he'd no longer play the fool for Maria. He'd always wanted a family of his own. He'd dedicated enough time and energy hoping Maria would fill that need. She'd proved him wrong.

Somewhere out there, his Maria waited. He'd find her. Someday. Meanwhile, the sea had soothed his soul once before, when he'd sailed to mourn the death of his parents. He'd lose himself on the ocean until he felt ready to return.

He laughed out loud. Sure. Escaping memories of Maria would be impossible. She'd left her mark on every corner of this rig. Her perfume still lingered in his cabin. He slammed the cabinet shut. A good dose of ocean wind would clear the air.

An engine rumbled in a ship heading to the docks, rocking the *Honora* gently at her mooring in Hope Town harbor. He checked his watch. Noon. The second ferry from Marsh Harbour, and again, no news. Hitting the button on his iPod, he turned it off.

Time to shove off.

He climbed into the cockpit. The breeze had freshened after the breathless morning. Overhead, the sky looked perfect. He'd leave the harbor under sail. A nice, quiet exit.

He climbed the cabin roof to prep the sails, and glanced at the ferry discharging passengers on the quay. A splash from the dock by the Inn caught his eye. Swimmers usually went oceanside, but one of the new arrivals probably couldn't wait. He surely understood. The sun already scorched his back. It wasn't until he moved to the bow when he realized the swimmer was headed toward the *Honora*.

He looked again, wanting to rub his eyes to make sure he wasn't hallucinating.

Maria.

He stood rock still. He wasn't going to play the foolish, gushing idiot. He wasn't going to react at all. He'd let her do all the talking. After all, *she* threw *him* out of their lives.

As she came closer, swimming with strong, easy breaststrokes, her hair streaming behind her, his pulse hammered in his chest. Her name shot out of his mouth before he could stop himself.

"Maria!"

Inwardly, he cringed. *Way to go, champ. Play hard to get. That'll show her who's boss.*

She pointed a finger at him. "Stay right there. Don't move."

Maria disappeared around the stern of the *Honora,* then slowly rose up the ladder, dripping wet. Venus rising from the sea. Her red tank top clung to her like a lover, her white shorts lay sheer against her thighs. She climbed barefoot over the lifelines into the cockpit, a siren, a mermaid, a dream come true, and Daniel stood frozen in place.

Forget her command. He couldn't move if he wanted. The sheer disbelief that she'd just boarded his boat stunned him into immobility. The hardened look in her eyes left him wondering if he was in for redemption or damnation.

Damn it all, he couldn't read her expression.

His voice was quiet, firm. "What do you want, Maria?"

Did he just *say* that?

She traversed the distance through the cockpit to the gunwales along the side, stopping halfway amidship. A new pain lit her eyes.

He wondered what she'd discovered.

She jutted her chin. "I want to know."

So, it came down to believing him. "Know what?"

She stepped closer. "I want to know what happened on the skiff in Little Harbour."

Daniel gestured to the cockpit. "Do you want to sit?"

She shook her head, water from her hair dripping on her shoulders, her clothes dripping on the teak.

"No. Just tell me. Straight out."

He inwardly counted to ten, unwilling to answer so soon. This could blow up in his face—one more time.

"Okay, I'll tell you."

Her hands fell to her sides. She stood like a warrior woman ready to take whatever blow he dispensed. Daniel ached to reach for her.

She lifted her chin a notch higher. "I want to hear every detail."

He inhaled a breath, refusing to release her gaze. This was it. The moment of truth. Now or never. No turning back. Every cliché in the book ran through his head as he struggled with where to begin. He didn't want to spook Maria again.

"You're ready to listen now?"

A snort of disgust escaped her lips. "I found Carmen's emails. What do you think?"

That explained the hurt in her eyes. He could only confirm what she'd already read, that was, up until the accident. Then she had to rely on him.

He nodded. "Okay. I'll tell you."

He walked closer, gripping the mast stay for support. He needed to watch her face as he told her the truth.

"The trouble started at Pelican Reef. You and I were snorkeling. Rosalinda and Carmen stayed in the boat, flirting with Ryan Sheppard and his friends in the ocean racer on the next mooring. Do you remember that at all?"

She shook her head. "I still don't remember snorkeling or seeing them."

His skin prickled like an acid burn at the thought of subjecting her to Carmen's foul play and her mother's infidelities. But he suspected she already knew.

"Sheppard and his friends followed us to Little Harbour. At one point, in the bar, Ryan tried to kiss you and pissed you off. He was pretty loaded. I suspect he thought you were Carmen. I demanded we leave. Carmen and Rosalinda wanted to let Sheppard take them back to Hope Town. I insisted he was too inebriated. We fought all the way back to the boat, while Sheppard yelled threats at me from the bar. It was an ugly scene."

Daniel inhaled a long breath. Retelling this story was

so damned difficult. He swallowed the knot rising in his throat. "Once we took off, Sheppard followed us. I could tell by the speed of his approach that he intended to swamp us. Our boat was slower, so all I could do was keep on course and take the drenching.

"He wanted to swamp us? Like Jack did?"

"Yes, but it went all wrong. Carmen was livid. I ruined her good time and she was going to make me pay. She kept screaming. Insulting me. Demanding I turn around." He opened his hands in a despairing gesture. "Every insult and lie she spewed was intended to upset you."

Maria's voice was a whisper. "Because she'd been trying to seduce you."

He dropped his hands, his frustration clear. "And I'd been dodging her. She'd been threatening for months to ruin us. I stopped saying anything to you because I thought I could handle her. I was wrong. Her revenge on me was going to be at our expense."

Maria nodded in agreement. If what she'd read in Carmen's file was any indication of her intent, she understood Daniel's concern.

"So what happened?"

He shook his head. "Carmen knew how to push my buttons, Maria. I started yelling back. Your mother thought it all amusing. Her laughter made me angrier. Sheppard got closer, and all I could see was red because I knew how Carmen's taunting tortured you. Then you started screaming at me and I honestly thought I was going to knock Carmen out cold, right then and there.

"Without warning, Carmen pushed me backward. I lost my balance. She grabbed the steering wheel and jerked the boat off course. We veered right into Sheppard's path. He was too high, and his boat was too close and too fast for him to react. The racer crashed right through the center of the boat. You and I were tossed. Carmen and Rosalinda were crushed."

Maria blinked a couple of times before closing her eyes. Without opening them, she spoke. "Carmen caused the accident. She could have killed us."

Daniel waited until she looked at him again. "Yes."

"And you took the blame."

He shrugged. "I'm a licensed captain. The accident should never have happened on my watch."

He hoped she didn't hear the hitch in his voice. He'd dragged that guilt like a boulder tied around his neck for a year now. Elias had forgiven him, but it had never been enough. He needed Maria's absolution, her fearless, trusting love to set him free.

Maria approached him, just as he had approached her on the bow the day they met Traci and Brad for the first time. Maria had been so terrified when Traci called them lovers. She'd been frozen in place, and Daniel offered a kiss to help her remember. Did he now have that same deer-in-headlights terror in his eyes? He sucked in a sharp breath as she laid a hand on his chest.

"You tried to tell me, and I refused to listen."

"I did."

"Can you forgive me for not believing you, Daniel?"

The tears in her eyes had him closing and opening his fists, fighting his own tears. The warmth of her hand reassured like a promise. He wanted desperately to take her into his arms. But no. He still needed to hear those important words he'd craved since Maria regained consciousness.

He wondered if he could speak around the lump in his throat. "Can you forgive me for killing your mother and sister?"

"Oh, Daniel. You didn't do it."

Her perfume managed to reach his senses. He inhaled, briefly closing his eyes, his chest tightening with the hope of redemption.

He covered her hand with his own, grateful for her touch. "I don't know if I can ever believe that."

She pressed a finger to his lips.

"I believe it, Daniel. I am so very sorry for the burden you suffered at the hands of my sister and mother."

A rush of air escaped his lips. How he'd craved hearing those words. "Thank you, Princess."

Before she could snake her arms around his neck, he crushed her against him. Her willing body offered all the redemption he required. Her wet hair doused his shoulder. Her shirt and shorts drenched his clothes in a baptism of the purest sort. She was in his arms, forgiving him.

The guilt dropped from his heart like a loose anchor, sinking down into the deepest ocean. He swung her in a circle, howling.

After he set her on her feet, he asked, "Will you wear my dolphin ring again?"

She wet her lips, as if enjoying the sight of his grin. "On one condition."

"What's that?"

"Are my paint supplies still on board?"

He was almost embarrassed to admit the truth. In all his anger, he couldn't toss them as he kept telling himself to do. Instead, he'd stowed them in a locker.

He nodded. "They're below."

She began leading him from the bow. "Good."

"Why?"

She leaned over and kissed him, a soft, seductive kiss, igniting him.

"I have one final canvas to paint before I answer your question."

"I was about to set sail."

She glanced down at the high waterline along the docks. "Tomorrow's another tide."

"Want to sail with me?"

Her laugh, rich and throaty, teased his libido. "You're not going anywhere in this wide world without me again, Captain. Is that understood?"

He smiled his appreciation. "Aye, mate."

She tugged his hand once again. "Come on. My easel calls."

"Don't you want to get out of those wet clothes first?"

"Good idea. I'll paint naked."

"Nice!"

She hummed low in her throat. "You owe me. I've had an inexplicable urge to paint you in the buff ever since the first night on this ship."

He laughed out loud, letting her lead him out of the glaring sun and into the cool shadow of the companionway.

"I always pay my debts, Princess. Only, this painting won't get sold."

She peeled off her tank top. She was braless. Goose bumps rose on her wet skin in the cabin's air-conditioning while the fire in her eyes seared him right down to his soul. "Will hanging your portrait over our bed at Reefside be a good place for it?"

He pulled her into his arms, letting heaven close in as her damp breasts and skin found purchase against his chest. God, she was so soft to touch. He ran his hands down her spine, resting his palms on her hips. "Are you proposing?"

She pulled away, burying her hands under his shirt slowly lifting it over his head. She teased her fingers through his hair, her raised arms making her breasts rise. "Didn't you propose the first time? I can return the favor."

He pushed away damp tendrils of her hair to kiss her neck beneath her earlobe, along her collarbone. Her soft, fragrant skin incited ideas of his own about painting.

"Suddenly, I'm not so disappointed you can't remember our engagement. I like this much better."

She unfastened her shorts, letting them drop to her feet, then peeled off the lacy thong. She reached for the waistband of Daniel's chinos. Her gaze roamed his body and stopped at the bulge beneath the zipper. She pressed against his hardness with the palm of her hand before easing the shorts off his hips.

"Nothing about you disappoints me, Daniel."

His grin faded into desire as he reached for her.

She placed a hand on his chest to stop him. "Now, my supplies, Captain?"

He scooped her into his arms, covering the short distance to his cabin.

"Later, Princess. First, you have to convince me to be a willing subject."

Laughter lit her eyes. "What if my memory fails me?"

He laid her on his bunk, the primal urge to conquer this woman battling a desire to slowly draw out every possible moment. Did she know what the sight of her did to every inch of his body? His words escaped deep and husky as he brought his mouth close to hers.

"Memory doesn't matter anymore, love. No more past. Only here and now. You. Me. And the rest of our lives. Can you handle that, *mi querida?*"

She pulled him down, wrapping her arms around his neck, entwining her legs with his, setting his blood on fire.

Her hands wandered the length of his body, matching his own hungry, heated exploration. He rolled onto his back, taking her with him. She captured his face with her palms, her dark eyes hot and alive, her ebony hair falling about her shoulders, brushing his face. Pressing her lips against his, she whispered, "Bring it on, Captain. I won't forget a thing."

* * * * *

HEART & HOME

Heartwarming romances where love can
happen right when you least expect it.

COMING NEXT MONTH
AVAILABLE FEBRUARY 14, 2012

#1758 BETWEEN LOVE AND DUTY
A Brother's Word
Janice Kay Johnson

#1759 MARRY ME, MARINE
In Uniform
Rogenna Brewer

#1760 FROM THE BEGINNING
Tracy Wolff

#1761 JUST DESSERTS
Too Many Cooks?
Jeannie Watt

#1762 ON COMMON GROUND
School Ties
Tracy Kelleher

#1763 A TEXAS CHANCE
The MacAllisters
Jean Brashear

REQUEST YOUR FREE BOOKS!
2 FREE NOVELS PLUS 2 FREE GIFTS!

Harlequin®

Super Romance®

Exciting, emotional, unexpected!

YES! Please send me 2 FREE Harlequin® Superromance® novels and my 2 FREE gifts (gifts are worth about $10). After receiving them, if I don't wish to receive any more books, I can return the shipping statement marked "cancel." If I don't cancel, I will receive 6 brand-new novels every month and be billed just $4.69 per book in the U.S. or $5.24 per book in Canada. That's a saving of at least 15% off the cover price! It's quite a bargain! Shipping and handling is just 50¢ per book in the U.S. and 75¢ per book in Canada.* I understand that accepting the 2 free books and gifts places me under no obligation to buy anything. I can always return a shipment and cancel at any time. Even if I never buy another book, the two free books and gifts are mine to keep forever.

135/336 HDN FC6T

Name _____ (PLEASE PRINT)

Address _____ Apt. #

City _____ State/Prov. _____ Zip/Postal Code

Signature (if under 18, a parent or guardian must sign)

Mail to the **Reader Service:**
IN U.S.A.: P.O. Box 1867, Buffalo, NY 14240-1867
IN CANADA: P.O. Box 609, Fort Erie, Ontario L2A 5X3

Not valid for current subscribers to Harlequin Superromance books.
Are you a current subscriber to Harlequin Superromance books and want to receive the larger-print edition?
Call 1-800-873-8635 or visit www.ReaderService.com.

* Terms and prices subject to change without notice. Prices do not include applicable taxes. Sales tax applicable in N.Y. Canadian residents will be charged applicable taxes. Offer not valid in Quebec. This offer is limited to one order per household. All orders subject to credit approval. Credit or debit balances in a customer's account(s) may be offset by any other outstanding balance owed by or to the customer. Please allow 4 to 6 weeks for delivery. Offer available while quantities last.

Your Privacy—The Reader Service is committed to protecting your privacy. Our Privacy Policy is available online at www.ReaderService.com or upon request from the Reader Service.

We make a portion of our mailing list available to reputable third parties that offer products we believe may interest you. If you prefer that we not exchange your name with third parties, or if you wish to clarify or modify your communication preferences, please visit us at www.ReaderService.com/consumerschoice or write to us at Reader Service Preference Service, P.O. Box 9062, Buffalo, NY 14269. Include your complete name and address.

HSR11

Get swept away with author

CATHY GILLEN THACKER

and her new miniseries

Legends of Laramie County

On the Cartwright ranch, it's the women
who endure and run the ranch—and it's time for
lawyer Liz Cartwright to take over. Needing some help
around the ranch, Liz hires Travis Anderson, a fellow
attorney, and Liz's high-school boyfriend. Travis says
he wants to get back to his ranch roots, but Liz knows
Travis is running from something. Old feelings emerge
as they work together, but Liz can't help but wonder
if Travis is home to stay.

Reluctant Texas Rancher

**Available March
wherever books are sold.**

www.Harlequin.com

HAR75398

New York Times *and* USA TODAY *bestselling author*
Maya Banks presents book three in her miniseries
PREGNANCY & PASSION.

TEMPTED BY HER INNOCENT KISS

Available March 2012 from Harlequin Desire!

There came a time in a man's life when he knew he was
well and truly caught. Devon Carter stared down at the dia-
mond ring nestled in velvet and acknowledged that this was
one such time. He snapped the lid closed and shoved the
box into the breast pocket of his suit.

He had two choices. He could marry Ashley Copeland
and fulfill his goal of merging his company with Copeland
Hotels, thus creating the largest, most exclusive line of re-
sorts in the world, or he could refuse and lose it all.

Put in that light, there wasn't much he could do except
pop the question.

The doorman to his Manhattan high-rise apartment hurried to open the door as Devon strode toward the street.
He took a deep breath before ducking into his car, and the
driver pulled into traffic.

Tonight was the night. All of his careful wooing, the
countless dinners, kisses that started brief and casual and
became more breathless—all a lead-up to tonight. Tonight
his seduction of Ashley Copeland would be complete, and
then he'd ask her to marry him.

He shook his head as the absurdity of the situation hit
him for the hundredth time. Personally, he thought William
Copeland was crazy for forcing his daughter down Devon's
throat.

Ashley was a sweet enough girl, but Devon had no desire

to marry anyone.

William had other plans. He'd told Devon that Ashley had no head for the family business. She was too softhearted, too naive. So he'd made Ashley part of the deal. The catch? Ashley wasn't to know of it. Which meant Devon was stuck playing stupid games.

Ashley was supposed to think this was a grand love match. She was a starry-eyed woman who preferred her animal-rescue foundation over board meetings, charts and financials for Copeland Hotels.

If she ever found out the truth, she wouldn't take it well.

And hell, he couldn't blame her.

But no matter the reason for his proposal, before the night was over, she'd have no doubts that she belonged to him.

What will happen when Devon marries Ashley?
Find out in Maya Banks's passionate new novel
TEMPTED BY HER INNOCENT KISS
Available March 2012 from Harlequin Desire!

Harlequin *Presents*

USA TODAY bestselling author

Carol Marinelli

begins a daring duet.

THE SECRETS of XANOS

Two brothers alike in charisma and power;
separated at birth and seeking revenge...

Nico has always felt like an outsider. He's turned his back on his
parents' fortune to become one of Xanos's most powerful exports
and nothing will stand in his way—until he stumbles
upon a virgin bride....

Zander took his chances on the streets rather than spending another
moment under his cruel father's roof. Now he is unrivaled in
business—and the bedroom! He wants the best people around him,
and Charlotte is the best PA! Can he tempt her
over to the dark side...?

A SHAMEFUL CONSEQUENCE
Available in March

AN INDECENT PROPOSITION
Available in April